STOLEN GIRL AND AIDEN'S STORY

SILENT CHILD sequels

SARAH A. DENZIL

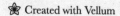 Created with Vellum

Also by the author:

Chapter One

EMMA

Even though September is here, the trees are still verdant green. We're all dressed in light clothing for the unseasonably warm weather, bare arms caressed by a calm breeze filtering through the trees. I can't deny that it's a beautiful day today, but inside my ribcage my heart is tapping away, quick as fluttering moth wings. Anticipation makes my skin prickle. I glance at the man to my right, who still seems like a boy; who stares out beyond with an inscrutable expression. He doesn't like to be touched but I slip my fingers into his and squeeze them, hoping those squeezes will convey my thoughts: *You're not alone. I'm here with you. I'll keep you safe. This is almost over.*

They built us a platform so that we wouldn't miss a single moment, and I feel strangely tall standing here in the woods, as though I'm on stilts. Below us there's a clearing surrounded by a metal fence, which seems out of place among the dark branches and lush foliage of the forest. But the fence marks out the location of the place we need to watch. I take it all in one final time as I breathe deeply to steady my heart.

On my left, there's a soft, sticky little hand in mine. 'Will it be loud?' says a small voice.

I glance down at my daughter, the owner of the tiny hand. 'It might be. Would you like some ear plugs?'

Gina grins. 'No, I want it to be loud.'

She's been looking forward to this for weeks. I, on the other hand, have been dreading it. And as for Aiden, well, I don't know how he feels, I can't even imagine, and when I ask, he gives me a shrug in return.

I turn my head to my son. 'Would you like them?'

He shakes his head. His body is rigid, his hand sweaty in mine. 'No, Mum.' Some tension leaves my body at the sound of his gentle voice. It means he's still here, still present in the world. When he disappears into himself, his voice goes away.

We're not alone on our platform, but no one else matters apart from Aiden and Gina. Their hands in mine. Their safety against this world and the darkness within it. I stare down into the woodland area, through the trees and tangles of thorny bushes.

'Get it over with,' Rob grumbles under his breath. Aiden's father. My ex.

I hear the cluck of Sonya's tongue as she gently chastises her son.

'Perhaps I should go and check everything's all right,' DCI Stevenson suggests.

'No,' I reply, worried that he'd miss it. He deserves to witness this moment as much as we all do. 'I'm sure it's just one of those things.' I smile at Gina, trying to keep the worry out of my voice. 'Like how the fireworks are always late on bonfire night.' Gina nods solemnly, remembering her own impatience last November, waiting outside a cold pub in Manchester.

It'll take a measly few seconds to demolish the bunker. After ripping out the internal fittings of it, the place has been fitted with explosives and the nearby trees have been cleared. A digger waits patiently for the clear-up. Another jarring contrast to the natural environment.

We were asked if we wanted to watch the demolition some months back. At first, I found it difficult to broach the subject with Aiden. He didn't answer right away, instead he went to his room and sat on his bed in silence. A few hours later, he came back down and nodded his head. He told me who he wanted to be here, and I began to hope that this could be a positive experience for us as a family. Closure for the trauma. For Aiden's trauma, and mine and everyone else's, but mainly for him. And here we are. Aiden, little Gina, Rob, Sonya, Peter, Josie and Stevenson, all shuffling our feet, sighing and sweating on a hot Tuesday in September, waiting and waiting.

They asked me if I would like to push the button, or whether Aiden would want to do it. He said no. I look at him now, the profile of his face, and try to imagine what he's thinking. I can't. There's no possibility of reaching into that mind and uncovering all the pain and suffering. It's the place he keeps locked away. It's a place I can never go to or feel for myself. And as a mother, that is horrifying.

There's a shout from one of the men, then a crack followed by a boom. A cloud of dust bursts upwards and it's over almost as soon as it begins. The ground sinks in on itself and soil falls away. Aiden's underground prison has been destroyed. It's done. I wait for it, the moment, the release, the acknowledgement that the worst part of my life is over. There's nothing.

On our way out of the woods, Aiden's hand leaves mine and he slips through the trees, fading from sight. A moment of panic constricts my chest until I remember that he's safe now. The bunker is gone. Hugh is dead. But even so, I find myself walking a little faster to keep him in sight.

'Too fast, Mummy,' Gina protests, yanking on my arm.

'Sorry, darling.' There's a glimpse of Aiden's red T-shirt between the branches of the trees. I wish he wouldn't wear red.

'Mummy, was that place where I was born?'

I scoop her up into my arms, remembering too late that at four she's becoming quite heavy for me to carry. 'Almost.'

'You blew it,' she says, referring to the bunker. There's a

3

note of disappointment in her voice that catches me off guard.

There was a limit to what I could explain to Gina about the bunker and what it means to Aiden. We told her that Aiden had some unhappy times there but that it wasn't all bad, because it was the place where my water broke, and she came into the world. The rest, we can't tell her. Not yet.

'Emma.'

I stop and turn around, realising that I've separated from the rest of the group. Everyone else is gathered around Rob, helping him along the path. My face warms with guilt. Since his head injury, Rob has had to learn to walk again, still relying on his cane. Much of his frame has withered away, but he's still tall and imposing as he struggles along the uneven path.

'We're going to the pub,' Rob says. 'Are you coming?'

'I don't know. What if we're being followed again?' All these years on and photographers still target my family. Still print our pictures.

Rob taps Gina on the nose with his finger and she giggles. 'Who cares? Let's celebrate.'

The word makes my skin crawl and I think I visibly cringe because Rob backtracks.

'Well, not celebrate, but you know what I mean. We're alive, the bunker is destroyed, Aiden is safe and those that deserve to be are dead.'

My eyes seek out Josie's face when he says that. But she's lost in her thoughts, gazing out into the woods.

'I don't know about Aiden. He's a little shaken up.'

'I want to.'

The sound of my son's voice makes my heart leap in surprise. I spin around so fast Gina has to grab hold of my shoulder.

'Sorry,' he says. 'I didn't mean to sneak up on you.'

I open my mouth to ask him how he managed to walk in one direction and then turn back without me noticing, but in truth, I'm beginning to get used to Aiden's cat-like prowling. Instead, I just laugh.

'It wouldn't hurt to spend a bit of time together,' Sonya says. 'As long as you're OK, Aiden?'

'I'm fine, Grandma.'

And with that, I'm swept away by the others as we head back to the car park. This time, Aiden stays by my side.

He's a miracle. The boy who returned. At one time I thought he'd died; I closed off a part of myself; sunk into the grief. Even after he returned there were those who thought he would've been better off dying than suffering through what he suffered. Even I thought it, fleetingly, guiltily. But he came through it, growing stronger than I could ever have imagined. More resilient than I could ever be. A miracle, and part of me. The best part.

I wonder whether I'll ever grow accustomed to him being above the legal age to drive and vote. He could live on his own or have an important job. There are other twenty-year-olds out there with children, careers, or studying for their university degree. But none of that has happened for Aiden yet. The scars are still there, of course, both physical and psychological. And for now, he lives with me, until he reaches the point where he can make his way out into the world. I hope that point isn't too soon. I'm not sure my heart could take it.

'She's lovely, Emma,' Josie says, as I let Gina down onto the tarmac. 'Hi, Gina!'

My little one hides behind my legs, her face poking out around the side with a big grin between her delicate ears. She isn't shy, but she knows that pretending to be shy gets her more attention. She waggles her fingers in hello.

'How old are you, Gina?' Josie asks.

She holds up four fingers before gripping my legs. I can feel her sticky skin against mine.

'Wow, that many?' Josie turns to me. 'Time flies.'

I nod.

'You should visit more, Em,' she says. 'I miss you.'

'I miss you too,' I say, thinking about Josie and what she's been through. Hugh fooled her, his wife, as much as he fooled us all. I know she still feels responsible for his actions, but she isn't, and she will always be my best friend, as well as one of the few people in the world who understands what Aiden and I have been through.

When Josie bends down to ruffle Gina's hair, instinct tells me to pull my daughter away, even though I trust Josie. It takes willpower to quell the urge. The sight of people touching my children does not get any easier.

'See you there,' she says, smiling sadly as she takes a couple of steps back. She felt my uncertainty, which means I'm not hiding my discomfort well.

Perhaps I never will. It might be a part of me that I'll need to accept going forward. *They're safe now,* I tell myself, lowering Gina into her car seat. *No one will hurt them ever again.* At least now I know what I'm capable of doing to keep them safe. That's some comfort to me, knowing that I will kill anyone who tries to hurt my children. After all, I've done it before.

Aiden obediently slips into the passenger seat, like he used to do during his period of silence. I can't stop myself dwelling on that time. It's this village, these woods. This air. I'm breathing in the past, exhaling the future, my mind obsessing over both but stripping me away from the present.

One by one the cars filter out of the small car park. I find myself checking the rear-view mirror as soon as I'm on the road. There's no one around, we're not being followed by photographers. The destruction of the bunker will be reported in the media, but we were firm that we wanted it to be a private occasion for those directly affected by what Hugh did to my son. We know the story is a public one, but the pain is private, and that's how it should remain.

The Blue Stoops is not as empty as the roads. It's Tuesday lunchtime and there's sun in the sky, which means locals are here to drink a few pints in the beer garden and eat a burger before they have to go back to work. I dab my sweaty forehead with a tissue before climbing out of the car.

'Are you both hungry? We can eat here, too, if you like,' I suggest, trying to brighten up a little. I hate them seeing their mother so serious all the time.

'Nuggies,' Gina cries.

Aiden smiles. 'It's nuggets, Ginny.'

She dramatically puts her finger to her lips. 'Nuff, Denny.'

While shaking my head at my two kids, I unclip the seat-belt and make my way around to the car seat to get Gina, but Aiden beats me to it.

'Ay-den.'

'Denny.'

'Ay-den.'

'She can pronounce it just fine,' I say. As Aiden brings her out of the car, I tickle her, and she squeals. 'She's just doing it to wind you up.' I place a hand on Aiden's shoulder and his body freezes. I quickly retract it and he lets out a quiet breath.

On a good day, he doesn't flinch at physical contact. But this isn't a good day for him.

'Sorry.' I take Gina's hand in mine and try to brush over the awkwardness.

The group waits for me before heading in, and this time I remember to slow down and walk beside Rob. He's a little out of breath heading up the steps to the door and it tugs on my heart. We owe him everything for saving our lives.

Stevenson hesitates at the bottom of the steps. I'd almost forgotten about him until he clears his throat. 'You know, you can say if you'd rather it be family only.' He pushes his hands into his trouser pockets and shrugs his shoulders.

Quietly, every face turns to him at the back of the group. I break the silence by leaning over and placing a hand on his upper arm.

'No. You need a drink as much as the rest of us do.' Even though it was Aiden who showed us the way to Hugh's bunker, it was DCI Stevenson who found me there and saved mine and Gina's life. Without him, she might never have been born.

'You've got that right,' he says, and his downturned expression breaks into a more natural smile. 'What a day.'

Peter, Rob's dad, holds the door open for everyone as we walk into the pub, appreciating the cool air away from the hot sun outside, and then offers to buy a round when we get to the bar. I order Gina some chicken nuggets, and sandwiches for me and Aiden, even though I'm not hungry. Peter, Stevenson and Rob all order a pint and Rob makes a joke about being drunk and in charge of a walking stick that we tentatively laugh at.

By the time we find a table in the corner of the pub, I'm beginning to unclench. When our food arrives, I'm almost relaxed, though I don't drink because I'm driving. As the tension leaves my body, I find myself ravenous, and tuck straight into my lunch.

'Why don't you leave your car here,' Peter says to Stevenson. 'Sonya's driving and can give you a lift.'

'Thank you, but no. I'll just have the one,' he replies. 'I live closer to York and it'll put you out.'

While the conversation goes on, I notice that Aiden isn't eating much. He sees me watching him and smiles.

'I'm fine, Mum. Just not hungry.'

'You tell me if you want to go,' I say, a little too firmly.

'I will.' He pats me lightly on the hand.

'Excuse me.'

We all look up from our table to a young woman, around twenty years old, standing next to us with her hands pulled behind her back, red-faced and nervous.

'Sorry, I didn't want to interrupt, but are you Aiden Price?'

I'm immediately on high alert. There's a slight shuffle next to me, Rob also focuses on the mystery girl.

'Yes,' Aiden says, managing a smile.

'I . . . I'm a fan of yours,' the girl says, blushing a darker shade of red. She quickly swipes the back of her hand over her forehead. She's pretty, with freckles and naturally golden hair. 'Could I take a selfie with you?'

There's tension running along Aiden's jaw as he grits his teeth. But nevertheless, he stands up and smiles.

'You don't have to,' I say, wanting to shove this girl away from my child. The memory of him in the hospital room flashes through my mind. The first meeting with the doctor, and the wretched, slopping sound as I vomited in response to what he told me about Aiden's injuries. The first time I saw Aiden's brown eyes staring up at me when he came home, so small for his age. My heart quickens again.

'It's OK,' Aiden says, before swallowing nervously.

'Thank you so much!' The girl takes her mobile phone and gets uncomfortably close to my boy. Thankfully, she doesn't put an arm around him. I watch the pained expression on my son's face with a sense of hopelessness. This is his life and there's nothing I can do to change that.

It's over in a moment and the girl retreats back to wherever she came from, but the incident only draws attention to us, because a second person approaches. A woman around my age this time, perhaps a little older, asking for an autograph on a beer mat. Aiden smiles politely as he signs it. I watch them both, my body still clenched. When will this stop?

'Could I have a quick photo, too?' she asks.

'OK.' He glances at me, lost, overwhelmed.

'We're actually trying to –' I start.

'Mum, it's OK,' he says, taking the picture using her phone.

This happens more than I'd like. It's the new normal, and there's nothing I can do about it. I can't imagine ever getting used to his celebrity status, and all I can think is how dangerous it might become unless I can control it.

Chapter Two

THE CHAPEL

The wind blew out the window again, which means it needs boarding up. My fingers catch on the nails while rummaging through the toolbox. I place one between my teeth as I hold the wood in position. It's strong MDF that I found in someone's skip. Heavy enough to make my arms ache as I keep it in place. At night, I scurry around the village roads, like a rat in the shadows. Sometimes I turn off my headlights, so no one knows I'm there. If you asked me why, I wouldn't know. It doesn't matter so much if they see me, I just don't want to be seen.

When the wood drops an inch underneath my grip I instinctively bite down on the nail and let out a curse through throbbing teeth and a cut lip. The pain strengthens my resolve. I shove my shoulder against the wood, banging in the nail as hard as I can. The second one secures it enough to allow me to get in a third. And then a fourth.

Today is a hot day, and my clothes are drenched through by the time the job is over. On a day like this I miss showers and electric fans. But I make do by removing my top and working in my underwear. Next, I move the mattress to underneath the hole in the roof, lie down, and let the breeze cool my hot skin.

This is a lonely place, but I don't care. When I speak, which is rarely, my voice echoes around the rafters. It frightens the spiders back into their corners. But I don't care.

It was a chapel once, before nature covered it. Now that it's abandoned, I'm the evil thing that lurks in this once-holy place. But I. Don't. Care.

There was a rich family who lived somewhere close to here who built this private chapel on their woodland. It ended up in disrepair after they sold their properties, along with an old mansion that was demolished to make way for a new road. Now their old chapel is haunted. I'm the thing lurking in the shadows.

There's no cooling down on a day like today. The high winds that blew out the window at the front of the building have gone, and I'm still as hot as I was before. I wouldn't have bothered with the boards but I didn't want any nosy trespassers to lean in and see me here. The covered windows tell them to keep walking. *Leave the ghost well alone or you'll be sorry.*

My lip stings a little, and I allow my tongue to trail the length of it, tasting the blood. I sit up from the old mattress and stretch, feeling the aching deep down in my bones.

Outside the chapel, I make my way to the vegetable patch I've been cultivating. Lettuce, strawberries, tomatoes. The tomatoes are the hardest because I need to buy plant food for them, and I don't like going out into the world. I don't like the noise or the faces.

I'm pleased to see that there's a squirrel in my trap today. I unclip the trap and take it back to the chapel. I have a knife there along with wood for a fire, though I'll have to wait until nightfall for the fire. The last thing I need is some nosy do-gooder seeing the smoke and calling the emergency services.

I can't have any attention drawn to me now. This is my time to hunker down and work things out in my mind. There are tasks to complete before I put my plan in motion.

I put the squirrel down on one of the old pews with the veg, which will need washing. Luckily, purification tablets help me when I don't have running water. Before doing any of that, I kneel down by the mattress and retrieve a tin box from near the old altar. It squeaks as I remove the lid. Good. It's still there: the last of my money, withdrawn from my bank before I came here.

No matter how hard I try, I can't escape society. I still need that money because it's essential for what I intend to do next.

With a sigh, I sit back down on the mattress and push the lid back on the tin wondering if what I want to do is worth it. I stare up at the cracked stained glass above the altar. I'm not sure who it depicts, but I think it might be Mary. I remember learning the nativity story. Back when I hid myself behind masks. Like how I hid my feelings deep down, down, down where no one could touch them. Mary was this woman with a destiny to bring a great good into the world. She still is the female ideal for the world, the virgin mother, the woman the world wants all women to be. A vessel waiting to be filled with purpose.

And I am who I am. Empty.

Alone.

But I don't care, because I have work to do.

Chapter Three

EMMA

When I say that I'm fine, I'm lying. I'm saying the words people want to hear. No one wants the truth when they ask you how you are; they want to go through the motions of checking in, to prove to themselves that they care, when they don't. The word *fine* is part of the dance we perform with each other. I'm not fine at all, but I *am* better.

It's a slow process that comes from within myself and extends out to my family. Each night, the nightmare fades away more than the night before. The picture of Jake's face dwindles away like an insignificant, unloved relative. The image of Hugh's dead body is obfuscated by time. The mental images slowly drift away.

But whether I'm healing with each day, or whether I'm simply forgetting the details, is a question I can't answer.

What I do know is that we've found some peace here. We don't like it in Bishoptown-on-Ouse anymore. We live in a three-bedroom apartment in the suburbs of Manchester overlooking a park. The selling point for me was the garage we open up in the afternoon sun. A good place to paint.

After the court cases ended and it was decided that what I

did was in self-defence, I inherited Jake's house as his widow. But I immediately sold it in order to buy back my parents' cottage. No matter how I feel about Bishoptown, I know I can't quite let it go.

In our Manchester apartment, we wake, eat together and run errands. I spend a lot of the day taking Aiden to his appointments because he hasn't learned to drive yet. Aiden still has weekly therapy sessions, speech therapy and physio-therapy. He has regular check-ups, too. I have a calendar with them all written down. When we're not going to Aiden's appointments, we read and learn together. Aiden missed ten years of school, but he's bright and eager to learn.

As much as I hate to admit it – I have to because it's a fact – while Aiden was in the bunker, Hugh bought books for him. Hugh was the one who helped to advance his reading and writing. He gave him history books, world maps, the occa-sional science textbook. While Aiden lost many, many things in that bunker, he never lost his desire to learn about the world.

It's early on Saturday morning and both Gina and Aiden are asleep. I have my hands wrapped around a cup of coffee, though the day is warm enough already that I don't need to hold it so close. I just like the comfort.

By the time I've finished my drink, Gina wanders into the kitchen, bleary-eyed and in her teddy pyjamas. She clutches Walnut the Dragon, a gift from Aiden.

'Mummy, I had another accident,' she says, rubbing her eyes.

Sure enough, the crotch of the teddy pyjamas is darker in colour.

'That's OK, sweetheart.' I brush a lock of her hair away from her face and gently pinch her in the part of her belly that usually makes her squeal. Today she silently wriggles away from me. No matter how hard I try to make sure she doesn't feel shame when she's wet the bed, somehow kids always sense that they've done something wrong.

'Where's Denny?' she asks, as I begin stripping her for the bath.

'Still asleep.'

'Can I wake him?' she asks.

'No, sweetheart. You know we talked about that.'

'Denny doesn't like it when I jump on the bed.'

No, he does not. Though I wish it was for a normal young man reason, and not because being woken abruptly pulls him out of his nightmares.

It doesn't take long to get Gina washed, dried and in clothes. She's a relaxed child who tends to go with the flow rather than fight me at every turn, very unlike Aiden as a boy. As I'm putting her bed linen into the washing machine, Aiden comes down the stairs.

'Denny!' Gina cries.

I glance up at my son. This is my morning routine. I need to gauge how well Aiden slept to know how to handle him for that day. If he has dark circles and is holding himself tightly, I know I need to make sure Gina gives him some space. If he doesn't have his hands balled into fists and there are no dark circles, then he's OK with conversation straight away. Today, he's tensed.

'Tuck into your breakfast, Ginny, before it goes cold.'

Obediently, she dunks a soldier in her egg and tucks in, smearing yolk around her mouth. Food tends to be a winning distraction for Gina.

Aiden sits down at the table and silently gazes out of the window. This kind of behaviour doesn't worry me as much anymore – I know that he retreats within himself when he's feeling overwhelmed. It has only been four days since the bunker was destroyed and he's still recovering from that change.

'What would you like for breakfast?' I ask, quietly.

'Can I have a glass of water please?'

'You can get that, remember?' I remind him.

He nods, and I sense a part of him coming back. Sometimes he needs to be reminded that he can do things for himself. Something simple like getting some water or making a meal is important for him. I've also been teaching him how to cook, since he never got to watch me cook for him as he grew up.

'Did you decide about the school?' he asks.

For a moment I'm not sure what he's referring to, because I'm so surprised to hear him talk without me asking a question. And then I realise he means Gina.

'I think it's best to school Gina at home.'

Aiden turns on the tap and the water comes gushing out. With his back to me I can't see his facial expression, but I know he'll be annoyed because we've had this chat before. Aiden thinks Gina should go to school. He doesn't want his abduction to be responsible for her not having a normal life. But I can't bear the thought of her out there in the world without my protection. It was a schoolteacher who gave my son to a paedophile. Amy Perry, one of the people I trusted most in this world, called her paedo boyfriend Hugh and told him where to kidnap my son, and how to make it look like an accidental death. Unfortunately, Amy is still out there, in the world.

Who knows who else might be waiting to do us harm? I can't help the way I feel about the darkness in people, and there's a chance I'm allowing that to seep into my parenting style. Gina already knows how to call the police because we've role-played it together. She never gets the opportunity to talk to strangers because I'm with her all the time. I know deep down that most people in the world are fundamentally good, but I can't stop thinking about the bad ones, and what they've done to me and my family. I'd keep Gina away from them forever if I could, but perhaps I'll have to settle for the next few years as a start.

Aiden walks over to the table with his water. 'It's not right, Mum. She should go.'

'Go where?' Gina says. 'The park?'

'Yes, we can go to the park.' I stroke her hair and she smiles.

'I'm going to paint.' Aiden pushes his water away and stands. His hands are balled into fists again. He's angry with me. A pained expression travels across his face, one that I'm familiar with and understand to mean he's keeping his temper in check. A technique he's been working on with his psychologist, Dr Anderton, for the last four years.

'Are you OK?' I ask.

He nods.

'It's for the best, you know that.' But as I say the words, I'm not sure whether I'm trying to persuade myself. I glance down at Gina. She's so *small*. I can't bear the thought of her being away from me for hours at a time. My heart tugs, and an aching pain opens up in my belly. Scar tissue from my grief.

The doorbell sends a jolt down my spine. Because I'm so close to Gina it also makes her jump and then she giggles.

'It's just the *bell*, Mummy. Silly.'

My four-year-old is comforting me. But of course she is. I'm forever blown away by how self-possessed she is for her age.

'I'll get it,' I say, hurrying to catch up to Aiden. I know he hates answering the door. Small talk is not something Aiden excels in, and we have a chatty postman.

I press the buzzer, establish that it's a delivery, and let the man into the apartment block. My heart always beats a little harder in these situations. *Who am I allowing in?*

It isn't the chatty postman, but a private courier who needs a signature for a heavy box. I heave it into the flat and see that the box is addressed to Aiden, not me.

'Can I open it?' he asks.

'Did you order something?'

'No, but I know what it is,' he says.

I stand back so that he can tear away the tape, realising what he means. He pulls the cardboard open and reaches inside. For the briefest of moments, I think it's going to be a bomb or some kind of airborne poison, until I force my thoughts to come back to reality. That kind of thinking is what I incurred in the moment I killed Jake.

Aiden is smiling as he pulls the first book out of the box. I lean closer for a better view.

'It's heavy,' he says, holding it with both hands. The bright colours catch the hallway light, making the glossy exterior shine.

'Bring it to the table so Ginny can see it,' I suggest.

He does, but she's more interested in her eggs.

'Your first book,' I say to Aiden, daring to rub his shoulder.

He nods and opens the pages, flicking through to check the quality.

Since Aiden escaped from the bunker, he's taken up painting again. We often paint together. My work is OK, and I love doing it, but I don't possess the talent that Aiden does, and with his 'celebrity' status after the bunker, Aiden found an agent and sold some pieces. Since then, a publisher contacted him, asking if he would like to release a coffee-table book filled with his art. These are the advance copies.

The pages are thick and smooth. The art jumps from the page in swirls and strong geometric shapes. Lots of primary colours mixed with a darker, gloomier aesthetic. They are his interpretations of the bunker. I like to think of the lighter, brighter pieces as interpretations of us, his family. But Aiden never explains his art. He puts it out into the world for others to take whatever meaning they want from it. Somehow feedback, good or bad, doesn't affect him at all.

'I need to tell you something, Mum,' Aiden says, lifting his face from the pages of the book.

'What is it?' My skin cools as unstoppable panic seizes my heart. Those are not words I often hear from my son.

'My agent called yesterday. She wants me to go on a chat show to talk about the book.'

I almost laugh out loud. 'A chat show?'

'Yes,' he says.

You're not chatty, Aiden. I want to reply, but I don't because I don't like to discourage him.

'I want to do it,' he says. 'I think it'll help sell a few copies.'

I take a seat in the chair next to him. 'They'll ask you questions about the bunker.'

'I know,' he says.

'How do you feel about that?'

He shrugs. 'I guess I'll find out when I get there.'

'Is it going to be live?'

'I don't think so. But there'll be a studio audience. They've suggested you do it too.'

The idea of talking about what we went through as a family makes my stomach churn. I'm suddenly filled with energy. I stand up and begin clearing Gina's breakfast plate.

'Egg!' she shouts.

'I don't know,' I reply, creating noise with the plates, scraping eggshell into the bin. 'I'm not sure this is a good idea.'

Out of the corner of my eye I notice Aiden's fingers grip tightly around the hard cover of his book. 'What isn't a good idea? Me moving on with my life?'

'This isn't moving on. It's rehashing the past with an audience there watching.' I stop piling up the breakfast plates and sigh. 'I'm worried . . . I'm concerned that they might take advantage of you. That they'll want you to talk about the bunker rather than promote your book.'

'I can look after myself,' he says. He gives me a defiant look; one I've never seen on his face before. One that takes me aback and makes me realise that I'm not going to win this argument.

But the entire situation fills me with dread. I can't stand the thought of letting the outside world back into our lives after working so hard to shut it out.

'I can do this,' he says.

Maybe he can, but I'm not sure I can.

Chapter Four

AIDEN

We go to my dad's on Sundays for a crowded family dinner. Grandma and Grandad's B&B gets crammed with people: Grandma and Grandad, of course, Dad, who lives with them, and then Mum, Ginny and me. We end up squashed into the living room, loud voices growing louder as everyone tries to be heard over one another. It's so noisy that I usually dread Sunday coming around. But if we don't go, I miss not being there. I don't understand how that works, but maybe I shouldn't second-guess my feelings.

It's taken a while to get Grandma to stop fussing so much, but now she understands that I only want water and a small meal. I'm pretty sure she thinks I'm ill and that I'm about to drop dead at any moment. She checks that Mum is making me wear sun cream and sunglasses in sunny weather, that I do my physiotherapy, that I get enough calcium. Sometimes I see her peering at me through squinty eyes and I think she might be assessing how I look, whether I've put on or lost weight, or have dark circles under my eyes.

It's exhausting, but Mum says that's what love is. The never-ending urge to fix whatever makes a loved-one sad.

I don't think I'm ill, not really, but I have spent a lot of time trying to figure out what I am.

At night, in my comfortable bed, my mind wanders its way to him. To Hugh.

The shadows of the bars fall across his face.

'I brought you books to read,' he says, slipping them through the steel.

They are school textbooks about maths, science, nature.

In the early days, I thought there was a great big search party out there that wouldn't stop until they found me. But after a few years I realised that I was never going to be saved. When I was older than twelve, I began to wonder how Hugh even managed the practicalities of what he was doing. Didn't anyone notice him buying me things? Didn't his wife ever see his bank statements? His receipts? Clothes. Food. Toilet paper. Even the occasional new mattress. Maintenance for the bunker, like new air pumps and generators. Rat traps and electric lamps.

Though I've often tried to explain what it was like to my therapist, Dr Anderton, I don't think she could ever grasp how the strangeness was normal for me. Hugh and I would have mundane conversations with each other. I'd ask about Mum and Dad, what they were up to. What was going on in the village.

'Your mum's getting married,' he said once. 'To a teacher at the secondary school. Jake Hewitt. He's rich, apparently.' He paused, mid-bite of an apple. 'I like him.'

Then, several months later, he dug his phone out of his pocket and brought it closer to me. 'It was the wedding this weekend. A beautiful day. She wore a long white dress. I think it had lace on it. Here, let me show you the photographs.' He swiped his finger across the screen, revealing photograph after photograph of my mother beaming with joy. There was an older man I didn't know by her side. Jake. 'They released balloons in your memory.'

I felt like a ghost then. A white balloon floating up into the sky, weightless. At the time, the idea was comforting, but now it terrifies me. What if, despite the Sunday lunches at Grandma's, I can never tether myself to the real world? I might not be dead like Jake is now, but there's such a thing as being dead inside, and maybe that's the same.

The car journey is fairly quiet because Gina has one of those toy computers for children. Mum buys us the odd expensive item every now and then, like my painting tools and laptop. She'll rarely acknowledge it, but we're basically living off the substantial inheritance from Jake.

Ginny sees me looking at her in the mirror, screws up her nose and pokes out her tongue. Mum pokes out her tongue back and giggles. A half-hearted laugh catches in my throat, but I don't let it out. Even in this car with a happy family, my mind has a tendency to drift to the past.

Was that the worst moment? I don't know.

I think the worst moments come to me in my nightmares, because when they were happening for real, I went to another place.

I should be grateful that I'm free, but the truth is, I don't feel free. And that's because of her pain. I glance across at Mum as she concentrates on the road. It's not that I blame her for her feelings. If I was a father, which I can't ever imagine, and my child was hurt by another person in the way Hugh hurt me, wouldn't I want to shelter them from the world? Palm to my heart, could I say I would be different?

It's something I think about a lot when I'm angry with her. Because there are times when I look at her face and all I can see are the happy photographs with Hugh's pale finger swiping through them. She was happier when I was gone. I think that a lot. Over and over until it hurts. *She was happier when I was gone.* But that isn't true, is it? When I'm alone with Dad he tells me about Jake and how he controlled everything. 'Controlling people are toxic,' he says. But that's kind of confusing, because I think Mum is controlling me a little bit.

I take a deep breath as we pull onto Dad's street. Dad helped us with his testimony at the trial, though Jake's storage unit spoke for itself. Mum was acquitted for the way she fought back against her abusive husband, and my crime was considered self-defence against a kidnapper. We had sympathy on our side. Mum did what she had to do to save her child. But I still remember the blood on her mouth, the wild look in her eyes. Can this person calmly driving this car really be the same person that bit into a man's arm? The world is strange to me. I don't know how to make it feel more familiar when nothing makes sense.

What I know is that the world pities me. I still have messages on my phone from famous people and letters from politicians telling me how inspiring I am.

I'm not even the slightest bit inspirational.

That's why I'm glad I have Faith to talk to. She isn't what Mum calls a 'sycophant', she's someone who listens to me and gives me real advice. She was being honest when she said that I shouldn't always listen to my mum because being a mother doesn't make you right. She encouraged me to get an agent and sell my art. She says I should be out in the world more, and maybe she's right. I spent so much of my life locked away from it.

Dad hovers in the doorway of the B&B when we arrive. Hugh never showed me any photos of Dad when I was away. Seeing my father again was the biggest surprise for me. I'd forgotten his face. Since then he's physically changed again, withering away because he tried to defend us against Jake and was hurt in the process. Faith also tells me not to feel guilty about that, because that's what a father does for a child.

Before I open the car door, I reach inside myself to see if my mind will go to that silent place it sometimes goes. If I notice it before it happens, I can usually stop myself. But today I'm still thinking of the book delivery and the promise of a future. My stomach flutters with anxious energy, but there's no darkness building up.

'Hiya, mate.'

Rather than hug me, Dad holds up a hand and we high-five. I'm twenty now and I know this game has gone on too long, but it's better than being pressed up against someone, even my dad.

'You OK?' he asks.

'Yeah.'

'Good, good,' he says, still standing there awkwardly. 'How about you, Em?'

Mum forces a tight smile. She's been making that expression a lot since I told her about the chat show.

'Bob!' Gina cries, pointing.

'Hello, Ginny-minny-skinny-bombinny.'

She slaps him on the leg. 'No, Bob. It's Gee-naa.'

All right, I'll admit it, she makes me laugh. Dad grins.

Mum stands proudly behind her daughter. 'You know how to say Rob, Ginny.'

'Oh, I know she does,' Dad replies. 'Come in. Mum's just put the Yorkshires in.'

'I'm going to eat all the puddings,' Gina announces to no one.

Mum gets her settled on the sofa with her toy computer while I sit awkwardly in the armchair and check my Instagram DMs to see if Faith has been in touch today. She sent me a smiley face this morning.

The room is bright, with the late-summer sun filtering through the windows. All of them are open but there's little breeze and the stifling air makes me think about the bunker. Though I don't want to, I imagine the naked lightbulb that would attract moths and throw shadows up the concrete walls.

Gina needs help with one of her games, and I force myself to be patient and talk her through the buttons she needs to press. Computers have been tricky to learn, but I'm getting the hang of them now and even have my own Instagram account for my art, something that bugs Mum.

The adults – I still think of myself as a child, I can't help it – stand around making small talk and setting the table. Grandad picks Gina up and gives her aeroplane rides around the living room for a little while. It's happy family time.

'Are you coming to the table, Aiden?' Mum asks.

I hadn't noticed myself slip away. By the time I come back, Grandma's carrying dishes of veg to the table.

Mum's features are all bunched up, so I know she's worrying about me. I make sure I get up quickly and hurry to the table at the back of the living room. It sits next to a bay window that gives us a view of the garden. My world is so vast now.

'Mum says your book is ready.' Dad starts the conversation as usual. He's good at this. 'You got the proofs, didn't you?'

'We brought a copy, but I left it in the car,' Mum says. 'I'll go and get it.'

'Oh, lovely.' Grandma clasps her hands together. 'Peter, have you got your glasses?'

'Yes, all ready.'

Mum shuffles her way around the table and leaves. I feel all of the eyeballs directed at me.

'My agent wants me to go on a chat show,' I blurt out, and then regret it.

The table is silent for a moment. My body drinks it in, craving silence. Until I realise there are faces staring at me. This isn't a *good* silence, it's a *bad* silence.

Dad speaks first. 'Is that a good idea, mate? It's a lot of pressure.'

'It's a wonderful opportunity to sell your book,' Grandad says carefully. 'But these people are more interested in selling themselves. They'll ask you all sorts of things.'

I hear the sound of the door opening and closing. Mum is returning.

'I want to do it,' I say.

'Well,' Grandma says. 'If he wants to do it . . .'

'Mum.' Dad raises his eyebrows at her. He's lowered his voice, signalling that this isn't meant for my ears. 'He can't seriously —'

'Can't seriously what?' Mum asks, slightly out of breath from hurrying back from the car.

'They agree with you,' I say. 'That I shouldn't do the interview.'

'Oh,' she says.

Dad lets out a low sigh. 'You're an adult now, Aiden. All we can do is give you our advice.'

'OK,' I say. 'And that advice is don't do it. I understand.'

There's another silence.

The rest of the meal continues on without much more discussion on the subject. Mum passes the art book around and everyone makes pleasant noises about it. Grandma even begins to cry. *I never thought he'd have this*, she says into Grandad's handkerchief.

Mum, Dad and Grandma clear the plates away while I play with Gina in the living room. Her imagination fuels my art. Today I'm a monkey and she's a fairy and we live on the moon. She shouts at me because I can't do the monkey right, delegating the role to Grandad instead.

As Grandad pretends to live in a crater on the moon, I slip out to use the bathroom. I don't like to announce my comings and goings. I don't like to be watched when I need to leave.

It's on the way up the stairs that I hear the sound of voices carrying from the kitchen. Someone has left the door open, and even though they speak in hushed tones, I can hear them.

'I'm not saying we should be together. But I miss you,' Dad says. 'I miss all of you. I know Gina isn't mine, but . . . well, I think of her as related to me, you know, like a daughter.'

When Mum speaks, I imagine her expression, her eyes wide and glossy. Mouth pulled down with emotion. 'It's too complicated. The way I feel about this village . . . is . . . I just don't think I could live here.'

'And I need to be here,' Rob says. 'Because I need the help my parents can give.'

'I know.' I imagine Mum placing a hand on his arm. 'I wish things were different. You know how grateful I am for what you did to help. I'm sorry, for what it's worth. I married a weak man. If I hadn't married Jake, you'd be walking without a cane. I –'

'Emma, don't. It's not your fault.'

I hear the catch in Mum's throat. She's crying again.

'I mean it. You didn't do anything wrong.'

I go up the stairs to the bathroom so that I can't hear her crying anymore. When the bathroom door is closed, I take my phone out of my pocket and type a message.

ME: Mum's crying again.

FAITH: It's not your fault.

ME: Wish I could change it tho.

FAITH: If she was a good mother, she'd pull herself together.

ME: She doesn't want Gina to go to school, or me to go on the chat show.

FAITH: That's not OK. She has to let you both be your own people.

FAITH: I think you're so awesome. I just wish she'd let you be you.

ME: Me too.

Chapter Five

EMMA

I tell myself over and over again that this is what he wants. This is his choice. I can't make it for him. Aiden is twenty years old and he has a right to be able to make his own decisions.

But I can't deny the heaviness in the pit of my stomach, and the quick patter of my heart within my chest. I clench and unclench my hands, desperate to scratch the worn patch of skin I ruined when Aiden first came back from the bunker.

The three of us – me, Aiden, Gina – arrive at the studio at an ungodly 6 a.m. because this gives everyone time to have make-up applied, hair styled; to be fixed up and made perfect. We need to look like polished versions of ourselves in order to seem real to the viewers. Every flaw is magnified when you're inside a television. Every deviation from the norm is seen as an indication that something isn't quite right about you. I never noticed this kind of thinking until I was thrust into the public eye.

I'm dressed in a grey suit with a cream blouse. Aiden has on smart trousers and a light-blue shirt. Gina is in her usual leggings and T-shirt. She has Walnut in her hands. I'm pretty sure she smeared crayon on my blouse this morning. Maybe it'll be one of those flaws discussed in a Twitter thread afterwards.

Whether I'll join the interview hasn't been decided, by me anyway. As long as I'm sitting on a chair in front of the cameras, I'm not by Gina's side, which is difficult for me.

As soon as we arrive, a smiley assistant called Becky buzzes around us, directing us where to go. We're bundled into a room and sat down in front of a mirror as a make-up lady applies powder to my face.

'Mummy doesn't like make-up,' Gina says, unhelpfully.

'That's not true,' I mumble, letting out an anxious laugh.

'She says she can't be arsed.'

The room erupts with laughter and one of the women, Claire, says to me, 'I can't believe what you've all gone through. To fight off that man while you were pregnant?' She shakes her head and bites her lip. 'You're a warrior.'

'Any other mother would do the same thing.' It's my standard response, but I mean it. I believe they would.

But Claire shakes her head. 'We all think we would. We hope we would, anyway. But I'm not sure if it's true. Anyway, we think you're amazing.'

Even as she says it, I cast my mind back to the microphones shoved in my face. The headlines that decided I was a bad mother. The public comments that criticised me for being too stupid for not seeing through the façades of evil men.

'Thank you,' I say, trying my best to smile. 'It means a lot to hear that.' I glance over at the make-up assistants preparing Aiden. 'Oh, Aiden doesn't like to be touched.'

'I'm fine, Mum,' he says.

'We think you're amazing too,' she says to my boy. 'You're both warriors.'

A few hours later, the audience begins to filter into the studio while we stand together at the back. I can see that the set has two chairs facing one chair. The single chair is for Stacey, the host, and the other two are for me and Aiden. I haven't actually told them I'll be doing the interview, but I suppose they've decided I am.

'Here are the questions,' Becky says, giving me a wad of cardboard rectangles.

'Thank you.' I take the questions and have a quick scan through.

'Can I look?' Aiden holds out his hand.

'Of course you can.' I pass them over, a little hurt that he thought I might not let him.

The questions are actually fairly tame. There are, of course, a few about how he is coping after being incarcerated and how he deals with the trauma of it all. There are some about me and how I support him, that kind of thing. What I don't want is for them to ask him about the sexual abuse or the escape. I don't want him to have to relieve those moments.

And I'm afraid they'll slip that in without warning.

At least this isn't a live broadcast.

'It's hot in here, Mummy,' Gina says, squirming under my grip. She's tired and fed up of hanging around on the set.

'I could take you to the canteen if you like,' Becky suggests.

'She's better off with me,' I reply. 'I think she might run rings around you!' I try to keep it light, but I'm secretly terrified of the thought of her being out of sight.

'I want to goooo,' Gina protests.

'Later, OK? Be a good girl for Denny.'

'Oh, she's adorable.' Becky gazes longingly. 'I can't wait to have kids.'

I would normally jump at the opportunity to talk about my children, but the audience is in place and Stacey is on set. My heart won't calm down.

'How are you feeling?' I scan Aiden's face, checking for signs of tension. Is he paler than usual or is it the lights? Is that sweat because he's afraid? Or is it the heat? His hands aren't balled into fists. The light layer of make-up covers his dark circles. It's hard to tell what he's thinking at the best of times but now I have no clue.

'I'm OK, Mum.'

I long for more than three words, but it's the best I'm going to get.

'So, no pressure or anything,' Becky says. 'But it would be incredible to have you both in the interview. And, honestly, it might make you both feel a lot less nervous. Andy, the director, asked me to have a chat and see if you feel comfortable with it. I'll take care of Gina and I'm great with kids. If you like, we'll stay right behind the camera so you can see us.'

My eyes are still fixed on my son. If I don't agree to this, he'll be out there alone. He'll be facing those questions by himself. But if I go with him, I can protect him.

'It'd be great if you could keep Gina where I can see her.'

'Absolutely.'

And with that, Becky leads the way. The director shakes Aiden's hand and talks very fast at us. Stacey hugs me and crouches to Gina's height to make her laugh before gushing at Aiden's bravery. She flicks through a copy of his art book, tells us how everything will happen, and all the while I can't take anything in. My hair is curled and perfect, but I keep touching it and a stylist has to brush it again. I'm told to stop touching it. Stacey has clips in her hair that are taken out and another spritz of hairspray goes on.

I stand as close to Aiden as I dare, hearing the sound of his heavy breathing.

'You don't have to do this,' I remind him. 'It's only a TV show. If you want to leave, we can.'

'I'm fine, Mum.'

'You control this,' I remind him. 'You tell them to stop at any moment. Look at me, Aiden. Listen to me.'

He turns.

'You control this. You can stop it.'

He nods his head, slowly.

I want more from him, but at least I know he's listening.

I take a deep breath for myself and we step out on the stage. There's a swell of applause for us both, and out of the corner of my eye, I see Gina placing both hands over her ears, tears in her eyes. *Make this be over.*

31

'What an incredibly warm welcome for my guests today,' Stacey says, a glossy mouth moving in exaggerated motions. It feels as though her bright white teeth are constantly showing, even when she isn't speaking. It reminds me of Amy Perry when she appeared on television, soaking up her fifteen minutes of fame, her teeth bleached, her hair highlighted. 'Aiden and Emma Price, I don't even know where to start. You're both so strong and inspirational. The pain you've suffered. I mean, for you Emma, you thought that Aiden had died. You grieved for him. You even registered his death. What was it like when he came back?'

The lights are hot on my face and the chair is hard against my back. I don't know what to do with my legs, whether to cross or uncross. My heart beats so loudly that I barely hear her question.

'It didn't feel real at first,' I manage to force out of my lips. 'I didn't want to get my hopes up. I thought they'd made some sort of mistake, matched the wrong set of DNA or something. And then I walked into the room and I saw him and knew that he was my son.'

'It was that instantaneous?' she asks, raising her eyebrows in faux shock.

'Yes.'

'Mummy!' Gina's voice cuts through the brief gap in conversation. The audience laughs and awws.

'Oh, that's your adorable daughter right there,' Stacey, the ultimate pro, waves towards Gina. 'Born the night Aiden took you to the bunker.'

'That's right —'

'Mummy, I'm hungry!'

The audience laughs again but it's getting awkward now. 'We won't be long, Ginny.'

'I'll take her to the canteen,' Becky says.

This time, even though I hate it, I agree, and Gina happily places her hand in Becky's. They toddle off together, the dragon toy tucked into her armpit, and I find myself forced back to Stacey and her questions.

'Talking about resilience,' Stacey says, jumping straight

back in, 'Aiden, you've managed to turn your horrifying experience into a positive one through art. Tell me a bit about how you've managed to do that.'

Aiden swallows and his body tenses. It always takes him a moment to speak.

'My art is . . . a . . . personal experience,' he says, tripping over his words. His teeth gritted. 'It's my way of expressing . . .' He lifts his hands as though trying to find the words. 'Everything.'

Stacey nods along. 'Do you think that's the result of you losing your voice after your escape?'

'Yes,' he replies.

'What was it like for you, Emma, when Aiden couldn't speak to you?'

'I just wanted to hear his voice. More than anything, I wanted him to tell me what he was thinking.'

'It was a hard time for you?' she prompts.

'Yes, it was. But I was still so happy to have him home.'

Stacey opens her arms in a manner that reminds me of Oprah. 'It was a miracle.' The word draws a murmur from the audience. 'But it was still emotionally tough for you. You were married to a controlling man, heavily pregnant with your second child –'

A high-pitched wail cuts Stacey's question. Her animated expression freezes and she turns to her director. 'What's going on, Andy?'

'It's the fire alarm,' he says.

I don't often grab Aiden, but I do then, taking his hand in mine and holding it tight. There are a few moments of uncertainty. Aiden's brow furrows as he gazes out towards the audience. They too seem unsure about what they should do, turning their bodies towards the exit, waiting for the instruction to leave. Behind the camera, people rush around speaking into their headsets. Stacey smiles tightly.

'I'll see if I can find out what's going on,' she says. Her skirt ripples as she stands up and heads over to one of the producers.

Eventually someone announces. 'There's smoke. It's a real fire.'

I pull Aiden up from his chair. 'We need to find Gina.'

Chapter Six

EMMA

The audience moves at a maddeningly slow pace, politely following the orders from the crew. I decided not to be polite, instead pushing my way through the crowd, keeping Aiden in my grasp. If there's anything worse for him than being touched, it's being in a crowded space with bodies pressed up against him. The best thing I can do is get him out of there as quickly as possible.

Once we're off the set and into a corridor, I see the smoke for myself. There isn't much of it, but the sight still makes me catch my breath. There's a real fire here and one of my children is out of sight. Is there anything more terrifying?

I grab one of the make-up artists as she hurries down the corridor. 'Which way to the canteen?'

'It's in the opposite direction to the fire exit,' she says.

'I need to find my daughter.'

'It's down the hall and on the right. You can't miss the double doors.'

I quickly nod my thanks and hurry through the steady stream of people. Not everyone is as polite as the studio audience; there are many panicked crew members with walkie-talkies or headsets, either rushing up and down the corridor or shepherding people towards the exit.

Before we reach the double doors, Becky rushes up to me. The first thing I see is the dragon toy in her hands.

'Where's Gina?'

The sight of that toy in her hands is an ice-cold spear to my heart. *Where is Gina?*

'I'm so sorry.' Becky hands me Walnut. Her face is pale, eyes rimmed red.

I've seen this expression before. I remember it well from the day of the flood. The headteacher of Aiden's school had stood in the entrance of the building waiting for me to arrive just so that she could break the bad news to me.

'You lost her,' I say. There's a rushing sound in my ears, like fast-flowing water. My legs turn to jelly and as a light-headed sensation takes over me, I think I might faint. With one sharp pinch of my thigh I bring myself back, forcing myself to concentrate.

'I turned away for a second and she slipped away from me. It was just a second . . . I . . . I'll help you find her.'

We start to move.

'Where did you last see her?' I ask.

'We went to the canteen and I bought her a cookie. We stopped and ate it, but she needed the toilet, so we came back out. Gina was right next to me. I swear it. But I bumped into someone I knew. I stopped, talked to my friend. Gina was right behind me. And then . . .' Becky stops. 'We were right here. When I turned around, Gina was gone.'

Aiden nods to the door next to the place where Becky says she last saw Gina. 'There are some stairs here.' The door is already open, with people filing out towards the fire exit.

'Have you been down the stairs?' I ask.

Becky nods. 'I went down to the next floor, but the fire alarm went off and everyone started coming out. I decided to come back here to tell you. I did find the dragon, though. On the stairs.'

I want to scream. I want to throw this girl and her headset down the stairs. I shove past her and hurry to the stairwell.

36

'Ginny! Ginny!'

The stairs clang and complain from the sheer amount of people clamouring to get out. The crowd of panicked people makes me want to scream in frustration, but I squeeze my way through them, determined to find my daughter. She could be trampled underfoot by this mob. Images of her broken body rush through my mind. A snapped leg. A broken arm. Or worse.

'Gina!'

Off the stairs now, I run through the corridor on the next floor down, opening doors, scanning rooms, screaming her name until my throat is raw. In the panic I can't even see Aiden. Did he stay on the floor above?

'Mum!' It's his voice. He's here.

I spin on my heel to face my son. 'Have you found her?'

He shakes his head. 'She might've gone outside with everyone else.'

But I don't think she would. I think she'd get scared and hide somewhere. This is a huge building and the alarm was loud. Any four-year-old would run and hide in a safe place. An empty room, a cupboard, a toilet.

'Let's try the next floor down.'

He nods.

I haven't seen any smoke since we came off set, which gives me hope that the fire wasn't serious. If the building was ablaze, she could die of smoke inhalation, but we know she isn't on the floor with the smoke.

'Where did Becky go?' I ask as we move through the corridor.

'I don't know, I just left her there,' he says.

'I never should have let her take her out of the room,' I say. 'We never should have come.'

'We'll find her,' Aiden says.

Our search isn't systematic, it's frantic, but I can't control myself. I can't stop my thoughts from drifting to the past. The rushing sound of the blood in my ears is the gushing of the Ouse. Becky is Amy, a woman willing to give my child away.

There could be some other dark presence waiting to hurt my child. Anything could happen to her.

Soon firefighters begin to filter into the building. One catches me on the elbow and tells me to leave via the fire exit.

'My four-year-old daughter is missing.' I blurt out her description and he nods, listening attentively.

'Don't worry, she can't have gone far,' he says. 'We'll be working through the entire buildings so we'll find her, you can be sure about that.'

'Her name is Gina, but she goes by Ginny too, OK?' I almost hand over Walnut the Dragon as a promise for him to bring me my child. But I don't, because he might need both hands to carry her.

'She's going to be just fine. The fire was started by a cigarette in a toilet bin, completely extinguished and harmless now. There was barely any damage and she won't have been hurt.' He pats me on the arm, but it's no comfort to me.

When I emerge from the building with Aiden, a silent car park of blank faces watches us. Many from the studio audience. Are some of them Aiden's strange fans?

I begin appealing to the crowd, asking as many people as I can if they saw her wander off on her own. No one saw her.

'Actually, I saw a woman carrying a girl about four years old out of the building.' The man was young, no more than thirty, in a shirt and jeans. 'I saw her from my office window. It was just after the alarm went off.'

My world narrows. 'A woman? What did she look like?'

'I'm not sure, I didn't see her face. But she had red hair. Slim build. About your height.'

'The girl she was carrying, did she seem upset?'

'It was too far away to see,' he says.

I pull up a photograph of Gina, my hands shaking. 'Was it her?'

'Maybe,' he says. 'Look, I only caught a glimpse so I can't be completely sure, but the girl in the picture had the same hair colour if that helps.'

'Which way did she go?' I ask.

The man points away from the car park, towards the main road.

'I'll go, Mum,' Aiden says. 'Wait here and see what the firefighters say.'

The hot, mid-morning air forms a clot around me. Every inch of my skin burns and my heart pounds. Am I drowning? Is this drowning? Pulled into the boiling, syrupy air?

'Maybe you should sit down for a minute.' A pair of hands lead me to a bench.

I bend my knees automatically, like a wooden mannequin guided into position.

'Someone has taken her,' I whisper, more to myself than anyone else.

A voice, calm, female, says, 'You don't know that yet. Try to breathe.'

'I can't breathe until they're back,' I say quietly. 'Both of them.'

When I close my eyes, I see the gushing river. I see the red coat fished out by a long pole, and the image of my son, six years old, bloated and pale. I see the nightmares I had after Aiden went missing, tendrils of dark hair pooling around a pale face, me in the water, being pulled deeper and deeper down into the depths. I see darkness.

Sweat drips from my nose and the kind woman peels away my suit jacket.

'There's crayon on my blouse,' I say, my words slurring slightly.

'That's all right,' she says. 'Deep breaths now.'

I'm having a panic attack, I realise. My daughter is missing, and I need to find her, but instead of doing something useful about it, I'm having a panic attack.

'Has anyone got a bottle of water?'

No, I think. I don't want the water. It reminds me of the river.

Hands dragging my son out from the current. Holding him close. Taking him to a car.

And then . . .

Amy.

Of course.

The red-haired woman must be Amy Perry, the school-teacher who gave my son to a monster. The woman who hates me with every ion of her being. She will have dyed her hair, kept her face away from the security cameras in the building. Did she set off the fire alarm to cause enough chaos to snatch a child?

The firefighter makes his way over to the bench, no tiny girl running along next to him, or carried in his arms.

'We checked every room, Ms Price. We've called the police for you.'

No, she won't be in the building.

I stand up and walk a few steps.

'Emma. Ms Price. Maybe you shouldn't . . .' the kind woman says.

I left it too long to chase her and now she'll be gone. What a fool I was to leave Amy alive. I killed for my family, for my own survival, but I left one threat alive, thinking she was too weak and pathetic to come after us. I remember her trembling beneath the knife I held to her throat, the high pitch of her voice when she confessed her part in Aiden's kidnapping.

I take my phone out of my bag and scroll through my contacts.

Stevenson answers after three rings.

'What can I do for you, Emma?'

'My daughter is missing. Someone took her.'

'What?'

'I'm at the Studioworks in White City. I . . . I'm in London. Amy Perry took my daughter.'

'Amy Perry? Hold on, Emma. What's going on? You're in London?'

'You need to come. Help me find her. You owe me this.'

'OK. I will. Have you called the police there?'

'Yes.'

'I'm on my way, Emma. Give me a few hours.'

As I'm hanging up, Aiden is walking towards me, his shirt drenched in sweat and clinging to his torso. He's been running all this time, and my boy has a weak body. He doesn't have the sunglasses he needs for a bright day like today. He should have them. Did I forget to pack them? He leans forward and puts his hands on his knees, body convulsing with breathlessness.

He's alone.

Chapter Seven

EMMA

The sunlight through the blinds casts stripes against the walls. On the desk are a number of stacked documents. The door is open and people come in and out. I feel eyes on me at all times, recording my reactions.

I'm in a building full of reporters and TV personalities. All of them want to see me react to this *big news*. An alert from the BBC app has already gone to thousands, if not millions, of phones with details about the investigation. A description of the red-haired woman carrying my daughter away. Mine and Aiden's names along with our background as the boy from the bunker and his mother. It happened at eleven am at BBC Studioworks, it says, a place and time I'll never forget. It sinks down deep, the realisation. My daughter is missing.

The local police are canvassing the area. Someone is pulling the security footage from the building. I'm being force-fed water and tea. Aiden paces the room. I tell them not to shut the door, he doesn't like it. Every now and then, I realise I'm either wringing or scratching my hands.

The kind woman from the car park turned out to be a

producer at the studio and has lent us her office to sit in while the search goes on. Now that the building has been cleared, many of the workers, and the studio audience from the show, are combing the surrounding area, calling Gina's name. At the same time, police are questioning everyone.

'We'll find her, Ms Price,' everyone says to me, or variations of that statement.

She can't have gone far.

We can follow the CCTV footage.

Everyone in London is looking for her.

But I know how this goes. The bad person takes my child. The bad person hurts my child.

When DCI Stevenson arrives, I realise that Gina has been missing for over four hours.

'It's all right, Emma,' he says. 'Stay as calm as you can, I know it's hard.'

'I should be looking for her,' I say.

'You're doing the right thing by letting the police work,' he says, but I don't agree. 'I'm going to go and liaise with them now. They might not let me help, because this is beyond my jurisdiction, so there may be a limit on how much I can do.'

I nod. I've already spoken to the detective at the Metropolitan Police Service and she has organised the search so far.

'I should go back out there,' Aiden says.

'No, I want you with me.' I reach out and take his hand. Squeeze it.

When Stevenson leaves, Aiden turns to me, his eyes slightly narrowed.

'You know who took her, don't you?' he says.

'I think it was your old primary school teacher. Amy. She was involved in your abduction but there wasn't enough evidence to convict her. I was stupid. I decided to handle it my own way and now I think she's getting revenge on me.'

'Hugh talked about Amy sometimes,' Aiden says. 'But I never saw her in the bunker.'

I cast my mind back to my final conversation with Amy,

the one where I told her to get out of the village. *I came into the bunker and watched him sleep.* Her words send a shiver down my spine. I had her life in my hands, and I allowed that repulsive human being to live.

I think back. Two weeks after I'd threatened her, I drove past Amy's house and saw her car gone, the curtains closed. I'd even asked a neighbour, who said they thought she was on holiday. They said she'd quit her job as a teacher and gone on some long vacation. It'd seemed like enough at the time, because I didn't expect her to come back. Later I learned I was wrong. We were in the process of searching for a new place to live and left for Manchester not long after. I'd kept what I did to her a secret because I knew I'd broken the law, but also because I'd been convinced that my threats had worked. That Amy Perry was gone for good.

She wasn't. One day, it came up in casual conversation with Sonya that Amy had been living at her house in Singer Lane the entire time and I'd had no idea. The spineless cow had pretended to move on when she'd actually sneaked back into the village as soon as my back was turned.

But by this point I'd been living in Manchester for three years with my family and I'd begun to move on. My once murderous rage had fizzled down to a low roar. All I did when I heard the news was park my car outside her house and look at her through the window. She'd seen me all right.

Six months ago, I heard through the Bishoptown grapevine, via Rob's family, that she'd moved on for good this time. It'd seemed like a victory then, but it wasn't.

Now I wondered. What if I'd done more? What if I'd handled it better?

I think back to that moment in her house when I'd drawn blood with my knife. What else had she said to me that day? That she'd admired Hugh's twisted desires? What kind of a woman says that? And if what she said was true, what does she have planned for my daughter?

I pull Aiden closer to me and he doesn't resist or squirm for a change. His expression has a resolve to it that I've never seen before. 'Anything you can remember about her could be important.'

Aiden sits down in the chair next to mine and our hands break apart. 'I don't always remember. I went away when I was in there, sometimes when he was talking.'

'This is for Gina,' I remind him, not that I need to.

His dark eyelashes rest along the delicate skin beneath his eyes. He nods his head.

'Hi Ms Price.' The detective for the Metropolitan Police Service walks into the room. A woman in her forties with thick curly hair to her shoulders, introduced to me as DI Khatri. 'I wanted to talk more about Amy Perry. I know you mentioned that you believe she may have abducted your daughter.'

'That's right,' I reply. 'She was involved with Hugh Barratt who kidnapped my son, as you know.'

'We'd like you to review some CCTV footage if you can. Perhaps you can identify Amy from the video.'

I rub my sweaty palms along my trousers as we sit waiting for the footage to move to the appropriate section. Aiden and I are sat closest to the screen, leaning over it. Stevenson stands behind me; DI Khatri to our right.

'This is the clearest image we can find of the red-haired woman,' Khatri says.

The video continues for another few seconds before a woman comes into view and my heart begins to race. *Gina.* I can't help it, my attention goes straight to my little daughter, and I almost forget to look at the woman. DI Khatri pauses the image so that I can take my time. It's a good thing she does.

'That's definitely Gina,' I say, and Aiden nods in agreement.

The woman, though. She has her head down, with hair covering her face. Most of her body is obscured by Gina, who she's holding against her hip. Gina's chin rests on the woman's shoulder. I don't see any discomfort in Gina's posture, but then Amy used to be a primary school teacher and she's good at putting children at ease. My stomach flips at the thought of Amy being around so many young children. *A wolf in sheep's clothing.*

I allow my eyes to examine every part of the image, from the long hair, to the body, to the hips and legs. I think about how Amy held herself, how she moved.

'Can you press play?' I ask.

I watch Amy walk along the lobby. I watch her walk out of the building in plain sight.

All the time I try to remember her gait, the angle of her shoulders, the way she moved when I knew her. Did Amy slouch? Did she stoop? None of that is obvious with her carrying Gina.

'I can't tell,' I say eventually, letting out a long sigh. 'Without seeing her face it's hard to know. Gina covers most of her body. What about you, Aiden?'

'I can't say for sure,' he replies.

'We have more footage of her,' Khatri says.

The security guard leans over my shoulder and brings up a different recording. This time the woman is alone. She's walking through the lobby of the building with her head down again. I notice that she's tucked herself behind a group of people, probably pretending to be with them, when she hands over a ticket to the guard. Even during this process, she keeps her head turned in a different direction, as though distracted. What she's really doing is making sure the cameras don't manage to record a good shot of her face.

I scrutinise every part of her. It certainly could be Amy. She's the right height. Her build is slimmer than I remember, but then she could have lost weight. I see now that there's a heavy fringe over her face. She's dressed in jeans and a plain top, nothing easily identified, and she carries a medium sized bag, large enough for a change of clothes.

'It could be her, but I can't say for sure. She's the right height, but Amy had mousy hair with blonde highlights, not red. She was always a little dumpy, but she could have lost weight. She could have dyed her hair, too.'

'We believe this woman started the fire,' Khatri says. 'We have footage of her coming out of the ladies' toilet a few minutes before the fire alarm went off. We think her plan was to wait until there was enough chaos to snatch Gina, but it just so happened that she was able to do it while Becky was distracted, a few moments before the alarm went off. That gave her a better head start and is making our job harder. But rest assured, Ms Price, we're scouring the area. She's going to show up on more CCTV. This is London.'

'What was the ticket for?' I ask.

'She was a member of the studio audience for your interview,' Khatri says in a matter of fact voice.

Next to me, I'm aware of Aiden lowering his face into his hands. Amy planned all of this. She saw the announcement that Aiden and I would be giving an interview, she applied for the ticket, she turned up and she took my child.

'Then you can trace her ticket? Find out if it's her?'

'There's no Amy Perry in the records. If it is her, she used false contact details to download the ticket. We're looking into it right now.'

'What else are you doing?' I ask.

'We're going to check Ms Perry's house in Bishoptown-on-Ouse and we're gathering as many witnesses as we can.'

'As far as I know she moved out of that house about six months ago, but I don't know where she went.'

'Well, we'll look into it. We may also ask you to do a press conference if it's needed.'

If it's needed means if Gina doesn't turn up today. She could spend tonight somewhere cold and dark with a woman she doesn't know. Frightened and alone.

'Do it all, DI Khatri,' I say. 'Do everything in your power and then do more.'

She nods.

'I mean it. Because I'll do everything in my power too.'

A flicker crosses her face. I'm not sure if it's doubt, or fear.

Chapter Eight

AIDEN

Stay strong.
> *We're thinking of you.*
> *She'll be found.*
> *Your family is cursed.*
> *You probably deserve this.*

Staring at the comments on my Instagram posts turns the words into strange poems. Soon they imprint on my mind. *Your family is cursed. We're thinking of you. Your family is cursed. Stay strong. You probably deserve this.*

I move into my direct messages.

FAITH: I'm so sorry.
> FAITH: My heart is broken.
> ME: It's all my fault. I should've listened to Mum.
> FAITH: Why would you say that?
> ME: The kidnapper was in the audience.
> ME: It's because of my interview. I pushed for this. It's all my fault.
> FAITH: You are a wondrous human being. No one has

more light in them than you. It's not your fault and it never could be.

ME: I wish I could believe that.

I put my phone away as the police move us from the studios to a Holiday Inn about a five-minute drive away from the area. We check into the same room. Mum puts on the TV and we watch the news. There are a few words about Gina scrolling along the bottom of the screen. That's it.

The newspapers will tell a different story. Mum has been asked to provide photographs of Gina to help the investigation, and I know which ones she's chosen. Gina in the park, sat at the top of the slide, her hair in two pigtails. Wide smile. The papers will print them in colour because those pictures will break people's hearts. She has Jake's eyes, and they're bright with happiness.

I lie down on the bed and stare up at the ceiling. I never tell Mum this, but I remember the coldness of the water on my skin after Jake pushed me into the river. I remember swallowing it, and my lungs burning. I remember being grateful for the hands that pulled me out and feeling that I was finally safe.

How long did that feeling of safety last for me?

How long will it last for Gina?

'I'm taking you to your mummy.' I can imagine the kidnapper saying that. Then she lifts Gina into the air and places her on her hip. *Shall we find her together?*

Gina loves people. No matter how hard Mum fights to keep Gina just for us, she loves nothing more than to be doted on. Was I like that? I remember snippets of my time before the bunker. Blurry faces. Bright paint. Lots and lots of smiles. So much attention from everyone.

Sometimes Mum gets the photo albums out and we flick through them to see me as a child. I'm like Gina, grinning, climbing, running.

The bunker took it all away.

I can't stop thinking about what could be happening to

her. It's late now and I know that Gina is going to spend the night with a stranger in a strange place.

Mum shuts the curtains against the dark, and any photographers with a long lens who might want to take our picture. We have to protect ourselves as much as we have to protect Gina. You can't leave the door open at a hotel.

'Aiden,' she says. 'Do you think it's Amy, too? Do you think Amy took Gina?'

I look at her, at the panic in her eyes, and the way she wrings her hands. 'I do if you do. I never really knew Amy.'

She paces the room. 'I keep thinking about the trial and the investigation after you came home. Remember how much they asked you about whether Hugh mentioned other children? About whether Hugh might have wanted to or was planning to kidnap more children?'

My spine straightens. 'I remember.'

'What if he did? And what if Amy is following some old plan of his?'

I shake my head. 'I don't know.'

She chews on a thumbnail and mumbles to herself. 'I can't stop thinking about it.'

This room is around the same size as the bunker. How many steps was it? Ten? Twenty? Perhaps twenty when I was younger and ten as I grew older. The details are already beginning to slip away.

My life is in two halves now. The ten years outside of the bunker. The ten years inside.

Another reference to Gina scrolls along the bottom of the screen. *Four-year-old Gina Price is missing in the White City area of Hammersmith, London. She is the younger sister of Aiden Price, the boy from the bunker.*

That was the title of the book they wanted either me or Mum to write. *The Boy from the Bunker.* Or *The Boy from the Woods.* Both snappy titles.

I don't want Gina's life to be a book title. But if it is, it's all my fault.

The comments keep popping up on my posts and in my direct messages. Nearly all of these people are complete strangers, aside from Faith. There are a few fans I recognise, too. Regular commenters. Since I decided to start a more public persona, I've had to accept that there are people out there wanting to follow everything I do. But there are some that comment so often that I frequently wonder whether to delete my profile altogether. But then I wouldn't be able to contact Faith, and I'd miss her. When I think about it, I know so little about her. I don't know what she looks like, because her profile picture is a black circle. I don't know her last name, because she's never told me. But what she *has* told me is that she knows how I feel, she hears what I have to say and she supports what I decide to do.

Faith and I first bonded over art and photography. She used to comment on my pictures, and I enjoyed her strange, modern style of photographing creepy old buildings with creepy abandoned dolls. Then one day she sent me a private message and our conversations started.

I glance over at the second bed where Mum is on the phone to Dad. He's offering to help, but not able to do anything and she's losing her patience with him. She's completely distracted while I read through my messages.

FAITH: Aiden my heart is breaking.
    FAITH: Your precious sister. Let me help you. Please.
    FAITH: I can be a shoulder for you to cry on.
    ME: I'd like that.

A love poem.

51

Chapter Nine

EMMA

I take every single newspaper and lay them all out over the hotel bed. Each and every one of them has a picture of my girl on the front page. There she is, smiling, hair in pigtails, dressed in a top with little pictures of cats all over it. I gave a selection to the police, choosing a variety from different angles, hoping that it might help the general public find her. But one constant is her smile. Every parent thinks their child is a treasure, but I know it of her. She's special. Right now, this is as close as I can be to my daughter without her being here.

With each newspaper, it surprises me who they've found to interview. Many chose to gather quotes from eyewitnesses at the scene, others called 'friends' in Bishoptown. But they aren't real friends. Most aren't even people I talk to. One plucky reporter managed to get a quote out of Sonya. *Our hearts break for Emma.*

Her words are no comfort, they merely remind me that I'm almost completely alone in this. Gina doesn't have a father or any grandparents, unless you count Sonya and Peter,

Rob's parents. I don't, though, because although they're supportive, they aren't related to her. She has me and she has Aiden, and that's all.

And who do I have? Perhaps, before Gina's kidnapping, it could be true to say that I began to pull away from Rob. Our relationship is a complex one built on rocky foundations. First love remains alluring no matter what, but that doesn't negate the pain we went through when we thought Aiden had died, and the way it pushed us apart. Part of me wants to open my heart and let him in, which is something I know he wants, but I've never quite got there. But where does it leave me? Alone.

I haven't slept, and I'm sure that's obvious to Stevenson when he turns up with coffees and pastries.

'You need to eat something,' he says, using a tone of voice that I imagine he uses on the young offenders, the ones that need to grow up and get out of crime.

Or maybe it's because he's a dad.

I take a croissant and bite the end, brushing crumbs away from the newspapers. I can't bear the thought of the pastry crumbs and coffee rings that will inevitably spread across pictures of my child all around the country.

'This is Tina,' Stevenson says, gesturing to a slim, blonde woman hovering in the doorway. 'She's your family liaison officer. Come in, Tina.'

'I brought you a few things,' Tina says, holding out a plastic bag. 'Mostly essentials, like toothbrushes and shower gel. I got Aiden some paints as well.' She glances at my son, who's sitting on his own bed scrolling through his phone again. 'I thought you might find it therapeutic. Well, both of you.'

'Thank you, that's very kind,' I reply. My voice sounds distant, the edges fading away. I want to disappear with it.

'I'll put these away.' Aiden begins to organise the contents of the bag, taking the toiletries into the bathroom.

I eyeball Stevenson. If he'd had news, he would've led with it. I knew as soon as he walked through the door that he had no fresh information for me. I know his face now, and I know the various expressions that mean *I don't know where your child is, and I don't know where to look.*

'The Met is still examining the CCTV footage all around the area.' He pulls the desk chair around to face me and perches on it, his long limbs too big for the cheap frame. 'We know that the woman took Gina through the car park and onto the main road. She turned off the main road into another car park where she exited onto a grassy area between council estates. It's here, I'm afraid, that we lose her. We think she walked across the grass to a vehicle somewhere in the area. She planned this carefully, researching a place to leave a car that's away from cameras. However, we are asking the private residences around there if they have any security cameras set up. People have doorbell cameras now, and you never know what they might've captured. If we can figure out the make and model of her car, we might be able to track her journey.'

'Are residents likely to hand over their camera footage? I'd imagine trust in the police around housing estates is pretty low.'

'You'd be surprised by what people will do for a missing child,' Stevenson replies. 'They're on your side, Emma.'

I glance down at the papers. Heartbreak is the word of the day. I'm heartbroken by the kidnapping of my child. The kidnapping of my *second* child. But lightning doesn't strike in the same place twice, does it? How long are they going to stay on my side? And if they aren't on my side, then they're not looking for my daughter.

I nod cautiously and take another bite of my croissant.

'Would you be willing to do a press conference later today?' Stevenson asks. 'It'd be with DI Khatri, not me. But I thought I'd come to ask because you know me.'

'Of course I will. Anything to help her.'

'Good. I'll let them know.' He pauses. 'Listen, I'm not PR and I'm not an expert, but I've learned a couple of things watching other high-profile cases. First, don't court the press. And second, don't smile. The media will follow the money.'

My fingers tighten around the pastry in my hand, crushing it. 'If you're the best story, that's where they'll go. Don't be anything other than the grieving mother. Don't be beautiful. Don't be religious. Don't be political. Be the grieving mother.'

The part that makes my stomach churn is the fact that I know he's right. Tina stands there with her mouth flapping open, staring at him. I assume he isn't supposed to be saying this to me.

'They're going to talk about Aiden,' he continues. 'And that conversation is going to insinuate that he's dangerous.' He leans forward. My heart is pounding now but I stay still, listening, taking it in, letting the words sour. 'There may even be experts that will suggest he could have been irreparably damaged by what he went through in the bunker. They may believe he could do to Gina what was done to him.'

I flinch away from him and throw the pastry down on the bed in disgust. 'No. They wouldn't dare. Aiden was in front of a camera at the time of her disappearance!'

'It doesn't matter,' he says. 'He could've had help. There will be a ton of conspiracy theories thrown around and you have to brace yourself for the worst.'

'What?' Aiden strides back into the room from the en-suite, hands balled into fists. He walks purposefully towards the detective and I have to stand up and physically block his way.

'It's not something I believe,' Stevenson says hastily. 'I'm preparing you both for what might be coming.' His voice remains calm, and if he was perturbed by Aiden's aggression, he doesn't show it. 'Like I said, they'll go for what sells the most newspapers, and that's probably going to be Aiden. Don't let them. I think Aiden should be at the press conference supporting you, Emma. Holding hands. Show the press some emotion.'

'I don't like the thought of my son being forced to perform for a crowd,' I say.

'It's OK, Mum. I'll do it,' he says. 'I would've done it anyway.'

I turn to face him and place a hand on his arm. His eyes are focused on the patterned carpet of the hotel room. The anger I saw a few moments ago has fizzled out as quickly as it came.

'I'll give you a call when they're ready for you,' Stevenson says before leaving.

Tina hesitates by the door. 'I'll be in the hotel lobby for a little while. If you need me, give me a call, OK?' She hands me a card with her phone number before disappearing through the door.

'I don't trust him anymore,' Aiden says. 'I think he said all of that to see how I'd react.'

I'm not sure what to think. A numbing sensation spreads over me. My thoughts are all jumbled up. I'm both exhausted and wide awake. Adrenaline won't allow my body to relax.

'He's not our friend,' Aiden says, and I'm inclined to agree with him.

At eleven, I realise that Gina has been missing for twenty-four hours and my heart skips a beat. Most children don't come back to their parents alive after the first twenty-four hours. This is the point where police – and parents – are forced to admit that their child didn't wander off; their child was taken.

I've been here before. The red coat in the Ouse.

I've lost hope before, too. I won't do that again.

Tina goes out to buy us some new clothes before the press conference, and the entire time I think about Stevenson's words. *Be the grieving mother*. It implies that Gina is dead, and I hate that, but I understand the concept. It's who I am anyway. I think about Gina every moment of the day. But it isn't all that I am. No one can cry all day and all night. I'm also a woman with opinions and ideas about how to find my daughter, but no one wants that from me. They don't want me to be active.

'The blue shirt, Aiden,' I say. 'It's similar to what you were wearing yesterday. Maybe it'll jog people's memories.'

I decide on a cardigan over a plain dress. I don't style my hair; I leave it limp and lifeless. I sit down in the chair and crumple the dress. People can't know that it's new. I can't be thought of as someone who could go shopping the day after my daughter was kidnapped. The press needs to focus on Amy. Any small detail about me could detract from the real culprit.

'Do you need anything to eat or drink before we go?' Tina asks.

I shake my head, the thought of eating just makes me want to throw up.

'Can I have some water, please?' Aiden asks. He's sitting on the edge of his bed, his shoulders slumped forward. There's paint on the tips of his fingers.

'Wash your hands,' I say, nodding to the paint. 'They can't think we're doing anything normal.'

While Tina takes a bottle of water from the mini-fridge, Aiden goes to wash his hands.

'I'm sure they won't notice,' Tina says.

But I shake my head. 'They'll notice everything.'

By the time he comes back, I'm pacing the length of the hotel room. 'Are you OK?' I ask.

He nods.

'I know what Stevenson said, but you don't have to do this if you don't want.'

'This is all my fault,' he says. 'So I do have to do this.'

I stop pacing and face my son. 'No, it's not.' I take his face in my hands and force him to look into my eyes. 'What makes you think that?'

'Because I insisted on doing the interview.'

I pull him into a hug and for once he wraps his arms around me. 'It's not your fault. None of this is. I promise you. OK?'

His head moves against my shoulder.

'We're going to get her back. Amy isn't going to win.'

He nods again.

'I promise, Aiden.'

He pulls away. 'Don't make any promises.'

'OK, I won't.'

'I'm sorry to interrupt,' Tina says. 'But it's time to go I'm afraid.'

My face is wet with tears that I desperately want to wipe away, but I don't. I let them dry on my cheeks.

Chapter Ten

EMMA

'There are some reporters outside the main entrance,' Tina warns. 'We can either go out the back of the hotel where it's quieter, or we can go through the reporters. Which would you prefer? I'll have the car brought around whichever.'

'The front,' I say, and then glance at Aiden to check that's fine for him too.

He nods.

I turn to Tina. 'I don't want them to think we have anything to hide. But we won't say anything to them.'

'OK.' Tina makes a quick call, and then we make our way out of the hotel.

'Would you like me to hold your hand while we do this?' I ask Aiden.

'Yes.'

Gently, I take his hand in mine and follow Tina out of the hotel. She has a couple of male police officers with us, who open the door and stop the journalists from getting too close. As soon as we set foot outside, I feel the camera lenses on me. I feel the weight of them leaning in. But it's just a few seconds before we're in the back of a car.

'You'd think they'd all be at the conference, not here,' I say, half to myself.

'Many newspapers are doing both,' Tina says by way of explanation. 'I think some wanted more candid photos. We've asked for privacy, but they never listen.'

The press conference is held at a small town hall not far from the studios where Gina was taken. Tina leads us through a corridor where we meet DI Khatri and a PC.

'Good afternoon, Ms Price,' she says. 'Did you manage to get much sleep?'

'No.'

'No one ever does in this situation,' she says. 'I promise you, we've been working hard to find your daughter. This is a good step. You can appeal for information and get the general public to help you. The eyes of the country are searching for your little girl, which gives us a lot to go on. Can I take a quick peek at your statement?'

I hand her a piece of paper and she scans it.

'Good, yes,' she says. 'Can I just suggest . . .' she pulls a pen from the top pocket of her jacket and scribbles out a few words. 'Let's not get too aggressive. No warnings for the kidnapper. Appeal for information. Appeal for anyone who might have taken her to give her back . . . That's really all we can say right now.'

'We know who took her, though,' I say, retrieving my statement. 'We know it was Amy.'

She cocks her head to one side. 'Do we?'

'Yes,' I reply, sensing her dismissing my theories as mere paranoia.

'Look, I understand how it might feel like that,' she says. 'You have a gut instinct and I don't blame you for having one. But I can't base any of my investigation on your prior history with Amy Perry. I need to examine the evidence. Amy is certainly a suspect and will remain one until she's eliminated.'

'What are you doing to find her?' I ask.

'We've been to her house on Singer Lane in Bishoptown and it's empty. According to a neighbour she moved out without warning and without leaving a forwarding address.

The house hasn't been put on the market as a sale or a rental property, so it seems that she still owns it. Where she is, we don't know.'

'That's pretty suspicious, don't you think?'

'Yes,' Khatri concedes. 'Trust me, she's a suspect. But let us do our job, Ms Price.'

And I should do mine, I think. *Be the grieving mother.*

The condescending tone of this woman brings out a bitterness in me. She makes me feel useless. Perhaps I am. I grit my teeth, biting back any possible retorts.

'Are you ready?' she asks. 'The cameras are all set up and the press are here.'

Many years ago, I did this for Aiden. I still remember the sea of faces. What I don't remember are the words I spoke. It was such a blur that the memory is more of a dream. Rob was beside me that time, now it's Aiden himself.

'Aiden?'

His skin is a pale shade of grey and there are purple bruises beneath his eyes. But he nods. It hits me, suddenly, just how unfair all of this it. Neither of my children should have been put through such terrible things. A small voice attempts to break through my mind, wanting to plant seeds of fear. That voice whispers all the disgusting things that could happen to Gina. I silence it and focus.

'Is Aiden going to speak?' Khatri asks.

'No,' I reply. 'He's here for support.'

'OK,' she says. 'That's fine. Shall we go out there?' She gestures to the door surrounded by PCs ready to allow us through.

'Yes.' I take Aiden's hand in mine and follow DI Khatri into the hallway.

The room is bright. There's a large picture of Gina next to the back table. It's a good picture, chosen from a selection I gave the police. She's at the top of a slide, grinning. They've cropped it so that just her face is visible.

Khatri strides confidently into the room clutching a bottle of water. She sits behind her name card. Aiden and I follow, each finding our seats.

There are camera clicks and murmurs. A microphone has been set up on the table in front of me. My body is pulled tight with tension. I glance at Aiden, who sits rigidly in his chair, eyes direct to the camera. *Please don't let him be the focus of this*, I think.

Khatri thanks the press for coming and explains the situation. In an emotionless voice, she tells the press that Gina was taken by a woman with red hair at eleven o'clock on Wednesday morning. She mentions that the woman may either have been wearing a wig or have since dyed her hair. She describes her clothing, then goes on to describe Gina's clothing.

Next to me, Aiden is breathing heavily. The camera flashes are frightening him. All of the doors to the room have been closed and I know he feels penned in with all these people. My son is a man, but he needs protection. I take his hand in mine and squeeze it, trying to bring him back.

'After this press conference is over, we will be showing images from the relevant CCTV footage,' Khatri continues. 'And we are appealing to the general public to get in touch if they recognise this woman. We thank you all for your co-operation. We also thank you for respecting the privacy of Ms Price and her son, Aiden, who are heartbroken over the abduction of little Gina.'

There's that word again, heartbroken. It suggests, to me, that Gina is already dead.

But she isn't, I refuse to believe that.

'Ms Price is going to say a few words now.' Khatri leans over and nods to me.

Eyes have been on me since the very beginning, but now is the moment I feel each and every eyeball. I also notice the brightness of the room. The pens tapping notebooks. The pounding of my heart. The sweat at my temples.

'I would like to say a few words on behalf of Aiden and myself,' my throat is dry as a bone, 'about the funny, smart little girl we both love. Gina is the light of our lives and we miss her more than anything. Please, if you see anything, report it to the hotline. Even the smallest detail could help the investigation. We just want Gina to come home safe. And if you did take her, if the woman in the CCTV footage is watching this right now. Don't hurt her. Bring her back to us.'

Khatri nods in a way that tells me I should shut up now. I let out a long exhale as she's wrapping up the conference. Some of the reporters have questions, but I don't hear them. All I can hear is the beating of my own heart. It isn't enough. What I said isn't enough. There wasn't enough time to adequately explain how much Gina means to us. This entire show feels formulaic, like I'm part of a reality TV programme. No one is being the real version of themselves, except perhaps for Aiden, who can't be anything other than real.

I find the camera and direct my gaze towards it. 'Amy.'

Khatri quiets. 'Ms Price, what are you –?'

'Amy, I know you have my daughter.'

'That's all we have time for –'

'Give her back to me. Give her back before I come and find you.'

Khatri tries to grasp my wrist, but I pull away from her. Out of the corner of my eye I sense her panic.

'If you harm a single hair on her head, I will kill you. I don't know why you took her, whether it's revenge or something worse. But I do know it was *you* who took my daughter. I know it was you, Amy.'

Hands hook beneath my arms.

'Amy Perry! That's who took my daughter. Find her!' I try to lean into the microphone but I'm being dragged away.

Aiden follows as I'm manhandled out of the room, his skin changed from grey to white. When the police officer lets go of me, he reaches out and touches my upper arm.

'Are you OK, Mum?'

'What the hell was that?' Khatri demands. 'Is that the image you want the general public to see? You taken out of a press conference by force?'

'It was your choice to pull me away.'

'No,' she says, 'it wasn't. You named and shamed a suspect on live television. Do you have any idea how much you've jeopardised this investigation? That was the stupidest . . .' She shakes her head, cheeks flushed, unable to find the words. 'I've never seen a parent do that before.'

Regret begins to seep in, but I push it away. She doesn't know Amy the way I do. Nothing I did jeopardised the investigation because Amy knows this is personal anyway. What I've done is rattled her, which might help flush her out from whatever hole she's hiding in.

'What you did has far bigger implications than this investigation,' Khatri warns. 'I could arrest you for inciting violence. If Amy Perry turns out to be innocent, you could have ruined her life. Do you understand that?'

'Well that's fine then,' I reply. 'Because she isn't innocent.'

Chapter Eleven

THE CHAPEL

Before I remove my earphones, I pause to observe my distorted reflection on the black computer screen. The dark hair takes some getting used to. As does the short cut, though I prefer that when I'm gardening. It's less hassle to maintain.

Amy Perry! That's who took my daughter. Find her!

I wish you could hear the feistiness in her voice! She's lost a little weight; you can see it in the face around the cheekbones. She doesn't wear make-up and her eyes are wet with fresh tears. She hangs her head in a dejected way. This role has always suited her. She's *the mother* to everyone.

But she should know how to play this game, now, the amount of practice she's had. What started with Aiden has happened to Gina. One might suspect that she's rather careless with her children. Losing one is unfortunate, two is a pattern, and you have to wonder what someone like that has done to deserve all of these bad things. I personally believe in karma.

Are some people born with *victim* stamped across their foreheads? If so, Emma has been marked. Perhaps it's the soulful eyes or the downcast mouth. But I'm not sure I buy the victim act. She's just getting what's coming to her.

It's time to leave the library – where I come to use the internet – but first I send a few messages using the internet access. Must keep in contact.

It's almost 5 p.m. and I should get back to the church before everyone filters out of their workplaces and heads to their sad little houses. I want to get back to you. I want to see your face again.

This time I decided to come to the library in the next town over. The village near the chapel is small, and I don't want to be remembered by anyone. This place isn't as tiny, but it's still a middle-England town with a small population and I don't want to take any unnecessary risks. But I need to go shopping.

This surprise September heatwave continues, which gives me a good excuse to wear a straw hat and sunglasses. I tuck my earphones into my bag and head to the Sainsbury's across the street.

Amy Perry! That's who took my daughter. Find her! Her voice is loud and clear in my mind. A smile plays on my lips. She'd walked into the room looking like a mess, but at the beginning she at least seemed in control. I enjoyed the moment when she suddenly snapped. Her accusations made her look like a crazy woman. Who could possibly take her seriously after that performance?

She's playing the game wrong again. The way Emma ensures everyone turns against her is a real gift of self-sabotage. I shake my head. She's talented at making sure she's completely alone.

I grab a supermarket basket and casually stroll up and down the aisles, enjoying the cool air-conditioning. There's a man in front of the cereal I want, so I wait patiently for him to move, smiling slightly as he realises he's in the way and apologises. Afterwards I head to the milk aisle. There's no fridge at the chapel, but this is a special occasion, don't you think?

Perhaps I can relax a little after the press conference. It's clear that the police have no idea what they're searching for or even where to begin. All Emma's managed to achieve is the undermining of her own suspicions. That unhinged performance will be all anyone can talk about over the next few weeks.

I add bottles of water, crisps, bread, butter, cheese and ham. Treats that I'm not used to buying anymore. But I need to get something for you, my little one, something that you'll love. I stalk up and down the aisles, searching each one for the perfect present. All the while I finger the cash in my pocket to pay for it all. There's no chip and pin for me anymore.

Next to the birthday cards is a section for children's toys. It's a small selection but my eye is drawn to the red dragon toy. I pick one up and toss it into the basket. You'll love it, sweet girl.

Chapter Twelve

EMMA

THE VIOLENT FEMME is the headline on the *Guardian*'s website. It's followed by the hypothetical question: *Should Emma Price be prosecuted for inciting violence?*

At least now I'm the story and not Aiden. I gave the papers the fuel they wanted and directed attention away from my son.

However, the sheer amount of vitriol still shocks me. My self-defence against Jake is brought up in every story. The photograph used is me with my mouth open, eyes wide, mid-diatribe. The picture that goes along with it is me being dragged away by DI Khatri.

'It's probably best not to read the comments,' Tina suggests as she hovers around the room, tidying things that don't need to be tidied. I get the distinct impression that I'm being watched. I remember it being the same with Denise, forever wondering what information she was filtering back to DCI Stevenson, before he became a friend to my family. And even now I wonder about the motives behind everything the police say to me, including Stevenson himself.

I remember the paranoia well. I remember how it stoked

the anger within, made me hate everyone around me. That fire is returning, and I don't know whether to bask in the warmth of the flames or extinguish it before it gets out of control.

I ignore Tina and scan the comments before reluctantly deciding that she's right. There's still some sympathy left for me, but there's more disgust. Right-wing types applaud my 'telling it like it is' approach of naming and shaming the person I believe kidnapped my daughter. There are pledges to find Amy and force her to reveal Gina's location. I conjure an image of a mob with their pitchforks, striding up to whatever hole Amy is hiding in, pulling her out. Then I shake my head and force the image away. Instead, I turn to Aiden, sitting quietly, scribbling in his notebook. Since the press conference he's either using his phone or drawing. I try to discourage him from using his phone because he has access to the internet, and therefore to the horrible comments left by people who don't know us. But he seems to be using it even more than before Gina went missing, and that worries me.

We've barely spoken today and I'm paranoid he's shutting me out. I don't think he understands why I did what I did, but that's OK. He doesn't need to know that I wanted to distract the press. I saw the way they were looking at him and I couldn't stop thinking about what Stevenson said, that Aiden could be a focus of this investigation. That he might be so damaged that he'd want to repeat what was done to him in the bunker. My stomach lurches just thinking about it.

When he goes to use the bathroom, I pick up the notepad and flick through the drawings, ignoring Tina's raised eyebrow. Almost all of them are of curls of hair. Gina's curls. I close the pad and go back to checking the news sites.

When Aiden returns, I finally address Tina. It's Friday afternoon. There has been no news about Gina. We've slept for no longer than four hours at a time, both of us waking up from nightmares, or waking the other up with our nightmares.

'We need to get out of this hotel room,' I say. 'We're going to lose our minds in here.'

'I'd advise against it, Ms Price,' Tina says. 'There are photographers everywhere.'

'My son needs to –'

'Mum, it's OK,' Aiden says calmly. 'I don't want to go out there with all those people watching me.'

My eyes fill with tears, but I nod my head and don't suggest it again. We stay in that stuffy room until the evening, when Stevenson and Khatri arrive. They walk in to find me pacing the length of the hotel room, jittery from too much caffeine. Going stir crazy.

'It's nothing to worry about,' Khatri says. 'But I would like to take your mobile phones. We'll give you a few minutes to note down whatever numbers you need.'

I stare at her, my jaw dropping open in disbelief. 'Are you kidding? What if someone needs to get in touch with us urgently?'

'You can buy new ones. There might be important evidence on the phones that can help us find Gina.' She shrugs, then shoves her hands in her trouser pockets. Disinterested in my incredulity, still sour about the press conference.

This is it, the beginning of what Stevenson warned us about. This feels like a subtle way of suggesting that Aiden is a suspect.

'It won't be for long,' Stevenson adds. I clock the way Khatri turns to him with an unsmiling expression. The Metropolitan Police are sick of our contact getting in the way. Even with his high rank in the force, he's beginning to outstay his welcome and I'm sure he knows that.

Both Aiden and I spend a few minutes noting down important contacts. Rob has been calling me every morning on that phone and will worry if I don't get in touch with him. My mind starts to drift to what might be embarrassing for police to see on my personal phone. My search history is all about human trafficking and paedophiles and what happens to children more than a day after they are abducted.

We drop our phones into a plastic bag, along with a note for our passcodes.

I had assumed that they wouldn't suspect me. Would

they? It's never the mother; it's usually the dad, or the uncle, or the older brother . . . Aiden is not that person. I know him. The idea is completely ridiculous to me. For one thing, he'd need help, and Aiden doesn't know anyone. Where would Gina even be taken? Why would he do it in the middle of promotion for his new book? I exhale slowly, trying to calm my heart. No, Aiden is *not* that person, no matter who suspects he might be.

'Is there anything else?' I ask.

'That's all for now,' she says.

'Actually, I wanted to add something,' Stevenson says. 'DI Khatri might agree with me here. You're both cooped up in this hotel room and the hotel is swarming with photographers. Whenever you're in central London, it's easy for them to follow you around. What if you were to go back to Bishoptown? Or even Manchester? DI Khatri can call you back down if there are any problems.'

Khatri gives Stevenson a sharp look. 'They're important for the investigation. We may need to question them.'

'You already have,' he points out. 'After Gina went missing. Ms Price has been extremely co-operative.' He's beginning to sound like a legal representative, but I'm glad for the suggestion. 'I don't believe either Ms Price or Mr Price are suspects. They were accounted for at the time of the kidnapping.'

'They aren't suspects, but –'

'Well, then. I think you can agree that they can't live like this. I can be your liaison officer in your own home if that's acceptable for you, Emma. Bishoptown would be better for me, as I live close by.'

Khatri offers Stevenson a wry smile. 'It would certainly be unusual for a DCI to be the family liaison officer.'

'I have a long professional connection to this case,' he says, and I can tell by the tone of his voice that he's pulling rank.

'Of course, sir,' she concedes.

'I'm sure everyone at the Met can continue their excellent investigation. Aiden and Emma will only be a few hours away by train if you need them.' His slow smile stretches from ear to ear. 'I can be your first point of contact for any information.'

'But what if you find Gina in London? I want to be here for her,' I interrupt.

'Emma, she might not be in London,' Stevenson replies. 'There's no point being uncomfortable here just for that reason.'

'What about our phones?'

'You might as well buy new ones if you can,' Khatri says, not smiling.

At least this means getting away from DI Khatri, who I'm starting to think may want to use her presence at the hotel as intimidation.

'What do you think, Aiden?' I know he has conflicting feelings about Bishoptown. 'Would you prefer to go to Manchester?'

'I just want to go where you go,' Aiden says. 'And where Gina can find us.'

'She can find us in the village,' I say. 'I know she can.'

Neither of us mean physically. My four-year-old couldn't walk to Bishoptown on her own. But it's a place that she knows with people she knows. Rob, Sonya, Peter, Josie. Suddenly I ache for them.

'All right,' I say, turning back to the detectives. 'Bishoptown it is. We'll set off in the morning, shall we?'

We agreed that Stevenson would drive my car up to Bishoptown for a couple of reasons. One being he came to London on the train, the other is because I don't think Khatri would let us go alone, and the final reason is I've barely slept since Gina was taken. It's a relief to be away from DI Khatri's looming presence. We even have to check in with her when we get there. Despite her claim that neither of us are suspects, I don't believe it. We were lucky to get out of that hotel room.

There's another reason why I agreed to this. My nightmare began in Bishoptown when Aiden was taken, and I have a feeling that it will end in the same place. The village connects me to Amy, from our school days to an adult friendship that turned sour. If Amy is going to contact us, it will be in Bishoptown. Amy isn't Hugh. I don't believe she has the same desire to harm a child. The reason she stole Gina is to get my attention and force me to face up to what I did when I drove her out of the village. She won't hurt my girl; she'll use my girl as bait. *My girl.* I close my eyes and can still smell her hair. That baby shampoo scent.

Pulling myself back before I start to cry again, I try to go over the facts in my mind. What I can't figure out is where Amy's keeping Gina. It isn't easy to hide a child away from the police. I think of all the lengths Hugh went to hide Aiden and my stomach roils. How is she living? How can there be no records of her renting or buying another house? The only thing I can think is that she's somehow created another identity, and she's using that to pay for wherever she's living. I hope, deep down, that Amy has at least put a roof over my daughter's head. That she's feeding her, making sure she doesn't get sick.

I take a deep breath.

'Are you OK?' Stevenson asks.

We're currently stuck in traffic on the motorway. Aiden has drifted off in the back seat, his chin resting against his chest.

'My head is all over the place,' I admit.

'Mine would be too.'

'How old are your kids?'

'Both teenagers now. Both girls.'

'No bathroom time for you then?'

He lets out a short laugh. 'They're as different as chalk and cheese. Jess can spend hours in the bathroom with all kinds of lotions and potions. Carrie would rather be outdoors walking, getting muddy.'

'Carrie. I like that name,' I say.

'My wife chose it after her favourite TV show. I guess people don't think of the film so much anymore.'

I make a *hmm* sound, but my mind is wandering again.

Speculating whether Amy can follow the news and how she'll find out that we've moved back to Bishoptown. How long can she physically keep a child without someone noticing? Surely any neighbours would notice the sudden appearance of a four-year-old girl.

'How certain are you that Amy Perry took your daughter?' Stevenson asks. Finally, the cars start to move again. It's now Saturday afternoon, sweltering, still suffocating inside the car despite the air-conditioning. Our early morning start turned into mid-morning by the time we'd managed to get organised.

'Ninety percent.'

'Not one hundred?'

'No,' I admit. 'But if I'm wrong, I don't have another answer. Amy, to me, is the one person with the motive to take Gina. She hates me and Aiden. Maybe she's always hated me, ever since school. Hugh, for some unknown reason, was the love of her life and Aiden took him away. I threatened her once, too. I held a knife to —'

'OK, Emma. Stop right there before I have to arrest you.'

I just shrug. 'You won't, though.'

He lets out a long sigh.

'She helped Hugh. I know that there was no evidence to connect her and him together, but I know she did. She admitted it to me.'

'While you threatened her with a knife?' he says.

I shake my head in frustration. 'You weren't there. She did it. She faked that Facebook status about Hugh in Las Vegas. She even sent Aiden down to the river and told Hugh where he'd be. She set it all up. She would have done anything for that man, she was in love with him. And then she hogged the limelight when Aiden came back, giving interviews on *This Morning* for Christ's sake. She has some sort of mental illness, I'm sure of it. Narcissism or something like that.'

'If what you suspect about her and Hugh is right, then I agree it makes sense to believe Amy is the kidnapper,' he says. 'But where would she take Gina? How would she hide her?'

I frown out of the car window, watching the yellowing grass fly by. 'That's what I'm trying to figure out.'

'What you did at the press conference was both smart and stupid.'

'I know,' I reply. 'At least she knows she has my attention now.'

Chapter Thirteen

EMMA

Back in Bishoptown, in my old childhood home, I dump a sad, deflated plastic bag onto the sofa and watch dust flutter into the air. Sunlight illuminates the particles as they float away. Gina would run around trying to catch them if she was here. She'd love this place; how shabby and unusual it is. How many times have I brought her to this house since we moved away? She was a baby when we moved out and wouldn't even remember living here. We've stopped overnight once or twice, but that isn't the same. I remember that she liked the colourful walls and the photographs last time we were here.

Stevenson has gone back to his house in York with his two teenage daughters and his wife. I have a picture of them in my mind: one in Wellington boots with short hair and a toothy smile, the other in a sundress, curled hair resting on her shoulders.

I have another picture in my mind. One of Gina, alone, chained to the wall, iron bars in front of her. I'm picturing her in Aiden's bunker, though I don't want to. I can never know, not for sure, how terrible it was for Aiden in that bunker, but that doesn't stop my brain from picturing it. The thought of Gina going through that is unbearable. It elicits pain – actual, physical pain.

But that won't bring her home. I catch Aiden's eye and see him stooped over, his jaw tense.

We begin tidying the house as something to do, because moving around is better than sitting and wallowing. He wipes down the kitchen and I vacuum the living room carpet. I catch two spiders from the cobwebs in the corners and throw them out of the window.

A couple of hours in, Aiden says goodnight before going straight to bed in the room that has barely changed since he was six years old. There were new owners for a short while, after I married Jake, but luckily they didn't do much with the place except for painting the living room and updating the kitchen. Aiden's bedroom had been largely unused. I flop down on the sofa and pull the small cardboard box out of my bag. On the way up to Bishoptown we stopped at a shopping centre and each bought a new smartphone. Seeing as Aiden has gone to bed, I stay up fiddling with it. Learning the new tech and installing the SIM card.

It's while browsing the news that my eyes drift and darkness takes over. An old claustrophobia nightmare of being stuck in a small space filters into my subconscious mind. I've had this same recurring dream since I was a little girl, which occasionally comes back to me even now. It's the same nightmare that haunted me once I realised what had happened to my son.

My eyes fly open, expecting to be trapped in that tiny space, my chest heaving up and down. It takes me a moment to remember where I am.

'Mum?' Aiden leans forward in the armchair across from the sofa. 'Are you OK?'

I pull myself upright and wipe sleep from my eyes, seeing the cup of hot tea on the coffee table.

'Did you buy milk?' I ask him, the thought immediately making me panic. It's stupid, but Aiden going out on his own still makes me uneasy, even if it is to fetch a pint of milk.

'No. I did.' Josie waves to me from the hallway. 'There'll be toast and jam for you, too.'

'How did you know we were back?' I grasp the tea, grateful for the caffeine.

'Aiden called at the crack of dawn,' she says. There's a springing sound from the kitchen and a metallic pop. 'That'll be the toast. I'll be right back.'

'I thought she might help,' he says. 'Was it the wrong thing to do?'

My muscles unclench, just a tiny bit. 'No. I'm glad you called her. How are you doing this morning?'

He shrugs. 'Everything seems quieter.'

I know exactly what he means. There are no constant questions or sassy comments. No giggles or little feet thundering across the carpet. Yes, it is quiet without her, and not the guilty relief of taking a break, more like the suffocating silence that signals an absence.

'Do you want some toast?' I ask Aiden. 'I can ask Josie for you.'

He nods.

'Actually, I'm not that hungry. But you have whatever Josie put in the toaster.' I remember this well, the chattering of my own voice, trying desperately to compensate for his silence. 'Listen, we're going to get her back. I know Amy and she isn't like Hugh. She never hurt you and I don't think she'll hurt Gina.' I pause. 'I'm sorry if that was insensitive.'

'No, it's OK,' he replies. 'I want to help so you should tell me what you think.'

I'm surprised by that. Aiden isn't usually so forthright about his feelings. 'I'm glad Stevenson suggested that we come here because this is where Amy and I grew up. She's connected to this place as much as I am, and I think she'll want to contact me if I'm here. The more I think about it, the more I'm convinced that taking Gina was a way to hurt us. A way to get my attention in particular.' I shake my head, feeling almost as though the idea is ridiculous now that I've said it out loud. 'What I mean is . . . I think this is personal.'

Aiden nods. 'But what's the point? Why not just attack you?'

'I don't know,' I admit. 'Maybe she's trying to lure me out.'

Aiden sucks in his breath and tenses. 'Then you need protection.'

'I can handle myself, kiddo,' I say.

'Hi, sorry.' Josie stands at the doorway holding out a plate of toast and jam. 'I didn't want to interrupt but the toast is going cold.'

'Aiden can have this round,' I say, passing the plate across. 'Do you mind if I give Rob a quick call?'

'Sure.'

On my way out of the room I pull her into a hug. 'Thank you for being here.'

'Anytime,' she says. 'You know that.'

We spend the morning eating toast while filling Josie in on everything that happened in London, and it serves to remind me I have a support system here that I'd forgotten all about. For the first time since Gina's abduction, I allow myself to be emotional around other people. I can't stop the tears from falling. Aiden sits quietly, his face full of sorrow. After lunch, we walk across the village to Rob's house. That's when we realise that some of the photographers have followed us here.

Perhaps they were with us the entire journey, a few cars behind on the motorway, waiting for their perfect photo opportunity. Got to get the exclusive of us napping while stuck in traffic.

Their presence is ever in the background, lurking in the shadow of the pub, or wandering the banks of the Ouse.

'Shall I say something to them?' Aiden suggests. The idea of Amy using Gina to inflict physical hurt has awoken some kind of protective instinct in my son. He stands up tall, trying to puff out that pigeon chest of his. The sight makes me want to cry again, but I just take his hand.

'Leave them be. We're going to see your dad. There's nothing wrong with that, and whatever they report is a waste of time for them.'

For the rest of the short walk, I even notice dogwalkers watching us with interest. I wish our faces could be anonymous. I wish we'd been allowed a normal life.

Rob opens the door, ditches his cane and pulls me into a hug. 'I wanted to come to London but . . . Well, I didn't want to be in the way.' His face is red, his cheeks puffy. One thing I can't help but notice about Rob these days is how quickly he's put on weight since he came out of hospital. Not only do I notice, but I feel responsible.

'You would never be in the way,' I say, and I mean it.

As he leads us in, I tell him that the photo of us hugging will probably be in the newspapers tomorrow.

He shrugs. 'Who cares. Nothing they say is true, is it?'

I don't know. Late at night when my mind is spiralling out of control, when I want to do nothing else but numb the pain with alcohol, I begin to wonder if they're right about one thing – about me being a bad mother. There was a comment on one of the news articles. Some anonymous poster: *once is unfortunate. Twice is a pattern.*

The pattern is me and the people I love. I harm everyone around me.

'Oh, Emma.' Sonya rushes over to hug me. 'How are you holding up? I've done nothing but hope and pray for the police to find little Ginny. I can't stop thinking about her. And you.'

'Thank you.'

'You look absolutely dead on your feet. Sit down for a bit.'

I sink into the sofa as she's planting a sloppy kiss on Aiden's cheek.

'Now, have you thought about hiring a private detective?' she asks, pulling a chair over to the sofa. 'I'm not saying that the police are incompetent, but Peter and I were talking about it, and we don't think they did a good job of finding Aiden. Well, they didn't, did they?'

'I . . . I hadn't thought of it,' I admit.

'Think on it, love,' she says.

I smile gratefully at Sonya. Since she's realised that I won't keep Aiden from her, the frostiness between us has thawed. It's nice to have them in my life; even though they aren't technically in-laws, they feel like it.

'Has Sonya told you about the private detective idea?' Peter asks as he walks into the room. 'Wouldn't be a bad thing to have another pair of eyes on the case.'

'Give her time to breathe,' Rob says.

'Don't listen to the papers.' Sonya ignores her son. 'They've already reported you coming back here. You've spent one night here!' She lifts her hands up in the air, exasperated. I can only nod along as the afternoon continues, exhausted.

Peter insists on driving us home, though I would have preferred to get a taxi. I suspect that he's been fantasising about dodging the paparazzi with impressive motoring skills in the five-minute drive from their house to ours. The reality is that there's no one around anymore. The photographers are probably watching from afar. Still, it saves us from walking.

I listen to my voicemail on the way home. Stevenson has left mail for me and Aiden at the house. A lot of letters were sent to the police, who have been through it for any clues and sent it on. Another reminder from the first time around. Kind letters from sympathetic members of the public, but also nutty ones, and cruel ones.

I hope they've filtered out the cruellest.

The stack of envelopes waits for us on the doormat. I bend down and scoop them up.

'Do you want to read these now or eat first?'

'Eat,' Aiden says.

We'd already agreed on the way home that we were

phoning for a pizza. And we'd decided on ham and pineapple because it's Gina's favourite. I dump the envelopes on the kitchen table and quickly phone the local takeaway place. I barely know the owner, though of course we've ordered many times before. Still, I'm surprised to hear him insist that our food is on the house.

'I couldn't possibly . . .'

'I mean it,' he says again.

Aiden and I sit at the table and find ourselves drawn to the mail while we wait. I start to sift through it, putting all letters addressed to Aiden in one pile, cards in another, and those for me in a separate pile.

'Remember not to take anything to heart,' I remind him. 'This kind of thing whips people into a frenzy.'

'I know,' he says, sounding more like a twenty-year-old man sick of his mother than ever. Whenever he surprises me with some normality, I want to grab him and hug him tight, but I know he wouldn't like that.

'Mum.' His voice sounds thin, an urgent whisper across the table.

'What is it?' I lift my head to find him staring at a piece of paper in his hands.

'This.' Aiden passes the letter across the table.

It's addressed to 'Emma and Aiden Price'.

YOU MUST PAY ME 50,000 IF YOU EVER WANT TO SEE HER AGAIN.

ANOTHER LETTER WILL BE DELIVERED.

WAIT.

DON'T GO TO POLICE OR SHE WILL BE KILLED.

Chapter Fourteen

THE CHAPEL

It rained for the first time in a week last night, but you already know that, don't you? I'm so sorry about the leaks. You must excuse this home; it isn't what I wanted for you. My bucket was a quarter full of rainwater. If I put it to one side to use with purification tablets, we'll have drinkable water. You see, there are many ways to live without relying on anyone else. This is how you survive.

Uncle Gregory used to show me how to do these things because I was his favourite niece. I was his only niece, but he liked to say that to me anyway. They didn't have children of their own and they welcomed it when I visited them. They would even tell me how special I was. Aunty Kim would plait my long hair and pin it to the top of my head like I was wearing a crown. She'd call me a princess.

But I was stupid enough to think I'd still be a princess once my visit became permanent. For a while everything was better, until it wasn't.

This is hard work, digging out veggies. You need a canvas sack, like this one, which helps to stop the potatoes from growing roots. There was a squirrel in the trap today, good thing there was, I've been craving the taste of meat. Perhaps you are too. I'll skin it and cook it for you. Uncle Gregory showed me how to do that too.

It was a thrill at first, receiving compliments from other people, and being taught a different way to live. I'm still grateful for my uncle, even though there were bad times. Whenever I think of them, I tend to think about the good times more than the bad. The excitement of knowing that a visit was coming up. But at that time in my life, anything was better than being with my mother. She wasn't good with compliments. She wasn't good at being a mother either.

You have to scrub the dirt from the root vegetables. First the potatoes. A good diet is a necessity. We must keep our strength up for what is to come. For the plan that will be put into action. And if I'm honest, I enjoy the manual work that comes with this life. It keeps my hands busy and allows my mind to wander. I have so many ideas going round and round in my mind all the time, like a washing machine on the spin cycle.

Right now, it's more important than ever to focus on the tasks ahead, but it's going to take a little while to filter through everything. Talking to you helps me figure it all out. Thank you for that. Thank you for being here.

You know, I hate to admit it, but I must: Emma is a good mother. She fought harder than my mother ever did. If I'd gone missing when I was a child, she probably wouldn't have noticed for days. In fact, it was my mother who would disappear for days on end. Every time, I convinced myself that this was it. She was never coming back this time and I would have to learn to fend for myself. In those dark times I'd jump on a bus, a young kid, about eleven, travelling all alone, and on the other end Aunty Kim would open her arms and say *princess*.

I made a decision long ago that I would rather be special than ignored. You can forgive a girl for that, can't you? Forgive me, please, for wanting to be special.

There was a boy I liked once. He was the boy all the girls liked. Good at rugby. Tall. Dark-haired. Brown eyes lined with long eyelashes. But he never thought I was special, not at first, anyway. He didn't even notice me. He was one of the boys at my new school after I went to live with Uncle Gregory and Aunty Kim.

I was right, you see. One day Mum didn't come back, and I was finally removed from her care. That was when I started a new school, a better school. The kind where the other kids judge what you wear and how you speak. None of them would accept me at that school. None of my clothes were fashionable, I didn't watch television and I'd clam up every time someone tried to talk to me. The teachers hated me because I rarely spoke. I sat in class completely silent. When it came to oral presentations, I stumbled through them with a face like a tomato. I had no friends or allies among the students or teachers.

It wasn't until I was in the final year of school that I discovered I could turn it all off: the embarrassment and anger. The loneliness. I stopped caring about any of it.

Shush now, hush little one. Don't cry, not for me. I won't have it. Do you hear me? I won't have it.

There, now you made me snap. Will you let me go on with my story? I have a lot more to say.

There was bullying at school and it was exactly what you'd expect. The most common insult was 'weirdo', but I came to accept it. I took in that word and decided it would mean something to be proud of. There were worse words, too. Along with the name-calling there was pushing and hair-pulling as well. Sometimes a few of them would wait by the entrance, grab my bag from my shoulder and toss it between them while I flailed around grasping at air. Or they'd lob it onto the highest locker so that I'd have to ask a teacher to get it down for me.

Once someone tipped my pencil case out of the second storey of the school. I ended up falling down the stairs trying to get to my pens before someone stole them. I broke my wrist and I didn't get the pens back.

That was the day that first changed me. After I fell, the nurse phoned my uncle and I went to hospital to have my wrist bandaged up. The drive home was so quiet, though I did let out a few sobs. I'm afraid to say I was a cry baby, a little bit like you. Neither my aunt nor uncle would look at me, the entire journey home.

That night I was told I would be paying for the pens I lost. It was the night I realised I was no longer Uncle Gregory's special niece. I was punished for losing my belongings. But looking back, that moment made me the person I am today. It made me realise that the world would never be kind to me, so why should I be kind to anyone else?

Now, please be quiet, I have an important letter to write.

Chapter Fifteen

AIDEN

'There's no envelope for this,' she says, putting it back down. 'Do you remember it being in an envelope?'

We're sitting at the kitchen table with the mail spread out around us. The ransom note lies on top of the mess, the block capital letters facing upwards. Scribbled in a biro.

EMMA AND AIDEN PRICE

YOU MUST PAY ME 50,000 IF YOU EVER WANT TO SEE HER AGAIN.

ANOTHER LETTER WILL BE DELIVERED.

WAIT.

DON'T GO TO POLICE OR SHE WILL BE KILLED.

While Mum was sorting them into piles, I'd been opening them. Most of the letters had already been unsealed by the police, and I'd been putting the envelopes together for the recycling.

'I can't remember,' I admit. 'But this is the stack it came from. Maybe it's in here somewhere.'

Mum begins to thumb through the envelopes, but it isn't clear which one might have contained the letter.

'We should stop touching things,' I say. 'They'll need to

87

look for DNA evidence.' I remember the police talking about DNA during the trial.

Mum nods. 'OK. You're right.' She sounds breathless. Her fingers are trembling. 'I should call Stevenson. How could the police miss this?'

'It says not to go to the police,' I say.

She stares at the note, transfixed, as though trying to make up her mind about something. 'No. We can't do this without them. We have to go to the police about this.'

'What if they hurt Gina?'

She presses her fingers into her temples. 'For God's sake, Aiden, I could do without you guilt-tripping me.'

'I wasn't, Mum.'

She reaches out for me, but I pull away. There are tears in her eyes and she bites her bottom lip so hard I think it might start to bleed.

'Aiden, I'm so sorry,' she says. 'That wasn't me, it was . . . We're under stress and I'm lashing out. I didn't mean to snap.'

'I know,' I say, accepting her apology, but still feeling the sting of her words.

She sniffs and reads the letter one more time before taking her phone out of her pocket.

On the television, when families are stressed, they argue with each other. In *Coronation Street* everyone yells. I know it's normal but I hate it. The change in someone's voice makes my body stiffen, waiting for the blow. I push away those thoughts and read the letter one more time. Where was the envelope? Then it hits me.

I don't know if Mum has had this thought, which makes me not want to say it out loud, but someone probably put the letter through our letterbox. They came to our house in order to deliver it by hand. There's a chance that Gina's kidnapper was right outside our house, just a few feet away from where we are sitting now.

I let out a long breath and hope that I'm wrong. I guess the police will have to check through everything to make sure.

Mum's right, we can't keep touching the evidence, but it feels like all we do is sit around and wait.

While she talks to Stevenson on the phone, I check my Instagram account. My heart quickens as the app loads. Every time I worry that I won't have any new messages, but I do. Faith has been in contact again, which is a relief.

Someone sent us a ransom note, I type, pressing send without giving it too much thought. The reply takes a moment or so. I chew the bottom of my lip waiting. Sometimes Faith doesn't reply for a few hours and it makes me worry she'll never reply again.

Fuck, she says. *What does it say?*

I tell her all about it and it's a relief to let it out. Mum isn't the easiest person to talk about. At least with Faith I can let it all go. And I trust her, too.

At least now we know what all this is about, I type. *I was worried Gina would be abused.*

Just be careful, Aiden. People send crazy things, she says. I pause with my thumbs over the screen, not sure how to reply, when I see that she's typing another message. *You know I'm for real, don't you? That I'm here for you.*

I smile to myself. *Yeah, I know.*

I'm always here. The one you can rely on. She sends me a big, grinning emoji.

Love ya, F. I reply.

Love you to the moon and back, A. When are we going to meet? Soon??

I pause before I respond, tapping the edge of my phone with a fingernail. *There's so much going on right now . . .*

I know but I could comfort you.

Do I want her to comfort me? Part of me, maybe. I reply back: *I dunno . . .*

'What are you up to?' Mum says as she comes back into the kitchen. 'You're smiling.'

'I . . . I just . . . I think maybe it's fear or something. I feel weird.'

She places a hand on my forehead like I'm still a child. 'Are you feeling ill?'

'No. Just a bit on edge.'

She nods. 'Me too.' She sits down in her seat, staring at the pile of letters on the table. She's red in the face, possibly from fear, I don't know. Worry? 'He's not coming. The police won't come to our house in uniforms and panda cars, apparently. They have to make it seem as though we haven't informed them.'

'That's a good thing, isn't it?' I suggest, still feeling naïve and like I don't understand the world. I missed a lot of it growing up.

'I don't know,' she mumbles. 'They're sending out an officer in regular clothes to pick up the letter and take it to be tested for fingerprints. He said we shouldn't worry because crazy people send this kind of stuff all the time. It's probably not even real.' She lets out a long, unsteady breath. 'I don't dare think it will be this easy. That we give them money and get Gina back. But I want it to be. I really want it to be.' Her eyes are unfocussed as though she's talking to herself. 'This doesn't feel like Amy, does it? She wouldn't want money and she knows I'd take the letter straight to the police. I feel like she'd contact me with a more personal note. Don't you think?'

'I don't know her as well as you do,' I point out.

She nods. 'I guess so. I wish there was another person I could talk to and get more information from.'

'I knew Hugh better than anyone.'

'Hugh,' she mutters. 'How could he possibly be . . . He's dead.'

'Isn't Amy the way she is because of Hugh?'

Mum's eyes shine and her fingers grip the tabletop.

'That's what he does. He creates monsters. Maybe we can understand Amy by understanding Hugh.'

I leave Mum at the table and stroll through to the lounge, trying to stop my thoughts from veering out of control.

She's right. This would be easier. I want it to be real. I want this to be over. Especially since the conversation I had with Mum about Amy Perry. About how all of this might be linked to Hugh.

If it's all connected to Hugh, then it's connected to me too.

I close my eyes and take a deep breath, still finding my thoughts drifting back to the bunker. Sometimes my thoughts get all jumbled up and the bunker feels like it's still happening. We've returned to the house where I grew up, but nothing about it feels familiar. Where did I become the person I am now? Here? Or in the bunker? In some ways, Hugh is the person who shaped me more than anyone else.

Which isn't something I like to admit.

My psychologist says that no one is all bad or all good, that we're a mixture of the two. Hugh was not all bad to me, and when I think that, I feel shame. He taught me to read and write. He brought me books so that I could learn. He used to tell me that one day I'd get to move to another place, one I'd be more comfortable in, but I wonder now whether it was a lie. He lied a lot.

Much of my time in the bunker is crystal clear in my mind, and a lot of it is so fuzzy that I feel it just out of reach. Beyond my fingertips. That's the part I don't want to reach, anyway. Like my broken leg, a punishment for trying to escape. The event is blurred around the edges, but the pain is as tangible as ever. Our conversations about the outside world. Some I recall completely, like the one about Mum's wedding day. Others I feel on the periphery of what I know.

Am I trying to remember something specific? My mind is as jumbled as always but part of me wonders if I'm trying to connect an old memory from the bunker with Gina's disappearance.

I wander back into the dining room and ask mum, 'Do you think Amy cares about money?'

Mum shakes her head. 'I don't know what to think.'

If Amy Perry really has taken Gina – and like Mum I think she has – then Hugh's legacy is all over this abduction. I can feel it. Amy was his pet project, aside from me. He liked to control her. What if she's following a plan that he concocted before he died? And what if he mentioned that plan to me while I was in the bunker?

If he did, it's inside me, but I can't find it.

But if this ransom note is real, I feel like Mum, I don't know what to think anymore.

The police officer stops by an hour later to collect the ransom note and take it away. As part of the ruse, he brings us food with him. Neither of us are hungry anymore, allowing most of it to go cold, but we manage to pick at a few samosas before putting the rest in the fridge.

We spend the night on tenterhooks, waiting for a sign that this is real. Mum sleeps on the sofa again. I don't know why she won't go to her room. She's constantly prowling the downstairs area like a guard dog. She's forever physically between me and the door.

Next morning, I wake from a restless sleep, with the echo of the bunker on my mind. The bright sun filters in through the curtains and birdsong chitters away. My stomach feels unsettled. Every now and then I wake and the air feels wrong. This isn't the right smell. The smell I know no longer exists, because they've blown up my home.

No. No that's all wrong. I can't help it, I hit myself, hard, on one temple. Stupid. That's wrong, stupid. The bunker isn't your home. Mum and Gina are your home.

And there are times, like now, when I'd like nothing more than to kill the chattering bird outside the window and staple the curtains together until it blocks out every millimetre of escaping sunlight. I want silence and I want dark. I want the smell of must and the spiders that somehow make it through the tiniest of cracks in the concrete. I want the familiar sound of the door clanking open and the smell of fresh food when Hugh arrives with dinner.

And I hate myself for it.

I see him stepping into the bunker. A plastic bag in one hand, a bottle of fizzy pop in the other.

'I got you a new toothbrush today, mate.'

I say thank you.

What else does he tell me? Hugh liked the sound of his own voice. He was one of those people who could convince you within thirty seconds that he was a decent bloke, just by making chit-chat. That was something Mum said a few months ago and it struck me as true.

But this morning, one throwaway remark keeps playing on a loop in my mind. There's nothing particularly remarkable about it, only that Hugh said it once and when I woke up this morning, I remembered it. 'Long journey up from London today. Sometimes I wish there was somewhere in between there and here. Halfway.'

Why is that important to me?

Mum's face appears at the doorway, ghostly pale and sickly. 'Good, you're awake. We should head down to the police station and speak to DCI Stevenson. I'm hoping they'll have some ideas about how to deal with this ransom.'

'Can you let me get dressed, please?' I say through gritted teeth. I can't meet her eyes. I don't want to be stared at.

She slips away silently.

I'm finally alone.

93

Chapter Sixteen

EMMA

Gina has been missing for six days. I haven't seen her face or heard her voice for nearly one hundred and fifty hours. I don't know that she's safe, well, properly fed and hydrated. She could be dirty, injured or starving. What if she's afraid? I keep picturing her crying herself to sleep or calling for me or Aiden.

But despite all of those things, I haven't lost hope that she *will* come back to us safe and sound, because Aiden came back to me once.

Six days is a long time, but it isn't ten years. We can find her. We can bring her home.

This ransom note throws everything I suspected into doubt and changes the way the police approach this case. It means we have to maintain a ruse, while also preparing ourselves for the ominous promise of further communication. We must live our lives as though we aren't in contact with the police.

Because we couldn't match an envelope to the letter, Stevenson suggests that we install security cameras around the outside of the house. If this person did hand deliver the note, we'll be able to pick them up on camera next time they come. He also assures me that there will be discreet surveillance around the house and on me and Aiden even if we don't see their physical presence.

'Are you ready, kid?'

Aiden raises his soulful eyes and nods.

'You won't need that jumper, it's boiling outside.'

He peels away the jumper and puts on a pair of glasses to protect his eyes from the sun. We had them made by a specialist. I press my own sunglasses onto my face, avoiding the mirror in the hallway. My roots are full of greys, my skin is blotchy. I can't bring myself to do anything for myself while she's gone. I can't apply moisturiser or condition my hair. Existence has halted again. I know this feeling well.

Rob meets us at the car. It's just another family day out, except that we're buying security cameras for the house.

'All set?'

I nod. 'Have you seen any photographers?'

'A couple,' he admits. 'But I think the media is starting to move on.'

I swear under my breath and lean against the car.

'Isn't that a good thing?' he asks.

'Not for Gina. She needs everyone in the country looking for her.' I wipe sweat from the back of my neck. 'Oh, I don't know, Rob. Maybe it is a good thing. They were just printing lies about me anyway.' I open the door and climb in. Aiden is already in the back, with his hands on his lap. He reminds me of the boy he was four years ago.

Rob presses the ignition switch. He has a specially modified car to help him drive with hand controls. Seeing him brake without a pedal jolts me every time.

'You're going to get her back,' he says. 'You have the money, right?'

'Someone from the police is going to help me withdraw it all in marked notes so that they can't use it. They'll put a tracker in the bag if it comes to an exchange. We don't even know if the letter is real yet. The police aren't convinced. They keep telling me not to get my hopes up.'

We make our way out of the drive towards the village. I decided to bring Rob with me while we buy the security cameras. He's more into this kind of technology than I am.

'And you still think this is Amy?' he asks.

I glance at Aiden in the rear-view mirror. 'If this is about money, then no.'

'If it isn't?'

'Then Hugh made his monster to be very cunning.'

It doesn't take long to buy doorbell security cameras, install them, and stock the house with food. Rob stays with us for all of that, often cursing that he isn't as physical as he used to be and can't help us with the heavy bags.

'I hate this,' he admits. 'At least I helped when we found out about Jake. I didn't do a good job of it, but at least I was physically able to. Now I'm just a useless lump.' He limps along with his cane, the strain visible on his face, a red flush creeping up from his neck.

The heatwave continues and we open up all the windows. I need to bring the fan up from the cellar, but I haven't had a chance yet.

I pull Rob to one side while Aiden is making us both a cup of tea. 'Listen, I know what you're going through, but I don't think it's good for Aiden to hear you talking like that.'

He frowns. 'What do you mean?'

'He's twenty now. He's an adult and he wants to be the one to help. It makes it sound dismissive, as though what he's doing isn't helping or protecting us. Do you know what I mean?'

'Yeah,' he says. 'Sorry, Em. I didn't think.'

'It's OK.'

The words aren't completely true, but I understand that this is what Rob needs to hear right now. He needs to be absolved of the instinct to take charge and be the man. But even though I care for him, it's a drain on my energy and Aiden's, when we need to be strong. I hate to even think it, but his insecurities are a burden right now. I place a hand on his arm. He pulls me into a hug. I rest my head against his chest for a while, just listening to his heartbeat. I still need him, no matter what. And then I pull away, remembering how I almost lost him.

We head into the living room with the mugs of tea, and for the rest of the day, we wait.

Stevenson calls me a few times during the afternoon and his advice is always the same. Waiting is the hardest thing to do in this situation. But it's what you have to do. *Give them the grieving mother*. It implies that my daughter is already dead.

Rob stays with us, and then Josie joins later to cook for us. We made the decision to tell them about the letter and no one else, because being stuck in this house on our own would be even worse. As it is, Aiden paces the floor, his hands balled by his side.

Today isn't a good day for him, I can tell. He withdraws into himself, retracting into that protective shell he created to block out the world. I hope he isn't going back there, to the bunker. He's told me before about how he allowed the memories to blur in order to distance himself, but they must be in his sub-conscious, forever lurking.

Finally, he settles on the sofa with the laptop. I drift into the kitchen, making more tea, because extra caffeine is exactly what we need to relax. Josie follows me.

'I hate this,' she says, pulling mugs out of the cupboards. 'I want to help you but I don't know how.'

I flick the switch on the kettle and sigh. 'You are helping, Jo.'

She flashes me a sad smile. 'Are you all right? God, sorry, I know you're not.'

'My head is a complete mess and I can't stop thinking of her.' I press my palm against the kitchen counter, pushing down as hard as I dare. And then I release. 'I keep trying to figure everything out but I know I shouldn't. I should leave it to the police.'

'No,' Josie says firmly. 'Your opinion is important, too. You know Amy really well.'

'I thought so. But this all feels wrong. The ransom. The impersonal note. What if it isn't her after all?'

She shakes her head. 'I just don't know.'

'Jo?'

'Yeah?'

'Do you think that Hugh had another plan? For another child?'

I watch the way her fingers fumble as she places a mug down on the kitchen surface. I see the tension running along her jaw and the grey tinge to her skin.

'I don't know.' She closes the cupboard a little louder than she intended and her body jolts with the shock of noise. 'Sorry, I . . . I couldn't possibly know.'

'It's OK,' I say, soothingly. 'I'm trying to figure everything out, but nothing makes sense. To be honest, I'm not sure the ransom note is even real.' I snatch a few tea bags from the tin. 'But what could make sense is if Amy had the structure of a plan to follow before she took Gina. If Hugh had another place set up for another child. It was something that came up in the investigation after Aiden left the bunker. They asked him about it in case there were other children trapped elsewhere.'

She leans over the kitchen counter, her chest heaving. 'It's . . . I find it so hard to think about.'

I reach out and place a hand on her shoulder. 'I know, and I'm sorry that I have to ask. But I need to find Ginny. If you can help in any way . . .'

'I'll look through his things,' she says. 'He had to buy the land in the woods surrounding the bunker before he abducted Aiden. Maybe he's bought other land, too. If he did, maybe there's some paperwork that was missed in the first investigation.' She straightens up, collecting herself. 'I don't know, though, Emma. Two children in two places? Logistically, how would that work?'

All I can do is shrug. 'I don't know either. He was planning to kill Aiden when he turned sixteen.' I close my eyes against the swelling rage that comes with these thoughts. When I compose myself, I say, 'He needed a replacement.'

'Why wouldn't he use Aiden's bunker?'

Behind me there's a rumbling and a click as the kettle boils and turns itself off. My heart leaps at the sound. 'You're right, I don't know. He had everything set up there. Unless he'd found a better location.'

Josie lifts the kettle and begins to pour. 'What has our life become that we have to think these dark thoughts. I still don't know how I could have married a monster like him.' Her hands shake so much that she spills some of the water and places the kettle down.

'Can I tell you something?' I rest my head against one of the cupboard doors, exhaustion seeping into every part of my body.

'You can tell me anything, you know that.'

'There are days when I miss Jake.' I tap my forehead against the wood. 'I know who, what, he was. A murderer. A predator. But for most of the time we were together, I knew him as the man who loved me. Is that sick?'

When I turn to Josie, I realise that there are tears rolling down her nose. 'I miss Hugh as well. I hate him. And I miss him. Whenever anything happens in my life my first thought is to tell Hugh about it, until I remember he's dead. And then I remember what he did.' She wipes the tears away with the heel of her hand. 'What's wrong with me? Why am I like this?'

We grasp hands, holding tight.

'There's nothing wrong with us, Jo. We're not the monsters, are we? Let's not feel guilty about this.' I take a deep, long breath. 'I think therapy is *long* overdue for us.'

She laughs. 'I think you're right.'

'I think we miss love, not them. We miss the people they pretended to be when they were with us.' I let her go for a moment and wipe away the rest of my tears. I won't waste any more on Jake Hewitt or Hugh Barratt. 'Come on, let's hurry up with these teas before the kettle goes cold.'

'Mum?'

Of course, we didn't hear Aiden's soft footsteps. The sound of his voice makes me audibly gasp.

'Sorry, love, you made me jump!'

'Mum,' he says again, and this time I hear the warning.

'What is it?' I cross the kitchen in less than five strides. He has the laptop in his hands.

'They've found out about the ransom note,' he says.

'Who?' Josie leans forward as I reach out to take the laptop.

The 'news' website isn't a particularly reputable one. It's the kind that sends out clickbait articles with a slideshow of twenty or more pictures of celebrities. I suppose Aiden and I are celebrities in our own way, in the sense that we're infamous. I scan the page filled with tacky adverts for liposuction and celebrity gossip. The headline reads, RANSOM LETTER DELIVERED TO PRICE FAMILY. Then it begins dramatically with: There has been a new development in the case of missing girl, Gina Price. Sources tell us a ransom letter has been delivered to the family, demanding £50,000 in exchange for her safe delivery.

It goes on, but I prise my eyes away from the screen. This jeopardises everything.

Chapter Seventeen

EMMA

It takes some restraint not to throw the laptop against the wall. How could this happen? No one knows about the ransom letter except for the police, Rob and Josie. I trust them both with my life. Neither of them would let anything bad happen to Gina.

'I don't believe it.' Instead of throwing it, I place the laptop down on the kitchen table and press my fingers against closed eyelids. 'Who did this?'

'Try to stay calm, Em.' Rob's voice barely penetrates the thick cloud of anger engulfing me. 'We're going to figure this out. Give Stevenson a call.'

I nod my head. The police need to know about this as soon as possible. I check the time the article was posted. It was barely an hour a go. Perhaps the police can scare the site into taking it down before anyone else sees it.

'How did you find it?' I turn to Aiden at the same time that I retrieve my phone from my pocket. He answers while I'm searching for Stevenson in my contacts.

'Someone on Instagram sent it to me.'

I shake my head. 'Aiden, you shouldn't be talking to people like that.'

'It helped us, didn't it?' he says quietly.

'You know how dangerous it is to talk to anyone who isn't in this room.' My fingers tremble as I tap on the icon to call Stevenson. 'You can't connect with these people. Did you tell anyone about the ransom note?'

His eyes drift to his feet. Rob moves closer to his son and places a protective arm around his shoulder. For a moment there I feel locked out of their paternal bond.

'Come on, Em. You know he's not stupid,' Rob says.

The phone is ringing. I take a deep breath.

'I'm sorry, matey,' I offer. 'I know it wasn't you.'

Aiden just nods his head, still avoiding my eye contact.

'It's not you I'm mad at,' I add. 'It's whoever leaked this to the press.'

As the phone continues to ring, my hand shakes with fury. Someone at that clickbait news site typed this article knowing that it could put a four-year-old child's life in danger. The rage that induces consumes me whole. It's physical, like a virus. But I can't let it spill out on the people I love.

'Stevenson.'

'The ransom note has leaked,' I blurt out. 'Some scummy pseudo-journalist has typed up every single fucking detail about the letter.'

'Tell me the name of the site.'

I reel off the details through my teeth, pacing up and down in the small kitchen while everyone else stands around me looking awkward. Josie bites her lower lip. Aiden stares at the floor. Rob grips his cane, knuckles white.

'Give me a list of everyone you told,' says Stevenson.

I tell him. Aiden, obviously, Josie and Rob.

'That's it?'

'Rob did you tell your parents?' I check.

'No.'

'Yes, that's it. It was one of your coppers. It had to be.'

'Let's not jump to any conclusions,' he says. 'The most

important thing to do now is to get this site to remove the article before any national newspapers decide to print it.'

'Is that possible?'

'I'll make it possible,' he says. 'No self-respecting journalist would print this. No one wants to be sued if . . .' he trails off, but I know the end of that sentence. *If the child dies.* 'This is the desperate act of a site wanting attention no matter the cost. I'm so sorry, Emma. I know this doesn't make you feel much better, but if this ransom letter turns out to be fake, it won't make any difference anyway.'

I know this is true, but the damage is done. Someone at the police did this, and now I know that I can't trust them.

Three long hours later, the article is removed. After an extensive web search, we accept that no one else has taken the information and written another article, but it was shared a few dozen times by various Facebook accounts. People have seen and read it. My nerves are drawn tight. The atmosphere in the house adopts the same level of tension and it begins to feel as though the walls are closing in.

Neither Rob nor Josie want to leave me alone, or maybe they don't want to leave Aiden alone with me. I snapped at him harshly when he told me about his Instagram account. But after regretting losing my temper, I agree he can keep it open in case anyone messages him with a sighting of Gina. I concede that it could actually be useful, but the idea of all that internet toxicity touching my son makes my stomach churn.

'You have to remember that none of those people are your friends,' I tell him. 'Unless you've met someone in real life, you don't know who they are. It's important not to let them too close, OK?'

But everything I say is tainted by the harsh words spoken before. I don't feel like he's even listening to me.

Evening turns into night. I manage to eat some toast, but I'm far too wound up to eat a real meal. I wish I had the ransom letter to look at but it's still at the police station. The only update I've had is that they're running tests on it, trying to find some DNA evidence that might give them a lead.

Eventually, Josie convinces me to go to bed and this time I use my old bedroom, rather than pass out on the sofa. The bones of me ache with exhaustion and I long for a way to stop the pain. During these drawn-out days I've craved alcohol more than ever before, but I can't allow myself to touch it. I feel like I'd start drinking and never stop.

In my dreams, Aiden is buried alive. I kneel on the soil digging with my hands, desperate to find him. The ghost of Gina stands behind me, laughing.

Morning comes and I wake with a start, expecting to find dirt beneath my fingernails. There's nothing, but I'm drenched in sweat after another hot night in this relentless Indian summer. I throw back the duvet and sit up, breathing in the heavy air. Wherever Gina is, I hope she isn't overheating. I imagine her tiny body covered in perspiration, flushed pink around her neck. She still carries baby fat, and her legs are chubbily cute. I miss them. Miss the smell of her.

Seven days.

One week ago, I spent the morning organising Aiden and Gina for the television interview. Aiden was wearing his smart blue shirt and I had on my grey suit. We drove to London, navigated the terrifying roads, arrived at the studio and had our make-up done. Gina charmed the assistants, producers and make-up artists. It feels as real as the nightmare I had last night.

And now all of that is over and I'm in agony.

I lie back down on the bed and wash the sweat clean with my tears.

'Emma! Em!'

Rob's voice doesn't hold the power it used to, but I hear the urgency as he calls up the stairs. Moving quickly, I wipe away tears and grab my dressing gown. News? Good news?

'Emma, we've heard from them,' he shouts. 'Aiden! Come down.'

My feet beat their way down the stairs, almost tripping. *Don't kill yourself now*, I tell myself. Stay alive for her.

'What is it?' I ask, running into the living room with Aiden a few steps behind.

'I just got off the phone with Mum. Another letter turned up at their house.'

'What?' I brush damp hair away from my face. 'But that makes no sense. Why would the letter go to your parents?'

'I guess the kidnapper figured out the police were watching your house. Or they saw us installing the cameras, maybe,' he suggests.

Whoever this person is, they're clever. After a full week, they haven't made any mistakes. They know where I live, where Rob and his parents live. Either this person has stalked us – which wouldn't be hard to do considering the amount of paparazzi photos of us online – or they know the village and they know me. Amy knows me. Amy knows the village.

'What does the letter say?' I ask.

'They're bringing it over,' he says. 'But she read it out to me on the phone. The letter gives details about a specific drop. They want the money on Friday, and they want Aiden to deliver it.'

I turn to my son and my heart almost beats out of my chest. 'Why Aiden?'

'I don't know,' he replies. 'Maybe we'll find out more when the letter gets here.'

'You're not doing it,' I say to my son.

'I will if it means getting Gina back,' Aiden replies. There's that steel in his eyes again. I remember it from the day his new book arrived at the flat in Manchester. One of the few times Aiden has argued back.

'It's too dangerous.' I shake my head, thoughts swirling through my mind. I want nothing more than my daughter home and safe, but this means putting my other child in danger. How can I do that? 'If something happened to you, I'd never forgive myself.'

'Why would you need to forgive yourself?' he says, his

voice cold as ice. 'This is my decision to make. I'm an adult, remember?'

'Hey, now.' Rob places a comforting hand on my shoulder. 'Let's speak to the police and see what they have to say about it. They might be able to come to a solution that keeps Aiden safe if he were to do the drop.'

'No, he can't!' I back away from them. 'I'll do it. I can't let Aiden do it.'

'But that's what they want,' Aiden insists. 'This is for Gina, remember? Have you forgotten her?'

'That's . . . that's unfair.' I say. 'Don't you both see that this was her plan all along?'

'Whose plan, Em?' Rob's voice has that soothing, patient edge to it that suggests he's humouring the crazy woman.

'Amy. She wants to draw Aiden out and then hurt him so that I'm punished for what I did to her. This isn't about money. She's going to try and kill him, I'm sure of it.'

'Come on, be sensible,' Rob says. 'How would she do that with police all around her? She's not going to be on a roof with a sniper rifle.'

'Maybe she's hired someone who can.'

'How?'

'I don't know. The dark web.'

Rob leans over me, reminding me of the power he once had. 'You're letting paranoia get the best of you. For all we know, Amy killed herself months ago and this is someone hoping to earn a few quid by taking a child from a high-profile family.'

I shake my head, infuriated that he's dismissing my fears so easily. 'That makes even less sense, Rob.'

The knock on the door pulls us both out of the spiralling argument and I'm glad of it. It's Josie who goes to the door, which surprises me because I hadn't even noticed her still in the room.

'Are you OK, Mum?' Aiden asks.

I place one hand on my chest, hoping the warmth will calm the pounding heart within. I nod my head.

'Emma!' Sonya's voice cuts through the brief moment of quiet. 'Why didn't you tell us?'

It's Rob who answers. 'It was my decision, Mum.'

'You don't trust us?' She storms into the lounge, her gaze directed at me. 'We've been pulled into this without any warning.'

'I know. I'm sorry,' I say, but the truth is I'm not. I couldn't predict that the letter would go to them. If they had to be pulled into this mess, so be it. Whatever it takes to get Gina back.

'Emma didn't mean for this to happen.' Josie slumps into an armchair, her voice and body exhausted.

'Did you put the letter in plastic?' I ask.

'Yes. I'm not an idiot. It's in a sandwich bag.'

'With the envelope?'

She nods. 'There's no stamp.'

Whoever delivered this did it by hand, and they know where Rob's parents live.

'Can I see it?'

She hands me the note, slippery inside the plastic coating. I examine it closely, taking in as much of the detail as I can. It's written in block capitals again. The paper is normal A4, folded into three sections to fit inside a regular envelope. On the other side of the paper, I see the Manila envelope with the address also written in block letters.

IT IS TIME TO DELIVER THE MONEY.

MIDNIGHT. FRIDAY NIGHT. THE ENTRANCE TO ROUGH VALLEY FOREST.

AIDEN MUST COME ALONE.

GINA IS WAITING FOR YOU.

Chapter Eighteen

AIDEN

It's Friday at 10 p.m. and the night is still warm. The kitchen windows are wide open and the air carries the scents of the village, from the faint woodiness of Rough Valley Forest to the smokiness of late-night summer barbecues.

We're sitting around the table. I have a bag of money by my feet. DCI Stevenson is on speakerphone, talking us through the details once again. Walk. Walk. Place money down. Wait for Gina. Walk. Walk. Drive.

Police will be with us in the shadows, their guns trained and ready for the kidnapper to show her, or his, face. It will be dark. I don't like my odds if I get in the way of a bullet.

Keeping the victim alive is their priority. Capturing the kidnapper is a lower priority, at least that's what they've told us.

Between Wednesday and now, Mum has prowled the house like a lioness in a contemplative stupor. She comes out of her fog and roars, and then she drifts back into her thoughts. There isn't much I can say or do to alleviate her pain, but I know one thing – I'm right there with her. I'm feeling every bit of it.

After Grandma and Grandad delivered the note, Mum called DCI Stevenson and we began to form a plan to deal with the new demands. Firstly, another non-uniformed officer called round. We gave him the letter and he took it for testing. Stevenson told us that two letters gave them a much greater chance of finding DNA.

At Mum's request, the police compared handwriting samples between Amy Perry's documents from when she was a teacher, with the written notes sent to us. The results were inconclusive. The only particles found on the letters came from surgical gloves. There was nothing to prove or disprove Mum's suspicions. With each blow I watch her paranoia grow. But my own suspicions dwindle. We're becoming more and more in opposition with each other. Faith says Mum isn't looking out for my best interests because she's in the middle of something called hysteria.

After the tests were completed, we met with a prepped bank manager to help us with the money. The police wanted to use marked notes to stop the kidnapper from being able to spend them. They also gave us a bag equipped with a GPS tracker so that they can follow the kidnapper after the exchange has been made.

'Listen,' Stevenson says. 'Kidnapping is uncommon in this country because these cases rarely go their way. Most kidnappers rely on widespread corruption to get away with their crimes. That's why abduction is rife in countries with shady governments.'

'What does that mean for us?' Mum asks.

'Well, another reason gangs in the Middle East get away with kidnapping is because the families are often too afraid of the police. Perhaps this kidnapper assumed that because of your background with Aiden, you'd be less likely to come to us. Or perhaps they're just stupid.'

Mum frowns. I don't think she believes that.

There's a buzz as my phone vibrates. I pick it up and check my messages.

. . .

FAITH: Good luck, Aiden. You can do this for Gina. I know you can.

ME: Mum is freaking out.

FAITH: Of course she is. She's unbalanced. Maybe even crazy.

FAITH: Just follow the instructions. I know you'll be fine.

'Aiden, are you listening?' Mum snaps.

I slip my phone into my pocket.

'Basically, all I mean is that we're most likely going to catch the person or people who have taken Gina tonight.' He pauses. 'Unless this is a hoax. But that means we're not losing anything. OK?'

'OK, thanks,' Mum says.

I hope he's right and we do catch the abductor because I want them to suffer. Last night I dreamed that I had the bat I used to kill Hugh and I pummelled the kidnapper with it until they were a bloody mess on the forest floor. The kidnapper had no face in my dream. Perhaps I'm beginning to doubt Mum's insistence that this is Amy. Even DCI Stevenson has his doubts. He's leaning towards the idea that organised crime has taken a role in this. Though he accepts that it's strange for such a high-profile child to be taken. On the other hand, people may assume that Mum has money now because of the strange celebrity status we've been given. Trauma rewards, I think of them. What a way to end up famous.

'I still don't like this,' Mum says. 'I don't like Aiden taking the money.'

Stevenson's voice is muffled through the speakerphone. 'I know, Emma. We're going to be right there with Aiden. Every step of the way.'

'You mean the same police that leaked important information?' she says.

'We found out who that was,' Stevenson says carefully. 'It wasn't a malicious act. Unfortunately, they had a family member who writes for the site and they happened to over-hear a private conversation. They've since lost their job,

Emma. And they're mortified about the breach. It's unfortunate that it happened, but the leak doesn't seem to have affected your case.'

She shakes her head, eyes hard and unsympathetic. 'It still shouldn't have happened.'

'I know,' he admits.

I feel differently to Mum, but I understand her reaction all the same. My mother has survived more heartbreak than most, which has hardened her in the same way my experiences have shaped me. I watched a movie about a kidnapping last year. The mother wailed through the entire two hours. My mother doesn't do that. She thinks. She works through problems and comes up with ideas. She'll do whatever's necessary.

'I want to be in the car that waits near the forest,' Mum says calmly.

'OK, you can do that,' Stevenson says.

He sounds so sure of himself. How can he be confident that everything will go well when he's never done this before? I glance down at the fifty thousand pounds in the bag. One small duffel bag. Marked notes.

We have another hour to wait before we leave.

The car headlights cut through the shadowy road towards the forest. We're in a car with dark windows, and I'm certain that the kidnapper will realise this isn't my mother's car. A police constable sits in the driver's seat, wearing a baseball cap to obscure his features.

The officer pulls into a layby about a five-minute walk from the entrance to Rough Valley Forest. I smell the pine and earth of the forest. Within those trees I lived my life in a cage.

'Are you all right?' Mum asks from the back seat. Her eyes are open wide, and they dart between me and the officer in the front seat. No drug could produce the kind of adrenaline she's running on right now.

'I'm OK,' I reassure her. 'Please try to relax.'

She lets out a slight whimper and then clamps her hands to her mouth. 'Can I walk with you?' Her voice cracks with emotion. This frightens me more than the money resting on my lap.

'No.' The officer leans through the seats to speak to Mum at the back. 'I'm sorry Ms Price, but the kidnapper requested Aiden to be alone and we believe it's best for him to walk alone. But look into the trees, Ms Price.'

I watch Mum turn her head to peer through the glass of the car window.

'You can't see them, but there are trained men within those trees. They will be with him every step of the way.'

She swallows down her emotions and nods her head. I knew that the trust between Mum and the police grew thin when she saw the article on the clickbait website, but she still trusts them just enough to allow them to guard me with guns. I guess they are the best she has right now.

'I love you, Aiden,' she says.

The words run through me, wash over me. I hear them often and they tend to leave me cold. There is a part of me that can't accept those words from anyone. I heard them a lot, spoken in a different voice. I have to remind myself that Mum is the one who means them, that she won't hurt me, that we love each other.

'Love you too, Mum. I'm going to be fine. Please try not to worry, OK?'

She reaches out and touches my shoulder. 'I know. I believe in you. But be careful, OK?'

A mother's prayer.

'I will. I promise.'

'It's almost five to,' the officer says. 'Would you like to set off?'

My fingers wrap around the handle of the duffel bag. 'Yes.'

Chapter Nineteen

AIDEN

Dr Anderton talks about survivor guilt. The responsibility that comes from surviving an improbable situation when others don't. How many children are returned after being abducted? How many aren't? I want Gina to come home more than anything. Her life is in my hands.

After a prompt from his walkie-talkie, the officer responds back and then turns to me. 'All right, you can leave now. Take it steady, and use your signals if anything goes wrong.'

My free hand finds the door handle. I thought I would be calmer than this, but my heart is pounding. *Dun-dun-dun-dun*.

Outside the car, the coolness of the night breeze tickles the nape of my neck. Because even the nights are warmer than usual, I'm just wearing a long-sleeved T-shirt with jeans. The shirt is bright yellow so that the police can see me.

Pine and earth drifts to my nostrils. I breathe it in with each step. It's the smell of the bunker. The smell of my child-hood. I follow the narrow road, and soon I'll turn right onto the track that leads to the entrance. There will be a sign in green saying Rough Valley, and a wooden stile. This is not a wood for joggers and dog walkers, it's too thick and unruly, but there is one easy path that dips into the trees.

Halfway there, and I begin to feel some excitement. If everything goes to plan, I'll see my little sister again. I'll know that she's safe and she can come home to live with us again. We'll show her that she can survive, like I did. We'll remind her what love is and she'll laugh. We'll laugh again. We'll be a family again.

If this goes well.

As the entrance to the woods comes into view, I slow my steps down. There is the stile, and the green sign. Inside, I'm shutting down, retreating into myself, slipping away . . . Until I pull it back. My hand squeezes the leather strap of the duffle bag. Palms sweat. I know what is inside that bag and what it means to my family.

As I climb over the stile, I use the torch app on my phone. There was nothing in the note about no phones. There was very little information, actually, which Stevenson seemed surprised about when we read him the note. Does this mean that the kidnapper is inexperienced? Someone for whom the ransom is an afterthought? A person who knows us? Or a random hoaxer who got lucky? I jump down and the soles of my trainers slip on a loose stone. My breath catches and I shine the torch around the floor by my feet. I raise the phone and hear the sound of my ragged breath.

The trees rustle and the breeze lifts the hair on my arms as I continue along the path. Where are the police officers? My mind wildly conjures the paranoid idea that Stevenson has set me up and there's no one guarding me. That I'm alone again.

'Hello?' I clear my throat and try again. 'Hello? Is someone here?'

I trip over a root and almost fall. Shouldn't the police have given me a torch? I suppose no one thought about it. I hold the phone aloft, still, my arm aching now. The light finds trampled, hardened soil, patches of grass, roots and stones, the bark of trees and, finally, a bench.

'Hello?'

My voice echoes through the darkness.

'Gina? If you're there, Gina, call out. It's Denny. I'm here to help take you home.'

I hold my breath as I wait for an answer, but the woods give nothing but silence.

Perhaps they want me to wait on the bench. The instructions said the entrance to Rough Valley Forest. There's nowhere else to wait. With my heart still beating hard, I sit down on the bench and wait.

Nothing.

I start to wonder whether the kidnapper has left further instructions on the bench. I drown the seat in torchlight, check underneath and in the dirt around it. There's nothing there. What if I'm being impatient? What if I'm fidgeting too much and they won't come to meet me? I decide to stay still for as long as I can, but there's an overwhelming feeling that someone is behind me. I stand up, shine my light into the trees behind me. The leaves rustle, but no one emerges.

I follow the sound, going deeper into the trees, convinced that someone is watching me. Why won't they reveal themselves?

'I have your money,' I yell. 'Give us Gina and you can have it. We don't care.'

My foot slips as the ground slopes below me. I tumble for a while, almost losing my phone, landing with the money beneath me for a cushion. When I climb back to my feet the sound of movement in the woods stops. I'm not even sure there was anyone there. If there was, it was probably the police. I walk back to the bench, which is still empty, and it dawns on me that Stevenson was right. This was a hoax.

When I get back to the car, Mum rushes towards me and pulls me into a hug, her wild eyes examining the scrape on my cheek, the dirt on my clothes. I still have the bag.

'What's going on? Where's Gina?'

I shake my head. My mind bursts with words. A noise. Scared. Gina. Lost. No one there.

'What happened?'

I swallow. My throat is thick. Every part of my body is tired. I'm sure I'm trembling all over, but when I look at my hands, they seem steady.

'Aiden?' She gently strokes my face, but I pull away and the hurt expression is back.

One of the officers comes to my rescue and explains everything. 'No one turned up. Looks like it was a hoax after all.'

'Maybe I did something wrong,' I say. 'Maybe they wouldn't come because I messed up.' I turn to the woods. What would happen if I went back there to live? Would I survive if I lived off the land like a wolf-child? I read about the stories of children raised by wolves. I read about them because I thought I might be one of them.

'Aiden.' Mum physically moves my head so that I'm facing her. 'This isn't your fault. We're going to get Ginny back, I promise.'

She leads me back to the car and all I can think is that I caused this. It's karma because of the success of my art. Why should I make money from the tragedy in my life? I feel sick. The car is claustrophobic, with that new plastic smell.

My phone buzzes.

FAITH: What happened? U OK?
ME: They didn't show.
FAITH: WTAF? Why not?
ME: Dunno.
FAITH: U OK?
ME: It's all my fault.
FAITH: No it isn't. You've never done anything wrong.
ME: K
FAITH: What about her, did she support you?
ME: Mum? Yeah.
FAITH: How?
ME: Just said it wasn't my fault.
FAITH: No, it's hers. She's the one people are after.

ME: What do you mean?

FAITH: Read the news. Everyone blames her.

FAITH: I know she's your mum, but maybe you need to face up to something important.

ME: What?

FAITH: That she isn't a good person.

I look up at Mum in the rear-view mirror. She's talking to the police officer driving the car, her expression pulled tight from stress.

'What happens next?' she says.

'Honestly, I'm not sure, the officer replies. You'd best check in with Stevenson.'

Mum leans back in her seat and closes her eyes. Then she turns her head and her brown eyes rest on me. 'I shouldn't have let you do this. I'm so sorry.'

I want to tell her that it was my choice, but I don't. My gaze drifts down to the messages on my phone.

FAITH: That she isn't a good person.

ME: No. You're wrong.

I'm about to put my phone away, but I notice Faith typing again.

FAITH: I overstepped. Sorry.

FAITH: It wasn't supposed to come out so harshly.

FAITH: U there, Aiden?

FAITH: Seriously, reply, I feel bad.

FAITH: Aiden, please. Just let me know I didn't fuck up.

Finally, I reply: *It's OK, I'm not mad.* And put my phone away.

Chapter Twenty

EMMA

He doesn't speak. He sits in the back of the car, trembling. I have to guide him when we get to the house because he doesn't seem to know where he is. All the time I have the vague sense that I should be talking to him, teasing out responses from him, but exhaustion means I can't move my lips to speak.

There's a ripe smell of old food when we walk in. I remember now that I threw away a few slices of pizza and the bin hasn't been taken out. Normally, I'd do that right away to get rid of the smell, but I don't. I lock the door and I lead Aiden upstairs. I want to make sure he goes to bed.

Outside his room, I turn him to face me. 'None of this is your fault. I know I've already said it, but I don't think you believe me.'

He shrugs.

'Talk to me, Aiden.'

He backs into his room, and, for once, closes the door. The sight of that sealed door sends a shiver down my spine. I'm lost to him, or he's lost to me. Is there a difference? I lean against the wall and close my eyes. Was it Gina who kept him anchored to me? That helped him speak? His first words to me were to warn me that Gina was coming. He pointed to the grey water on the floor and told me I was leaking. That was Gina forcing herself into our world and turning the shadows into light.

I stagger away from his room into my own. Ginny is still out there somewhere and we're no closer to figuring out where.

Now that I know the ransom note was a hoax, I can admit to myself that it gave me more hope than I thought it had. It never seemed real, but at the same time, it provided a motive to Ginny's kidnapping, and suggested I could get her home safe and sound. That's always the way in the movies. There's a reason. Then there's a transaction. Money for a life. But then the hero swoops in and takes down the bad guy so that the villain ends up with nothing.

Money is not the reason Gina was taken. I know that now. But who sent the letter? Could it be Amy, messing with my head, or am I fixating on her when I should be considering other options? Maybe Rob's right and she's gone.

DCI Stevenson's name pops up on my phone screen, but I reject the call. Nothing is going right. The ransom note ended up on the internet, and Aiden walked alone into a dark wood for no reason. Perhaps it's time to try things my own way.

I wake to the sound of the birds and the orange light seeping in through the slats in the blinds. I wake rigid. My arms and legs straight by my sides. The dream I was having is already ebbing away, but I sense that I was falling from a tall drop with the ground coming up close.

For the first time since Gina went missing, I feel a solid sense of purpose. Despite the aching muscles and the sweat beads around my hairline, I throw back the covers and swing my legs out of the bed. Today is the day I begin to take matters into my own hands.

After a shower, I dry my hair, put on jeans and a shirt, and head downstairs. Aiden's door is open again when I walk along the landing, but he isn't there. I hear the sound of the shower running and continue into the kitchen.

It's time to clear up some of the mess that has been accumulating since we moved in. I take out the bin, wipe down the counters, fill the dishwasher and dust the dining room. By the time Aiden comes down, I'm on to making coffee for us both. But he shakes his head when I offer him a cup.

When he rejects the coffee, he notices the widening of my eyes, the tension in my posture. He knows I'm afraid he'll never speak again, because he follows up with, 'Can I have tea instead?'

When I reach out to hug him, however, he reels away from me, and I retract my arms to hug my chest instead.

'You sit down in the lounge and I'll bring it over if you like,' I manage to say without croaking. He leaves as I flip the switch on the kettle.

As soon as he's out of sight, I grab hold of the counter, watching the blood fade from my fingers and the skin turn bright white. I need a release. I need to be on my knees with my head in my hands, crying so hard that snot comes out of my nose and the sobs can be heard down the street. I need to be a mess. But I can't. Instead I press my arm against my mouth and moan into the fabric of my shirt. The moan becomes a muffled scream of frustration, obscured by the loud bubbling water of the kettle.

The doorbell rings and I pull myself together, smoothing down the arm of my shirt, rearranging the collar, wiping away the dew from under my eyes. I take two deep breaths and head to the door.

A mousy-haired man of about twenty-five stands outside. I examine his smooth pores, the eagerness of his bright blue eyes, the way his mouth slopes up at the corners.

'I don't speak to reporters,' I say.

'Oh, no,' he replies. 'Didn't DCI Stevenson tell you? I'm your new family liaison officer.'

I close the door, put it on the latch, and come back into the kitchen to make Aiden his cup of tea. The doorbell rings twice more, and then there's a hesitant knock.

On the third knock, Aiden comes into the kitchen. 'Who is that?'

'Our new family liaison officer, apparently.'

'Aren't you going to let them in?'

'Nope.'

I pass him the tea before taking a sip of my coffee. The third knock appears to be the last one. Whatever-his-name-is has taken the hint and left. My phone rings again. I hold it up to show Aiden the screen. It's Stevenson.

'What's going on, Mum?' Aiden asks.

I shrug. 'We can't trust them, can we?' I think about DI Khatri forcing me out of the press conference, the leaked information about the ransom note.

'Mum, we can't ignore them.' Aiden places his mug down on the table. He's lost weight, I realise. He hasn't been to his physio sessions or to the gym. Aiden has been working on bulking his frame for quite some time now. It's the first time I've seen him looking gaunt again. 'They might have information that we need.'

My sip of coffee rests sour in the pit of my stomach. 'I know, love, but we also need to protect ourselves.' I nod my head over to the table, gesturing for Aiden to follow me there. 'I've been trying to work with them, but it's clearly not working. No one's on our side, not the police, not the press, not the people who message you on Instagram or the ones who send us cards. It's me, you and Gina. OK?'

Aiden lets out a short, sharp breath through his nose. 'What about Dad? Grandma and Grandad?'

'They're important,' I admit. 'But they're not us.'

He shakes his head and folds his arms across his chest.

'Aiden hear me out a minute. I know we didn't ask for any of this, but we're famous now. The media has printed our photographs so often, and told our story so many times, that people think they know everything about us. They think we're their friends. But we're not.' I pause to rub my hands together. The itching between my thumb and forefinger is coming back stronger with each day that Gina is missing. 'Any PC working on the case could sell our information. Any random on the internet could use your social media posts for their own personal gain. Do you understand what I'm saying?'

'You want me to stop using the internet?'

I lean back for a minute. 'Honestly, I'm not sure.' I think for a moment. 'No, keep your account's open. Once Gina's back you'll want to use them for your art. It's your vocation and you shouldn't give it up. But stop posting and stop replying to messages.'

His face crumples in. 'You can't control what I do like this. It isn't fair.'

'Well, playing fair won't bring Gina home, will it? I've seen you replying to people online. It could hurt Gina. Don't you understand that? Anything you pass on to another person could be used against us.'

'All right,' he says quietly. 'But what's the point in keeping them open if I can't post anything or comment?'

I rub my eyes and let out a long sigh. 'What I mean is . . . be careful. Don't engage with people. It's important. You know that, don't you?'

He nods.

'We're going to find Gina and we're going to bring her home.' I reach over and place one hand on the family laptop. 'I should've done this sooner. I'm going to find a private detective to hire. We need help.'

I can see Aiden's mind thinking things over. Eventually he nods. 'You still have to listen to the police though, Mum. They could have important information they can share.'

'I will, I promise. I'll call Stevenson back and see what he has to say. We're not having any more liaison officers, though.' I think of the forced conversation, the constant platitudes, the prying eyes and listening ears. No, I won't go back to that.

After we spend a little time researching potential private investigative firms, I give Stevenson a call back. He answers on the first ring, and his greeting is somewhat tense.

'Emma. Hi. I've been trying to get hold of you.' He coughs, possibly out of nervousness. 'Listen, my department is working with the Met more and more since the ransom and they wanted you to have a new liaison officer. I sent someone over to you, but it seems you stopped him from coming into the house.'

'You're our liaison officer,' I say. 'We're not going through all that again.'

'It streamlines the process and gives me time –'

'All you have to do is call me whenever there's an update,' I reply, trying to keep my voice calm. 'And make sure no one leaks information to the press. I'm sorry, but I have to protect Aiden as much as I have to find Gina. If there's someone in our house for extended periods of time, that means there's someone who could leak information about us to the media.'

'Look, Emma, I understand, but –'

'You're not talking me out of this. My mind is made up.' I pause. 'But that doesn't mean we won't help with the investigation in any other way we can. You know I've appreciated everything you've done for us, in the past and the present.'

'I'm glad to hear it,' he says. 'We're still a team. OK?'

I remember how he was there for me when Aiden showed me the bunker that cold night in the woods. I remember his calm words on the phone and the fact that he dropped everything to come and find me. 'OK.'

'I'm sorry the ransom note was a dead end,' he says. 'We're working hard on every lead we have.'

'What are those leads?' I ask.

'Some potential sightings,' he says. 'One in York, which sounds promising. Others, not so much. Devon. Aberystwyth, even Spain.'

'Will you keep me in the loop?'

'Of course,' he replies, and I note the disappointment in his voice. He knows I've hardened to him and the rest of the police. That I've turned my back on them.

'All right,' I say. 'Thanks.'

Aiden is waiting behind me as I put my phone back into the pocket of my jeans. His eyes droop sadly as I recite the news. Despite waking with purpose, the potential sightings leave me cold. There are far too many people out there who enjoy misdirecting the police.

We go back to the laptop, narrow down a list of potential investigators and then make lunch. More stodge. Most of it lies uneaten on our plates as we work. The day wears me down as it goes on, but doing something helps.

Rob and his parents pop in a few hours later. I'd already told them about the failed ransom exchange over the phone on the way home the night before. Sonya pulls me into a hug, but I don't feel it. Rob's eyes trail over me from head to toe. He notices the change in my demeanour, but he doesn't ask me anything while his parents are there.

We make tea. Aiden is silent as I describe how he went into the woods alone. Rob agrees with me about the family liaison officer and the private detective.

'The police have had their chance,' he says. 'They've failed too many times. They failed Aiden all those years ago.' We all nod. It's time to do things our way.

By the time they leave, I'm wiped out. Aiden goes up to his room as soon as night falls. I decide to watch bland sitcoms until I can no longer keep my eyes open.

I drift. Head bobbing up and down, chin almost landing on my chest. And then I hear it: the unmistakeable sound of a letterbox snapping shut.

I'm off the sofa in a second, thoughts of my sleepiness already gone. I sprint into the kitchen and snatch up the letter lying on the doormat. But I can't open it now. I need to find the person who put it through the door. I grab my keys from the hook on the wall and fumble through them to find the right one. A second or two later I fling open the door and run out into the darkness.

Chapter Twenty-One

THE CHAPEL

Yes, Emma is a good mother, I have to admit that. But she isn't a perfect woman. That halo of hers hasn't always been polished. There was a time when she was as petty as everyone else. Did you know that when I moved to Bishoptown to live with my aunty and uncle, she treated me like an outsider in the same way everyone else did?

Hush, little one. Let me tell you the rest of my story. Let me tell it now, and then we can leave. There's a place I want to take you, and things I need to do.

Out of everything that happened to me at school, the worst of it occurred at Wetherington House. We were sixteen and on a camping trip. This wasn't the first time that students had gone camping, but it was the first time I'd been invited. These camping trips were legendary. Half of year eleven would go with crates of Hooch and WKD. There'd be tales of drunken kisses and drunken sex. Afterward, these tales would spread around the school for weeks on end. Who had cheated on who? I'd listen intently, figuring out which relationships were doomed, and which were steady.

I never dreamed of going myself, until Emma invited me.

The week before we'd worked together on a group project. I can't remember what it was now, some sort of sociology experiment. Forcing the year seven kids to take a questionnaire or something like that. She hadn't been a bitch to me, like the others, and I took that to mean we were friends.

'It's no biggie,' she said. 'Just a few people chilling out near Rough.'

Rough Valley was close to the edge of the Wetherington House estate. I'd heard rumours that the camping trips often trespassed onto the Duke's land, and that we were supposed to be careful in case one of his groundskeepers shot someone.

Exaggeration, of course.

'Sure, I'll see if I'm free,' I'd said.

I remember the wry smile on her face because she knew I was free. It was obvious I was trying to play it cool because I was never invited anywhere.

That night I asked my uncle if I could borrow a tent so I could go camping. He fished out a load of equipment for me, including a camping stove, pans, a torch, mosquito repellent and many other gadgets I use in the chapel now. He lectured me on how to use each one.

'Will there be boys there?' he'd asked.

'It's just girls,' I lied.

'Maybe I should come with you.'

Horrified, I quickly dispelled all his worries and packed my belongings. He'd shown me how to put his heavy-duty tent together. I knew the instruction packet from start to finish on every single one of the gadgets. I was prepared for every eventuality.

When the night came, I got the bus to the woods, lying to Uncle Gregory that I was meeting Emma at her house and travelling with her mother. He wasn't particularly happy about it, but my Aunty Kim knew about some of the bullying and insisted that I go to make friends. I was sixteen after all; old enough to have sex and live on my own if I wanted to.

I had a ten-minute walk off the bus, dragging my heavy backpack and tent. The straps kept catching in my hair, which I wore in a long, messy plait down my back. Sometimes the boys would yank my plait in the middle of class, but I still couldn't bring myself to cut my hair.

By the time I got there, the others were already slightly drunk. At first no one noticed me arrive, until one of the boys saw me and pointed.

'Weirdo! Who invited the weirdo?'

Emma, sat on Rob's knee, a bottle of Orange Reef in her hand, said, 'I invited her. Leave her alone, OK?'

There was some snort-laughing, but I smiled gratefully at her before setting up my tent. As I did so, I imagined what it would be like to sit on Rob's knee. I wondered whether becoming friends with Emma would lead to me being friends with Rob, too, and whether I could then work out a way to get him to dump her for me. For a while my mind drifted to fantasies similar to the movies I watched. The nerdy girl who takes off her glasses and was beautiful all along.

'What the fuck's this thing?'

One of Rob's friends – Dan, I think his name was – kicked at my tent pole.

'It's an army tent,' I replied. 'I borrowed it from my uncle.'

'You guys have got to come and see this monstrosity.'

I self-consciously glanced around me at the trendy, colourful pop-up tents that everyone else was using. They were the kind you saw when the camera panned over a festival like Glastonbury or Leeds.

Somehow, during the laughter, someone shoved a beer in my hand. I sipped it – my first ever – and started to loosen up.

Having me there was something of a novelty for them and they decided to make the most of it. They asked me questions. Where I was from. Who I lived with. What my uncle did for a living. It was fun. Until the questions became more personal. Had I ever kissed a boy? Fucked one? Fumbled with one? I searched for Emma, but she was kissing Rob by the campfire.

'What's with the hair?' Dan asked.

I pulled my plait around my neck so that it draped over one breast. 'What do you mean?'

'I mean, why? Why not have it cut?'

One of the girls snickered and I knew then that my hair was disgusting compared to the other girls.

'My mum likes it long,' I said. I gulped on more of the beer. Saying that out loud hurt. I hadn't seen my mum for four years at that point. And I hadn't had my hair cut for that long either.

'Why don't you live with your mum?' someone asked. I can't remember who.

'I think I'm going to go to my tent now,' I said, standing up from the grass. The sun had just set, and I was cold. My cardigan was inside the tent.

'Going to bed already?' Dan joked. 'Bit early isn't it?'

'I guess.' I shivered and drank more beer. I kept searching for Emma, but she was still kissing Rob. They were entwined in each other. Lost within each other. I hated her then. She was wearing his jacket, warm and snuggled with the boy everyone wanted.

'If you're cold, come by the fire,' Dan suggested. 'Get a bit closer. You could sit next to me.'

I didn't like Dan. He had an air about him that I've come to know as entitled. Hugh had it too, but I could forgive it in him. There were lots of young people in Bishoptown who thought the world was at their feet because they'd been brought up with a little bit of money. Some learn empathy and grow out of it, others don't. I haven't seen much of Dan since school so I can't say for certain that he's still the same, but my instinct tells me he is.

Despite the fact that I didn't like him, I still moved closer. I wanted to be more popular. I wanted to make some friends. Maybe the best way to do that was sitting close to a boy for a few hours.

'I don't bite,' he said, opening one arm so that I could snuggle in.

The snickering girl was watching us intently, and I became worried that she was his girlfriend. I hadn't noticed anything between them at that point, but she had a strange expression on her face. Then I decided that if she was jealous, I liked it. I wanted the other girls to be jealous of me.

I was on my second beer and I wouldn't say I was drunk, but I was a little buzzed. My heart was racing. Adrenaline worked through me. I sensed a change stirring in me. I was slowly coming into a new kind of power. That night was the beginning, I could feel it.

'Are you glad you came tonight?' Dan asked, taking my empty can and replacing it with a fresh one.

'I'm really glad I got invited,' I said. 'I've never been to anything like this before.'

He made a bored sound. 'Eh, they're not that interesting. But then nothing about Bishoptown is interesting.' He drank a couple of sips of beer, watching me do the same. 'Hey, is that a spider on you?'

I stared down at myself in horror. 'Where?'

But Dan didn't answer. He pinned me down and shouted. 'Now!'

The snickering girl pulled a pair of scissors out from underneath her crossed legs. She must have been to fetch them while I was talking to Dan.

'Turn her over,' she said.

'What are you doing!' I said loud enough that I hoped Emma would hear. She'd invited me here, surely she could stop whatever it was they were about to do.

Dan flipped me on to my stomach with ease, pressing his body against me while I tried to squirm away. He was heavier than me. I had no chance of escaping.

The girl grabbed hold of my plait at the nape of my neck, pushing the cold edge of metal on my skin. There was a slicing sound as she hacked through my thick hair. Her heavy-handedness pulled painfully at the roots and I yelped as it felt like a hundred needles were piercing my scalp.

I sensed the murmuring of the others, along with foot-steps that told me people were coming over.

'You're not!'

'Fucking hell!'

'Dan, you absolute madman!'

'Oh my God, she's getting a makeover.'

'What the hell are you doing?'

The last voice was Emma, the girl who was supposed to stop anything bad happening to me tonight. The so-called friend who invited me here and suggested that I was welcome, who made me think that I would be safe. The girl who had spent all night kissing the boy I had an obsession with.

There was an elbow in my back. I felt the cold air across my bare neck. The girl made some sort of triumphant noise, which was followed by everyone else cheering.

The footsteps moved again and I heard people asking the girl what she was going to do with my plait. Emma was silent now.

Eventually, Dan let me up, and I wiped damp grass away from my face.

I wish I could say that I slapped him or punched him or did anything with agency. I didn't. I cried. Snot came out of my nose. Tears streamed down my face. I felt what was left of my hair curl up above the bottoms of my earlobes. What would my mum say if she saw me now? How was I going to explain this to my Aunt and Uncle?

The others were all standing around one tree. It was a vast oak tree with low branches spreading out into the field. In June it was a lush green, verdant with life.

Dan was with them, holding a tent peg and a pole. He was hammering something into the bark. The laughter echoed around me, coupling with the sound of my own blood pumping. I staggered up to the tree, wiping snot from my nose.

There was my plait. Pegged to the tree.

He laughed and began to chant. 'Amy Perry has no hair. Has no hair. Has no hair.' The others joined in.

No, stop crying. You have to hear this. You have to understand what happened and why I have to do this.

Chapter Twenty-Two

EMMA

There's nothing but the night air and the faint sound of a car. I run down the drive and up the road, trying to chase them down, but I'm merely enveloped by the deep blue of night. I pull my hand up to my neck, heart pounding, scalp prickling, nerves shredded.

The letter.

My steps back to the house are much slower. Now that I know the kidnapper is gone – was it Amy? Did I miss her by a hair's breadth? – I don't want to face what waits for me. I don't want to see.

Gently, I close the door behind me and listen intently to the sounds within the house. From the lounge there's the faint sound of a laugh track coming from the television. The rest of the house is quiet. Aiden is still in bed.

I make my way to the table, noticing that the sound of my breathing is louder than the sound of the television in the next room. A hammering heart punctuates my breaths. The white envelope sits askew on the tabletop. Waiting.

It says Emma on the front of the envelope in block capitals. The last letter didn't have an envelope, but it had been addressed to us both at the top of the letter. This one is, notably, just for me.

Amy. I can feel her, smell her, sense her presence. Sense the games she's been playing. What if the hoax letter was all about isolation? Forcing paranoia into our ranks, breaking us apart. What if Amy has been playing mind games with me all alone?

I know that she isn't physically here, but the mere thought of her occupies a space. Makes me want to wrinkle my nose in disgust or turn up a lip. Now I know that the hatred for her has seeped its way into my core. This is a personal hate that only two women can harbour. Long ago I tried to help her, and this is how she repays me.

Even though I'm desperate to rip the letter apart, I don't. Instead I put on clean rubber gloves and take a sharp knife from the kitchen drawer. Holding one corner with my gloved fingers, I slice open the envelope. It takes all of my concentration to ensure the knife doesn't slip and catch my finger because I'm trembling all over.

While I slide the piece of paper out of the envelope, I wonder what she has to say to me. We go back years. Back to when she first started school here. I'd felt sorry for her then, because she never had any fashionable clothes or a nice haircut. She was picked on and left out. None of that pity remains. I believe people can overcome their circumstances. I have to believe it, otherwise I would be condemning Aiden to a life I don't want to imagine.

I unfold the note, pulling in a deep breath to steady my heart. The handwriting is exactly the same as the ransom note. After reading the latest correspondence, I know, for certain this time, that Amy Perry has my daughter.

Emma, Emma. Pretty Emma.
 I like your hair that length. It suits you long.
 Do you remember, Emma?
 We were young, but not that young,
 I had hair like yours, once. Braided, though.

They took me to the tree. Sliced me open.
Do you remember, Emma?
Show me that you remember.
Come alone.
No police. I'll know.

I place the note back inside the envelope. I know what she wants from me.

I don't go to sleep, but I can't stumble out there in the dark, so I sit up and wait for morning. Just before sunrise, I slip quietly out of the house, leaving Aiden a 'back soon' note with the vagueness of a person avoiding the details of where they're going. I hope it doesn't worry him, but I can't think of a valid reason for me to leave without him. Hopefully I'll be home before he wakes.

The morning is muggy. I'm wearing the same clothes as the day before, stale sweat beneath my arms. Sleeves rolled up to the elbow. I have a duffelbag with me that I place on the backseat of the car before setting off.

My company for the journey is birds. Lines of them huddled on telephone wires and tree branches. Flocks swooping through the air. Outside of the car I imagine them singing the morning chorus, blissfully ignorant of the human world living around them, all the pain, emotional and physical, but also the love. I think about Amy's letter, which is folded and placed in my jeans pocket, and the bag on the backseat. There's a sliver of doubt worming its way through my insides. What if I *don't* remember the exact place? That's clearly what she wants me to do – remember what happened to her. She wants me to acknowledge her pain.

I felt sorry for her after it happened. For a long time, I half-heartedly tried to make up for my part in it by attempting to talk to her in the corridors at school. Most of the time she would walk away from me, eyes down, shuffling along like an anxious penguin. Then she began to come out of her shell, and I remember thinking, good for you, Amy. You're turning it around.

It was in year twelve that she started hanging around with me and Rob. There was a group of about ten of us who would hang out in the pub or Rough Valley Forest. Amy would be there. She seemed to have a different boyfriend every week. And then I fell pregnant with Aiden and I wasn't part of the group anymore.

I park in a small gravelled car park near to the campsite. It isn't actually a campsite, it's a field on the outskirts of the estate owned by the Duke of Hardwick. Or rather, the Duchess, now that the Duke is in prison for the child pornography on his laptop. I think of Maeve as I climb over the stile between fence posts. There's a chance that I'm trespassing on her land. It wouldn't be the first time.

Even at 6am, the air is warm enough that sweat forms on my upper lip from the effort of pulling my tired body over the stile with the bag. The material sags, pulled down by the weight of the hammer.

I stop and scan the field. Creamy clouds of sheep graze in packs, their bodies now growing plump with wool. There's a small group collected under a tall oak tree, sheltering from the warm morning sun beneath the canopy of the leaves. The sight of it reminds me of the sound of laughter along with the sound of tears. *You're seriously going to . . . You're mad! Holy shit.* By the time I went to see what the commotion was, it was too late. I remember Amy pinned to the ground. I remember the gathering around the trunk of the tree. I even remember the position of the bright coloured tents. Only Amy had brought a green, heavy canvas tent that seemed cheerless against the pinks and blues and reds.

I'd invited her here. A familiar stab of guilt hits me, but I push it away. She doesn't deserve it, not anymore. As I stride off towards the tree, Gina's laugh swirls around my mind. You took my daughter. You will pay for that.

But she isn't here. I wasn't sure from the letter whether she would be or not, but I had a feeling about what would catch her attention if she failed to meet me. I pull in a deep breath and concentrate.

Sheep skitter away from the tree as I stand there, facing the place Amy was bullied all those years ago. The orange glow of the rising sun partly hidden by the great boughs of the oak. I touch the bark, feel it rough beneath my fingertips. The camera stands out immediately. It's strapped to a low branch, the camouflage exterior fooling only the animals it's designed to record. Amy has set up a trail cam used by hunters and wildlife photographers. I don't know much about them. I've only ever seen them used in American horror movies when the gloomy green-black images show the monster or ghost hiding in the woods. My eyes flick up to the camera. Will these images be sent to her?

I drop the bag to the grass and pull my gaze away from the camera long enough to kneel down and take the scissors out of the bag. I knew what she wanted as soon as I read that note. With the scissors in my right hand, I stand up and stare straight into the camera. Is she watching me now? Does she have Gina with her? An ache forms in my belly.

Before I came here, I plaited my hair, surprised by how long it is now. Not as long as Amy's was when we came camping that night, though. I grasp it with my left hand, raise the scissors to show the camera, and then I reach behind my head, fumbling a little to get the blades of the scissors around the plait, and I begin to cut.

The thickness of my hair and the bluntness of the scissors – my regular household scissors rather than the sharp kind hairdressers use – means that it takes a while to get through it. Strand by strand, the braid comes loose, the gnawing of the metal shivering through my ears. I'm not gentle with it, pulling at the nape of my neck until it hurts. The blades struggle on, the pain radiates from the sore pores at the root of each hair, and I let out a frustrated scream halfway through. She wants this, I remind myself. She wants me to remember, to suffer what she suffered. But it won't be enough, because I'm not humiliated by it.

When the hair comes loose, finally, I pinch the top of the

plait, throw the scissors to the ground, and pull a hair elastic from my wrist. Once the hair is sealed at the top and the bottom, I retrieve the heavy hammer from the bag, along with a nail, and I line it up on the tree.

Past and present collide as I knock the nail into the wood. Rob wasn't laughing that day, but everyone else was. Fuck you, Amy. It doesn't justify anything that came after. Fuck you, Amy. I will get my daughter back.

There. This is what you want. It's done. The braid is attached to the tree. I'm tempted to pull down the camera and turn it around so that she can see my hair hammered onto the bark. I imagine her watching and laughing, amused by her own power. Instead, I stare up at the lens. I think of what I could say to her. Does the camera have sound? I'm not sure. Anything I say could provoke her into hurting Gina and I don't want that. I could beg her not to hurt my daughter, but that would be pointless.

Instead I gather my things back into the bag and sling it over my shoulder. The swing of the hammer hits me through the fabric. I hardly feel it.

Chapter Twenty-Three

AMY

You have beautiful hair. Soft, honey-hued, that falls over your creamy skin. There, let me tuck a lock of it behind your ear as you sleep. I'll be gentle. Sleep tight, little one. We have a long journey ahead of us.

Red sunlight filters through the tent. I'm stripped to a vest top and shorts but am still feeling the effects of the muggy atmosphere.

I haven't slept. Delivering the letter was a close call. I thought both Emma and Aiden would be asleep, but I was wrong. As I was walking away from the door, I heard movement within the house and I had to make a quick escape, driving a little faster than I should have.

Emma will know the letter is from me – all the letters have been from me – but I took precautions anyway. I parked the car further up the street, I wore a hood obscuring my features. There's a chance that my car will be identified on CCTV somewhere near the house, but Bishoptown is a small village, there won't be as many cameras as in a city. They won't be able to track my whereabouts with as much ease.

It was a stroke of luck that Emma decided to come back

to the village, but I had my suspicions that she would even before I put this plan into action. I knew the press wouldn't be on her side for long, that London would be intense, and that she would need to escape from the attention. It all happened sooner than I expected.

The cheap smartphone begins to buzz. I snatch it from where it lays on the sleeping bag. For my plan to work, I had to set up a new SIM card and pay as you go system. Luckily, this is one of the many interesting things I learned from Hugh when he was alive. He would sometimes set up cameras in the bunker to keep an eye on Aiden when he was away.

When I receive a notification, it means there's been movement near the tree. The camera sends me recordings from that movement. Most of the time it's bleating sheep, and I expect this to be the same.

It isn't.

I don't know why this image of Emma is so much more evocative to me than any of the ones in the newspapers, but it is. She stands beneath the tree, eyes focused on the camera. She knows I can see her. Because it's daytime, I get the footage in colour, and her brown eyes are like two hard pebbles inside her eye sockets. My stomach flips over with anticipation that the plan is progressing, but also some fear, too. I would be an idiot if I didn't consider Emma to be a dangerous enemy. She murdered Jake.

And yet everything I've done so far has worked – and not only that, it's controlled her from start to finish. The hoax letters worked especially well. As the information leaked to the press, her paranoia grew. I forced her to watch her precious, murdering son walk alone into the woods with a bag full of money. It's a shame there were too many officers around to do some damage to the bunker boy. Part of me had hoped I might get the chance there, but that's OK. I have other tricks up my sleeve.

Even though most of my plan has gone without a hitch, I can't get complacent. The most dangerous trait Emma possesses is her ability to keep fighting, even when she's losing.

I remember the cold blade she pressed against my neck. The warmth of the blood that trickled down to my collarbone.

Emma's hands lift to the back of her neck and I bring the screen closer to me, watching her move as my heart quickens. She does remember. She remembers everything. I knew you would, Emma. I knew it. I see her grimace as she attempts to cut through her thick hair with a pair of household scissors. I lick my lips and lean in. Emma always had beautiful hair. She tends to wear it long, past her shoulders. Brown, like Aiden's. Like Rob's. It never frizzed like mine did.

This isn't the same as what happened to me. She doesn't have hands holding her down into the dirt, or the laughter of bullies in her ears. She didn't grow up the way I did, unwanted by my parents, passed on like old clothes.

It isn't going to stop here. There's much more to do yet. I haven't even begun.

Chapter Twenty-Four

EMMA

As I step away from the tree, it occurs to me that the trail cam might have a limited range. Being close to the Wetherington Estate, signal generally isn't too bad around here, but could she be in a different part of the country and still receive the signal? She had to be in Bishoptown in order to post the note. She had to come and set up the camera. She must still be here.

I spend the next couple of hours hiking around the fields, checking in the woods, almost getting lost on several occasions. The nakedness of my neck is alien, but at least it helps to keep me cool as the sun rises. I'm all too aware of the fact that my shirt is sticking to my back.

Eventually, I traipse back to the car, with bits of grass stuck to my shoes, my legs aching from navigating the sloping countryside; thighs chafing against the denim of my jeans. I get into the car and pull down the visor to look in the mirror.

My hair is lopsided. On the right it's sheared close to my ear, and on the left it's an inch below. What am I going to say to Aiden? It's 8:30. My shoes are covered in soil and sticky grass. My shirt is stained with sweat. I've cut my own hair in an uneven, haphazard way. If any photographers take my picture now, I'll never be taken seriously again. I can't go home like this.

I put the car in gear and head into the village instead. My old hairdresser opens at 9am. I'm waiting outside the salon when she arrives to open. She doesn't ask questions; she just does what I ask.

Back at the house, I walk in, somewhat sheepishly, to find Aiden on his feet. There are shadows beneath his eyes.

'Have you been up a long time?'

'You went to get your hair cut?' He stares at me in disbelief. 'Why didn't you say? That note, it was . . .' He drifts off as though searching for the right word.

'I didn't intend to,' I admit. 'I went for some air and it was so hot.' I gesture to my stained shirt. 'I needed to get rid of the length. I'm sorry, I didn't mean to worry you.'

He shrugs, and his body relaxes slightly as though he's shedding away his tension. 'I'm just surprised, that's all.'

I know what he's thinking: what kind of woman has her hair cut while her daughter is missing? Who could be so tone deaf that they wouldn't think about how it might come across? That's something I will just have to accept as a consequence. They don't know the truth and I'm fine with that.

'Do you want me to make you some breakfast?' I offer.

'I had toast,' he says.

'OK, well, I'm going to shower and change then.'

His eyes follow me as I leave the room. I bow my head, wishing I could explain. But if I involved him, it could be dangerous for him. What if he becomes one of Amy's targets? What if he is already? I realise for the first time that I've been dealing with this very same anxiety ever since Aiden came back from the bunker. Sometimes it's a low-level hum in the back of my mind, not the muscle gripping, chest tightening panic that I feel now. But now I'm in the midst of these games with the person who kidnapped my baby daughter. I'm dealing with evil, pure evil. Anything could happen to us.

Anything could happen to him. What if he'd been attacked in the woods?

After I turn on the shower, I can't help but examine my new hair in the bathroom mirror. It's a nice cut, no longer wonky, with the ends tucked neatly below my ears. It's actually quite a trendy cut that I've seen a few young girls wearing. But I look at it and see all of my failures to keep my children safe. Not killing Amy or figuring a way to have her arrested when I had the chance. Allowing one of the assistants at the studio to take my daughter out of my sight, even for a moment.

I strip, throwing the stiff, sweat-stained clothes onto the floor. My body feels both thinner and puffier. I'm losing weight, but at the same time retaining water from eating too much salt. I carry baggage beneath my eyes, across my abdomen. I trace the stretch marks with my fingers. Gina had been a small baby and I'd carried a tidy bump, but pregnancy always leaves its mark. I close my eyes and think back to the night in the woods when I was chasing Aiden. Stumbling through the trees as fast as my body would allow. Feeling the contractions tearing through me. My palm reaching out to a tree for support. I can almost feel its roughness against my skin.

I step beneath the water and wash it all away.

Because it's a Sunday, Aiden wants to go to Rob's, but I can't face it. I ask him if he'd like to go without me, and his jaw drops slightly. He pulls his eyebrows together. I can imagine him wondering who this woman is. A far cry from the mother who never allows him to do anything of his own.

'I'll drop you off and pick you up,' I add.

He nods.

What he doesn't know is that I'm considering keeping him away from me. He'll be safe at Rob's while I try to find Amy. She has to be in the village. And if she is, then it means Gina is with her. Gina is somewhere near. While we're driving to the B&B I inhale, and I swear I can smell the baby shampoo I use on her hair. The one with the elephant on the packaging.

'I'll come by about four, OK?' I say as I drop Aiden off at the bottom of the drive.

'You're not calling in to say hello?' he asks.

I shake my head.

His brow furrows in confusion, and I can see him trying to work out what's going on. I know that Aiden missed a lot while he was in the bunker, like learning to read facial expressions and body language for instance. Right now, I can tell he's trying to figure out what I'm thinking.

'Everything is OK,' I reassure him, opening my face and smiling. 'I promise. The last week has been so hard on all of us. I just need a little time to myself. Is that OK?'

'I guess so.' There's no way for Aiden to hide his feelings. Though he's not the most emotive person, at the same time he struggles to lie or deceive others. He's both open and closed at the same time.

'I love you.'

Aiden's throat works. 'Love you too.'

He climbs out and I watch him make his way up to the front door of the B&B. I watch Rob open the door and immediately smile at the sight of his son. I watch Rob lift his head and frown at me. He waves, and I wave back. Before he can limp down the drive, I put the car in gear and leave, tears flooding my eyes. The road blurs and I hastily wipe them away. They are my family, but it will never be complete until Gina is home.

Now that I know Amy is close by, I need to figure out where she's staying. Being in or around Bishoptown would be risky. This is where the people know me the most. They pay attention to the news here. They will have examined Amy's face from the newspapers. Some know her anyway and would recognise her easily. So, she can't be staying in Bishoptown, but perhaps she's in one of the towns a little further away. Can I track her down somehow?

On the way home, I notice a car hanging back, but clearly visible. It's a dark grey Toyota, but I'm unsure of the model. I take a left, close to the local park, and then turn onto my road, deciding that it's probably a photographer. I'm alone, which I'm sure they've deciphered. They know which car is mine. They know the cars used by Josie, and by Rob's parents, too. They know everything about us, every little detail.

As I get out of the car, I'm vaguely aware of movement on the other side of the road. I was right, there is a photographer following me. A man, over six feet, broad across the chest, with thinning hair. I imagine that he uses his intimidating size to get the photographs he wants. I push my sunglasses onto my head to get a better view.

'Nice hair,' he calls out.

I ignore him and head into the house, already picturing the kind of criticism I'll endure once the world realises I had a haircut while my daughter is missing. Sympathy for me is already thin, now it will be non-existent. Perhaps it'll turn into suspicion. Someone somewhere will write a comment about how I had my own daughter kidnapped to get attention, or make money, or promote a book I'm about to write. I don't care. The words bounce off me now.

I throw my keys on the counter, grab my laptop and get to work researching all of the holiday cottages, B&Bs, small hotels that I can find within ten miles. I assume Amy has a car and some money to be able to fund this. Obviously, she has *some* money, otherwise she wouldn't be able to keep a child out of sight. My stomach lurches, but I concentrate and the nausea ebbs away. That's who I need to be. A woman capable of facing the realities head-on, without blinking. That's how I catch her.

After making a list of possible locations, I quickly call back some of the private investigators. Things are now moving faster than I expected and I'll need to examine these locations myself, but I'll also need help. Then I scroll through my contacts and allow my finger to hover over DCI Stevenson's number. *No police. I'll know.* The words are ominous. It brings to mind a great eye following me around as I live my life. Watching, constantly watching. But one police officer could slip by, couldn't they? The problem is, I don't know if I can do this alone. Should I call him? If I knew he could work independently from the rest of the police, then I wouldn't hesitate.

Closing my eyes, leaning against the hard chair, I wonder whether I'm making the right decision. Is this what Amy wants? Me isolated, away from the police? If it is, she's clever. Even when I moved back to Bishoptown she managed to pull my strings. How is she doing all of this and keeping Gina away from the world? My stomach flips over when a tiny part of my brain whispers: *what if she's already dead?* No, I won't think it.

Instead, I glance down at the list. Twenty potential places. That's a lot of work, and I worry that confidentiality policies will mean I won't manage to wrangle much information out of the businesses. But then I have another thought. There is one place, now empty, connected to Amy. Perhaps there's a way for me to do my own investigation.

Chapter Twenty-Five

AIDEN

Silence is what I know, and what soothes me. But there's hardly ever any actual silence. Even if I'm in my room alone, I hear the sounds of the house. Someone in another room, shuffling around, making the floorboards creak. Or the faint sound of a television. The clunking of pipes or the sound of a car on the road. The bunker was the purest silence I knew. I could turn off my thoughts and bask in it. Silence meant I was safe. It was when I heard a key in the lock that I began to feel afraid.

Grandma bustles around the kitchen, clattering plates. She hums along to the music on the radio, a song I don't know. It sounds old. Grandad and Dad both stare at the television. Cricket. Occasionally one of them will shake their head and mutter angrily.

The house is alive with noise and I should be happy to be here, in this safe place, but part of me won't stop craving the silence.

'So, your mum got a haircut?' Dad leans back on the sofa, his feet resting on the patterned pouffe.

'She was too hot with it long.' I feel the need to justify it. But whether it's to him or myself, I'm not sure.

He nods, but I can see the surprise on his face. 'Pretty odd priority to have at the moment.'

'She's entitled to a bloody haircut,' Grandad mumbles.

'All right, Dad. I just meant that it's not like Em, that's all. Not that it means she doesn't love Gina or isn't trying her hardest to get her back.' He frowns. 'Did she seem OK to you, Aiden? It was weird her not coming to say hello at least.'

It takes a moment to get my mouth to work. 'She wanted to be alone for a while.'

Dad nods slowly, returning his attention to the cricket as my phone vibrates again. Another message from Faith to add to the others. They've turned to pleading: *I'm so sorry for what I said. I know you said you weren't mad, but you haven't been in contact and I think you are mad at me. Please forgive me. Please reply. Let me know you're OK.* Scrolling through her messages produces a number of conflicting feelings. Sadness for her, and for me, and for the change in our relationship. A strange, queasy sensation in the pit of my stomach. Shame? Fear? An ache. Missing her. Missing the way she made me feel with her words.

'The food's ready.' Grandma sweeps into the room. 'Come on.'

Life goes on, I think. I give my phone one last glance before we walk through to the dining table. Shifting chairs, adjusting knives and forks. Moving on; living.

A thought hits me. Will Gina blame me when she comes home? She was most likely targeted because of me. She was taken at the TV studios because I insisted on giving the interview. When we get her back, will she resent me for the rest of her life?

'Roast potatoes?' Grandma holds out a serving spoon. Her eyebrows are raised high up on her face. I think she's showing extra concern for me because I'm being quiet again.

'Two please.'

She relaxes and drops two onto my plate.

After everyone starts to eat, I send a quick message to Faith.

I forgive you.

'What do you think she's doing?' Dad asks, as he spins his spoon around his bowl, collecting every molecule of melted ice cream. We had tinned fruit and a scoop of ice cream for dessert. 'Did she tell you, Aiden?'

I stir my melted ice cream into the slimy peaches. My stomach keeps cramping every time Dad mentions Mum. 'She didn't say what she's doing. Going home probably.'

'That's understandable, isn't it?' Grandad replies.

'I guess so,' Dad says, his voice almost sarcastic. Even I can tell he doesn't believe it. 'Don't you think it's weird, though? Have you ever known Emma, in the four years since Aiden came home, to let her kids out of her sight?'

'Oh dear,' Grandma says.

My head snaps up from the bowl of peaches.

'What is it, Mum?' Dad asks. He drops his spoon and reaches for the phone Grandma is holding aloft. After reading for a few moments he rolls his eyes. 'Oh, here we go. I knew this would happen. *Bunker Mum gets a haircut.* Jesus Christ, they've given her the title Bunker Mum as well.' He shakes his head. 'Fuck –'

'Rob!' Grandma glares at him. 'Not in front of your son.'

'Sorry, pal.' He reaches out and pats the back of my hand. 'I'm just so mad at this "journalist".' He waggles his fingers to create air quotes. 'This whole article insinuates Emma is a bad mother. They've even posted a picture of some model with the same hair style, as though Em walked into the hairdressers with a photo to get the same cut.'

Grandma nods sadly. 'They don't understand, these people. They don't realise how you have to do the small things to keep yourself sane.' She sighs and throws her napkin down on the table.

I stare down at my peaches, stirring the mixture together until the syrup and the ice cream merge. 'It's my fault Gina was taken, not Mum's. I insisted on going to that stupid TV interview.'

Grandad sighs. 'None of this is your fault, Aiden.'

'What if Gina hates me when she comes back?'

'She could never hate you,' says Dad. You're her big brother!'

'That's right, love,' Grandma adds. 'You're her Denny.' She sniffs and wipes away a few tears. 'Come on now. Let's have a nice cup of tea and calm down. Come on, love.'

She practically shoos us back into the lounge. I take out my phone and find the article for myself. It's exactly as Dad described it, calling Mum's hair 'on trend' and 'glamorous'. The photograph of Mum is one of her stepping out of the car, wearing the same sunglasses, jeans and red top she wore to drop me off at the B&B. The sunglasses are the ones she uses when she's driving and it's sunny. But in this photograph, it makes her appear as though she's wearing them to look cool. Even I can see that. I've read a lot of clickbait articles over the past four years and I can identify the style of them now. Mum explained to me that this wasn't proper journalism, that it was a way to get people to click on the article, and then click through to a product to buy. They make their money that way. I see various highlighted words, such as the make of Mum's car. I click on it, and it takes me to the car's website.

People are making money from our misery, which means there are moments when I truly believe that the world can be more painful outside the bunker than in it. The world outside is messier, more complicated and often more ruthless. Seeing that article gives me an idea. I open my Instagram account, scroll through photos of Mum and Gina, find a nice one, and then I began typing.

My mum has fought hard for our protection ever since I went missing fourteen years ago. She saved my life. She's a fighter. She loves us more than anything and she's doing everything she can to find my little sister Gina. Leave my family alone.

. . .

Someone will find a way to take my words out of context, to make me seem as unhinged as they make Mum seem. After all I'm the boy from the bunker and most people think I'm going to go on a killing spree one day. They think I'm damaged beyond repair. Who could survive it? That's what they all think. Who could live in that place for ten years and come out a normal person?

'You OK, mate?' Dad smiles at me. Smiles mean happiness. They don't, though; smiles cover up what you're really feeling. He's scared for me. Scared for Gina and Mum and everyone else. We're all scared beneath our smiles.

I tell him I'm fine, and then I write another message to Faith. *I'm scared.*

Chapter Twenty-Six

EMMA

The car thrums to silence as I hit the ignition switch. New technology can jar against old memories. I used to come here driving my mum's Volvo with the dodgy handbrake. It's not as though I came here often, but the recognition is strong. This is where Amy lives. This is the house on the way to the one pub in Bishoptown that served underage teenagers. Those bricks, this piece of land, are part of my history.

It was after the camping trip that I first came here. She'd reinvented herself as someone else. From a prudish, strange girl, to the one with a number of lads on the go. Her reputation spread as an easy lay, apparently. I didn't pay much attention to these rumours because I fell pregnant around the same time. Amy got to have a proper career and I resented her for that at times. She was the promiscuous one, but I ended up pregnant before anyone else at school.

It all seems pointless now. A typical way in which women drag each other down. That *you made different choices than me and I resent you for it* philosophy. I later learned she was jealous of me.

I get out of the car and peer into the house. According to

Stevenson, the police have already been here and found nothing. But what have they missed? What could I see that they didn't? I need to search this place for myself.

It looks like they secured the building with a new lock after the police search. I head around to the back of the property, not particularly caring about any repercussions from trespassing. The urgency of this situation has gone beyond an arrest for a petty crime.

At the back of the house there's a window into the tiny dining room. I've brought my hammer with me again. I pull it out from my bag, angle my face away from the window and smash as hard as I can. I researched this before I came out of the house. Double-glazed windows are most vulnerable in the lower corners. The outer pane smashes first, so loudly that I imagine most elderly neighbours will be twitching their curtains to find out where the noise came from. With the second and third blows, I get through the second pane and widen the hole to so I can climb through. I brought a thick picnic blanket to lay over the window to make sure I don't cut myself.

With an ungainly heave, I push myself over the windowsill and into the house. My Doc Martens boots grind the shards of glass into the carpet. They were worn specifically for this purpose, too. I can't say what will come next, because I don't know, but I'm certain I'll need to be physically strong and injury free.

The room is eerily quiet and empty enough that my footsteps create a faint echo. All the dining furniture is gone. Whether Amy moved her belongings out or sold them, I couldn't say. But there is clearly nothing in this room. I move to the kitchen.

I work my way through the cupboards, finding nothing but crumbs and dust. A large house spider sits in the sink.

Next, the lounge. The place where I backed Amy into a corner and put a knife to her throat. The second time I've drawn blood from a person. I still remember the taste of Jake's blood, and the surprise of how easily my teeth tore into him. Tooth and claw. Just as any mother would fight.

I take my hammer, turn it over and use the claw to pull up the carpet. Perhaps she has secrets hidden in the floorboards. Anything would help. But there's nothing. No loose floorboards. No hiding holes. I wipe the sweat from my forehead and move up the stairs.

At this point I'm concerned that someone could have seen the broken window and called the police, so I go quickly through the upstairs rooms. It seems that Amy has left some belongings behind. There are a few bin bags filled with clothes. Old books. Magazines. Some CDs of Nineties bands. Nothing particularly personal, like a photo album or framed pictures. She must have taken them with her, which suggests that she does care about other people, unless she threw them away. But then wouldn't she have thrown these old things away, too?

I do the same here, ripping up the carpet, sweating through my top and blinking away dust. There are no loose floorboards. There's nothing here. No dastardly plan with a map. Nothing.

My last hope is the attic. I reach high above my head and pull down the steps. My hands shake as the metal bars unfold. I don't know if it will be any sort of room, or whether it'll be nothing but insulation and beams. One wrong move and I could fall straight through the ceiling. I could break an ankle or give myself a concussion.

It's as I climb to the top of the ladder that the exhaustion hits me the hardest. Tired muscles complain and, in one panicky moment, I begin to feel slightly dizzy. But it passes, and I push myself up onto the floorboards in the attic. My fingers grope the air around me, and I swear under my breath. I should've thought about a torch. Then I remember my phone in my pocket and use the light from the screen to guide me. When I spot the dangling cord, I grasp it gratefully and a single bulb illuminates the room.

With the new light, I can see that the space has been partially converted, with proper flooring and a little bit of furniture. There's an old armchair and a table. Across from the old armchair is a wooden dining chair set up as though for two people to have a conversation. Who would want to spend time up here? I turn my body around, slowly taking everything in. I'm not sure whether the police have been up here, but there are some old books and photo albums scattered along the floorboards. Perhaps this is where Amy dumped her personal belongings. I pick up a photo album and thumb through it. Most of the photographs are of Amy with her aunt and uncle, but as I go back further, I find pictures of Amy with a young woman. A woman with faraway eyes, greasy hair and long, bony limbs. This must be Amy's mother. Whoever she is, or was, she had some issues and definitely looks like a drug addict.

There are some children's toys here, too. Teddy bears, a porcelain doll with perfectly plaited hair that makes my body tingle all over. Amy's face pops into my mind as she passed me the baby shower present on my last day of work four years ago, the day I received the phone call to say Aiden had been found. A perfect doll with a porcelain face.

The air in the attic is cloying. I feel the dust settling in my nostrils. A trickle of sweat worms its way down between my shoulder blades. I sit in the chair and lean back, allowing my weight to sink into it. Why are there two chairs here? Why are there children's toys here? If the attic was used for storage, I could understand it. But there aren't any boxes or stacks of tat that you'd expect. Could Amy have been keeping Gina here? No, the police would have found her. And this doll is clearly old. This was Amy's doll. This could be a place that Amy came as a child.

There's a heaviness building in my stomach. A worldweariness. Why would Amy be brought into a dusty attic as a child? There's no real reason for her to use this space as an adult. Two chairs. Someone would be in here with her?

The air catches in my throat and I move swiftly out of the chair and down the ladder. I can't stand to be in this place a moment longer.

• • •

It's a few minutes after midday when I emerge from Amy's sad old house, and the sun beats down overhead. This September heatwave is lasting too long, and everywhere I go, I see the frustrations of hot parents with irritable children. I get into the car and turn on the air-conditioning. After a few moments of leaning back into the headrest, a knock on the window startles me. I gaze wide-eyed out of the car to see Amy's neighbour, a woman in her seventies, small as a bird, with gnarled knuckles and misty eyes, through the glass.

I let down the window halfway.

'Emma Price, isn't it?' she asks.

I nod.

'You broke in?'

'Yes.'

'Well.' She sighs and stares at Amy's house. 'I don't blame you. I hope you get your daughter back.'

'I heard she left about six months ago. Is that true?' I ask.

'Sounds about right, yes,' she replies. 'Not that she ever put the house up for sale. We thought it was strange leaving it empty like that.'

'Was Amy doing anything suspicious before she left?' I ask, deciding to take the opportunity to learn more.

'Not that I could tell.'

'All her furniture's gone.'

'Before she left she had people collecting bits every now and then. The dining room table and chairs. Television, too. I figured she was hard-up and selling everything off.'

'Were they different people collecting the furniture each time?'

'Oh, yes,' she says. 'And I saw the charity van once or twice, too.'

'You haven't seen Amy with any children?'

She shakes her head. 'I'm sorry, love, but no.'

'But you don't seem surprised about me suspecting her?'

She works her tongue along her teeth, pausing before she answers, her gaze directed towards the window of the house. 'I used to feel right sorry for her before. With that man yelling all the time.'

'Her uncle?'

'Yes. He was a nasty beggar. But then there was something a bit off about her, too. Amy, I mean. Did you know her mother left her here? Far as I know, the mother just never came back.'

'You think Amy is so damaged she could do something awful?'

'Saw her with that fella a couple of times. The one that hurt your boy.'

'Hugh?'

She nods. 'I never liked him neither.'

I give the woman my number and ask her to call me if she remembers anything else, or if she sees Amy. When I check my phone, I see a few missed calls from DCI Stevenson and decide to call back.

'Emma, I'm sorry about that article, it's really unfair. It was, um, a strange time for a makeover though?'

I just sigh. 'What article?'

He explains but I find it hard to concentrate on what he's saying. 'Was there something you wanted?' I don't mean the words to sound cutting, but I can't focus on anything other than Gina right now.

'Sorry, I didn't mean to offend,' he says, perturbed by my dismissive tone. 'I just wanted to check you were all right.'

'I'm OK. Not to be rude, but can you only call me when there's news. Has there been any news?'

'Not right now but we're working on it.'

I hang up and suck in a long, deep breath. It probably isn't wise to hang around outside Amy's house, even though it seems that the neighbours aren't going to report the breaking and entering. At least someone is on my side.

I'm about to put the car in gear and drive away when I hear another knock on the car window. This time, a boy, about fifteen, probably taller than me. He's on a red bike, the handlebars angled towards the car like a twisted spine. I lower the window.

'Are you Emma?' he asks.

He's younger than I first thought. More like twelve or thirteen, with a voice that hasn't broken yet. He leans back on his bicycle seat.

'Yes.'

'The lady asked me to give you this.'

Puzzled, I reach out and take the white envelope from his hand. I tear it open and reach inside to find hair. Soft, honey-hued hair with a slight curl at the end.

Chapter Twenty-Seven

EMMA

A lump rises from my belly to my heart, clotted and thick, hot and all-encompassing. My eyes fill with tears. The boy on the bike pedals away from the car, and, as I see the blurry shape of him leaving, I realise what he said. *The lady asked me to give you this.*

I drop the envelope and the lock of hair into the seat and leap out of the car. 'Wait,' I shout. 'Wait! Stop!'

The boy, halfway down the street, presses his feet against the pavement and stops his bike. He waits for me to catch up, expression wary.

'How old was the lady who gave you this letter?'

'Like, your age, I guess.'

My breath catches.

I pull up a photo on my phone. 'Is this her?'

He frowns at the picture. 'I don't know, she had a hat.'

It has to be Amy. 'What did she say?'

'That you were friends and were playing a game or something. I dunno . . . I just delivered the note like she asked.'

Without another word, I turn away from the boy and start running up the road. I run around the corner, down the next road and then back. I do the same on the other side, snaking around side streets. How did she leave so quickly? I press my hands into my eyes and let out a scream of frustration. Fuck you, Amy.

On the way back to the car, the pleasant lady who answered my questions comes out of the house to check I'm OK. I tell her that I am, and then I get into the car, jamming the heel of my hand against the ignition. The brakes screech as I set off, and the boy on the bike stares with his jaw dropped open.

For the next ten or fifteen minutes I drive around searching the roads. The white envelope sits on the passenger seat, the lock of hair on top. I long to press it to my skin.

But it's not good enough. It's not my Ginny.

After twenty minutes I have to admit to myself that she's long gone. I know that Amy has a car because I heard her drive away after she delivered the first letter. I'd be better off going home and figuring out what to do next. I need to read the contents of this new letter. I leave, knowing I was within a few feet of my daughter.

I press the envelope to my chest, take a moment to breathe and then climb out of the car. How long was I at Amy's? An hour, two? I check my phone, it's 12:45. Everything is going so fast. It wasn't long ago that I was cutting off my hair and nailing it to a tree. Now I have a lock of Gina's hair in return. That's Amy telling me she's received my offering.

As soon as I'm in the kitchen I slide down to my knees and remain there as I lift the hair out of the envelope, dragging it against my cheek, feeling the softness. Then I take out the note. I gently place the hair inside the envelope so that I don't lose any of the precious strands and put it by my legs. My breath is ragged and raw as I unfold the piece of paper in my hands and read.

I'm glad you remembered, Emma.

*For what it's worth, I'm sorry it came to this. But I am willing to
hurt her if you don't do exactly what I tell you to do.*

Come to the tree. Alone. At 1 a.m.

Set your alarm, Em.

Don't tell Rob.

Don't tell DCI Stevenson.

Don't tell Aiden.

Come alone or I will send more pieces of your daughter to you.

A familiar heat pulses through my body, starting with my toes
and ending with a prickling scalp. It floods my veins, pushing
away sadness and dejection. This is the fire that helped me
save Aiden four years ago. The rage that kept me going. I
close my eyes and breathe it in, soak myself in it. Rage and
hatred. That's the only way I'll beat her. I can't give up. I
can't.

This is a trap. I know that only too well, but Amy has
what I want, and I can't get to what I want without playing
her game. Grabbing the envelope, I climb to my feet and
begin to pace the kitchen. I need to think this through. I need
help. There are the private investigators but could they start
in time to find her by 1 a.m? I put the envelope on the table
and decide to try.

For the rest of the afternoon, I make as many calls as I
can. I call Rob and suggest that Aiden stays overnight. Rob
persistently asks me if I'm OK, to the point where I hang up.
I call three investigation firms, willing to send them a deposit
if they can start now. They promise to call back if they have
the resources to start straight away. I call every hotel and B&B
on my list, practically begging them for any information they
can give over the phone. Some waver, but most are reluctant.
No one has seen anyone matching Amy and Gina's
description.

In the end, I stare at Stevenson's number on my phone.
Can he help me? Is he willing to go above and beyond what a
detective is supposed to do? What would he advise me?

My feet track the length of the kitchen. I play with Gina's

hair between my fingers. I don't know what to do. I don't want to feel this alone but I'm afraid for her. Would Amy kill Gina if she saw the police? I remember the uneasiness I felt about the ransom and how it was handled.

At 5 p.m. I pour myself a cup of coffee and allow the caffeine to jangle my nerves. Images of Gina's hand clasped by Amy's keep flashing into my mind. I close my eyes and see the knife I held to Amy's throat, only now it's held to Gina's throat and she's slicing through the delicate flesh. I can't bear it.

I shake my head, channel the anger again, and call DCI Stevenson.

'Emma, sorry about before −'

'Will you help me?'

He sighs. 'You know I'm doing everything I can −'

'Not the police. No one else. Just you.'

His tone changes. 'What's happened?'

'I can't tell you anything unless you promise that it will be you and no one else.'

I hear him exhale through his nose, and then I hear a rustling sound as though he's walking. I imagine him stepping out of a public place to go somewhere more private.

'Emma, listen to me. We believe Amy is in Bishoptown. There've been a couple of potential sightings in and around the village −'

'I know she's here,' I reply. 'Amy has been in contact with me.'

'Emma, you have to tell me everything you know.'

'My daughter's life is in danger,' I say.

'I know that. We want to help you.'

'We?'

'All right. Me. I'll help you alone if that's what you want.'

'I think you're just placating me.' I tap my fingers against the kitchen counter. 'I want to be able to trust you after how much you helped me the night Jake died.'

'You can trust me,' he insists.

'I don't know if I can. You're saying what I want to hear.'

'Tell me what's going on, Emma. Please. I can't help you if you don't tell me.'

But I know exactly what he'll do. He'll file it. He'll have a meeting about it and assemble a team. A plan will be made. I won't be alone. And Amy will kill my child. There's something else going on. I can see the shape of it but not the details. When I threatened her four years ago, I flicked whatever switch was keeping her together and now she's running on the same emotions as me. Revenge. Hatred. Grief. I don't know exactly, but I think it started in that attic many years ago.

'I need to go.' I hang up on him and place the phone on the table.

I have lots time before I need to leave, so I eat, and then I nap for an hour. When I wake, I check the house for potential weapons.

At 6:30 p.m. there's a knock on the door. I open it and Stevenson walks past me into the house.

'Whatever you're doing, I'm doing it with you.'

'You need to leave. Now.' I gesture wildly to the open door. 'She can't . . .'

'What?' His gaze trails along the counter to the knife rack and sharpener. 'Steak for dinner, is it?' He raises an eyebrow. 'Come on, Emma, you can't do this alone.'

'I have to. She has my daughter.' Stepping away from the door, but not closing it, I move to one of the chairs and grip the back of it with my fingers. Tension runs up my arms, shoulders, into my neck. 'Just go. You're making it worse.'

'No. I'm going to help you.'

I let out a long sigh and walk over to the door. With one, furtive glance outside, I close it and move back into the house.

Chapter Twenty-Eight

EMMA

I go unarmed into the darkness. The heatwave is on the cusp of breaking, and a long overdue gusty wind whips up the leaves in the high branches of the oak. Beneath it, several sheep huddle for warmth. As they hurry away from me, the wind carries the sickly sour whiff of their fresh dung.

I have an earpiece and a wire running down my chest. Stevenson is listening to everything. I'm sure that he can hear the sound of my heart hammering away. He is in the car, laying low on the backseat, which is parked in the same lay-by as before.

In the hours leading up to 1 a.m. we discussed the meet in detail. Amy isn't a professional criminal but she's outsmarted us at every turn because of her clever planning.

'She's in control here,' Stevenson had said. 'Because she has Gina and we don't know where Gina is.'

In the end, he persuaded me to involve the police. There are three armed officers positioned around the field. Will she be able to see us? Will she know? I'm on edge, consumed by questioning whether I did the right thing getting help, or whether I should've gone alone. My nerves are pulled tight, my throat feels strangled.

I have a GPS tracker strapped around my wrist, tucked under the sleeve of my coat. If Amy takes me somewhere else, the police will be able to follow me there. Surely this will work. The reasoning is simple: Amy takes me to my daughter, the police find me, and they come and arrest Amy. But while I'm grateful to DCI Stevenson for arranging this, I'm also aware it means he lied to me when he told me it would just be him.

And I hope I won't have to pay for that lie.

As I come a little closer to the tree, I can see there's a note attached to the trunk, nailed in the same place where I nailed my hair. I take my phone out and take a photo of it before I take the note down. I'm not sure why I do this, I wasn't asked to, but it seems important to document as much as I can.

The note is inside a clear plastic wallet. I reach inside to take it out when I notice there are two sheets of paper. One of these says, FOR YOU. I read this one first.

Come back. 3 a.m. Get rid of the police.

I fold this and put it into my jeans pocket.

The second one says:

You broke the agreement. I will not meet you. Gina's life is in your hands and you failed her.

I stuff this one back into the plastic wallet and make my way back to Stevenson.

. . .

'I have officers on the streets,' he says as he drives my car back to the village. 'She won't get far. I promise you that. We'll keep an eye on your security camera for you, too. Thanks for giving us access to the app.'

But I'm silent, because inside my head, I'm thinking about 3 a.m. My heart is pounding. How is Amy doing this? How is she keeping out of the way of the police?

'Emma, I know you're disappointed. But you did the right thing by calling me. Please, keep calling us every time there's a development because you can't do this on your own.'

I gently nod my head, and I think he takes this to mean compliance. What it actually means is that I'm distracted by thoughts about how to sneak back out of the house at 3 a.m. without the police seeing me. I'm now convinced that they're watching me. Amy could be a threat to me, she could come to my house. They know this. They want to catch her. But Amy isn't going to do anything if she knows the police are involved. Does she have a camera set up somewhere near my house? Another trail cam, perhaps? Or is she just following me?

It's just after 1.30 by the time I get home. I pace the kitchen, chewing my lip. I'll have to walk, it's the only way. Driving would attract too much attention from the surveillance team. But the walk will take at least an hour, which means I need to leave now.

I grab one of the sharpest knives from the kitchen and tuck it into a belt loop on my jeans. I put on a dark jacket with a hood and slip my phone into the pocket. The wire and earpiece have already been removed. But I remove the GPS tracker from my wrist and place it on the kitchen table. Then I slip through the hallway to the back door. There's one camera at the back of the house, but I know the range, and I know where to step to avoid being seen.

The garden nightlight has been broken for years, so I don't have to worry about that. Still, I hurry to the opposite end of the garden, staying close to the fence where the camera can't see me. It's at the wall at the end of the garden where I need to be the most careful. I pull myself up the wall. It's a five-foot drop onto the pavement below, not something I would normally have the nerve to do, but I let my body slide down while bending my knees as I land, taking the pressure off my ankles. Even with this method, the jolt sends me toppling forward and I almost fall to my knees. When I stand straight, I shake out both legs, paranoid about twisted ankles, but neither seems injured. I sigh in relief.

The village is silent in the early hours of the morning. Sticking to side streets, it doesn't take me long to find the path that leads around the woods towards the Wetherington Estate. For the first time in weeks I feel cold in my clothes, despite the hooded jacket. It's too big for me now, bought at another time, and I shiver inside the long sleeves that cover my fingers. I wrap my arms around my body and begin to feel as though this is happening to someone else. A character from a movie. Someone who can fight and win every time. A cynical part of my brain considers the possibility that I used up all of my luck when I saved Aiden from Jake.

Away from the road, I use the torch app on my smartphone. But I keep it directed on the ground to guide my feet, rather than swinging it around and attracting anyone watching. Then I stop. I'm barely five minutes away from the field, all too aware of how alone I am in this. My heart is heavy as I send Aiden the text message I'd planned before I left.

I'm meeting Amy at 3 a.m. on the Wetherington Estate.

If I don't come home, try to track my phone.

I'm going to get Gina back. I love you.

As soon as it's sent, I break into a jog. This gets my blood pumping and my body warm. Soon enough I'm climbing into the field and striding towards the tree. I daren't allow the light to pick out the great oak in case I see her, or worse, another note. Another hoop to jump through. I break out into a sprint, desperate for it all to be over. The sheep disperse in a panic.

The place is almost completely silent when I arrive. My

breath is ragged, and the leaves rustle above me, but there's nothing else.

'Amy,' I say breathlessly to the whispering leaves. 'Where are you?'

I'm here, I think *I made it. Give me my daughter*.

But there's no one here and no note. I take a slow, measured walk around the circumference of the oak. It confirms that I'm alone.

My fist thuds against the bark of the tree once. Twice. Behind there is a third thud; the sound of feet hitting the ground.

Before I can turn around, a skinny hand circles my arm. I attempt to twist away, but the person continues to grip my forearm. Before I can react, they push up my jacket sleeve and something cold and metal is forced against my skin. It pinches me and I let out a cry of surprise. When I look down at my wrist, there's a silver hoop around it. I try to pull it away and see the other arm connected to mine via a handcuff. In the split second before I find the person's face, I imagine that Stevenson has arrested me for disobeying his orders. But it isn't Stevenson. It's her, and she's handcuffed to me. The rustling of the leaves wasn't just wind, Amy was hiding up there in the dark, and she dropped from one of the branches to surprise me.

She yanks me forward. 'Come on.' I realise there's some wildness in my eyes when she adds, 'If you try anything, all it will do is delay being reunited with your daughter. Don't even bother.'

I grit my teeth. 'Where is she?'

'I'll show you if you walk with me.' She pulls me again and then stops. 'Wait a minute.' Her free hand pats down my jeans, from hip to ankle. It takes all of my willpower not to grab her by the throat, to try and take control, but she has my daughter in a secret location. If I hurt Amy I might never know where Gina is. Eventually Amy's hand discovers the knife. 'Still playing with knives, I see.' She removes it from the belt loop on my jeans and tosses it over to the tree. Then she pulls my phone out of my pocket and does the same. 'The instructions were pretty simple, Emma. But then I could never teach your son any listening skills, either.'

I bite my tongue and follow her as she begins to walk. The cuff binds us; we're fused by metal. Is hers chafing as much as mine? She doesn't seem to notice as we walk.

'Where is she, Amy? Have you hurt her? Just tell me she's OK. Please.'

The world isn't dark enough for me to miss the smirk that lifts the side of her mouth. The dread comes to me with a cold, prickling sensation that spreads over my skin. What has she planned for us?

Chapter Twenty-Nine

AMY

Every now and then our arms brush together, the waterproof
material of her jacket crinkling against mine. In this late hour,
every sound is amplified. It feeds my adrenaline.

Soon I'll bring her to you. That's the next step of the
plan. Soon Emma will understand why this has to happen,
why it was inevitable that we would end here.

But I must admit, I didn't expect Emma to go to the
police. When I saw DCI Stevenson enter her house, I knew I
had to adjust the plan. That was why I used the second note. I
knew Emma would come back alone if the first time didn't
work. But the police are on high alert now, which may make
leaving Bishoptown even trickier.

'Where is my daughter?' Emma asks. She yanks at the
cuffs, almost knocking me off balance.

I grab her by the jacket and pull her closer.

'Didn't I tell you to behave yourself?'

She cringes away from me, away from my lips at her ear.

Not even Emma will be able to get out of these handcuffs.
I have to remind myself that I'm still in control, that she will
be with you soon, that I've done everything I can to make this

169

plan work. And it will work, I have faith in it. There's a secret weapon in my pocket.

'We need to go,' I say. But before we go, I retrieve the switchblade hidden in my coat pocket and brandish it close to her ribs. 'If you try to scream, I won't hesitate.'

Emma nods.

Everything is under control. I place the knife back in my pocket.

I lead the way and we stumble along in the dark because I won't use a torch. I need my free arm to subdue Emma in case she tries anything. Physically, we're pretty evenly matched, though I believe I'm stronger from the gardening and hunting back at the chapel. Emma has lost weight, but she has the ferocious desire to save her child.

'Where are we going?' she asks.

I don't answer her.

'How have you done all of this alone? Do you have some little protégée under your wing, like Hugh controlled you? How have you organised this?'

Again, I don't answer.

Eventually, the terrain becomes slippery and Emma focuses her attention on making sure she doesn't fall. I keep my eyes on the trees, searching for the tiny clues I left myself when I planned this walk. Very thin swatches of yellow fabric, ripped from a shirt, tied around whatever will be visible to me in the dark. There's just enough moonlight to pick them out and allow me to follow my way to where I parked the car.

Emma is silent as we come out the other side of the woods next to the road. I see her head move from side to side as she searches for help.

'Remember that I will stab you if you scream. You'll never see your daughter again.'

My own heart is pounding now. The car is parked in the driveway of an old, unused property five minutes up the road. I decided to use that spot because not everyone knows it's empty. If I'm right, then the police would drive straight past the car, assume it belongs to the homeowner, and not even think to check it. But what I can't predict is whether the police will pull me over as I drive out of the village. I know the less travelled route, and I know the tiny country roads that they might not, but it still means relying on a little bit of luck.

'Whatever you have planned,' Emma says. There's a change in her voice, she's talking more smoothly, more quietly. It's not quite patronising, but it's close. 'It isn't too late to stop it. I know what I did to you and I'm sorry, for what it's worth. I went to your house and I saw the attic. I know that your home life was more complicated than anyone realised.'

I reach inside my jacket pocket and wrap my fingers around the knife.

'I think your aunt and uncle were probably horrible people, just like your mother.' She glances at me, expecting a reaction. I give her none. 'Listen to me, Amy. I can be on your side if you want me to. I'll help you get out of Bishoptown and away from the police if you let me and Gina go. I know that you're a product of your circumstances and I think that with some therapy you could move beyond this. You can get better.'

I shake my head. She's clueless.

'Aiden is improving every day. You don't see the struggles, do you? I'm with him and I see the nightmares. I see the flares in his temper and the way he doesn't quite understand people. He's not the boy he was when Hugh took him but he's a good person with a bright future. You could be that too.'

She's breathless when she stops talking, and her eyes flick across to me every few seconds. That was all she had, an attempt to reason with me. Now she's quiet because she's scared. She wanted to control this situation, but she's failed. I'm the one in control. Finally.

I see the crumbled wall and the mossy, cracked drive. We've walked a long way and now the world's colour palette is turning from black to a deep, royal blue. Soon the birds will start singing and the sun will rise. We need to move fast.

It takes us around twenty minutes to walk to the car, which is not easy to spot unless you know it's there. Emma seems taken aback by the vehicle tucked away. Perhaps she thought I was leading her to a hiding place in the woods.

'How long have you been planning this?' she asks.

I shrug. 'A long time.'

'Before Hugh died?'

I don't tell her that her guess is right.

'Is that your car?' Emma asks.

I nod.

'I saw you following me once. I thought it was a photographer.'

I can almost hear the internal conflict of her mind. She was *this* close to catching me. But also *this* far away.

A blackbird chirrups. A reminder to hurry up. I unlock the car and then gently reach into my jeans pocket. Jacket pocket for the knife. Jeans for the other thing.

With one hand, I thumb the cap off the top. Emma doesn't see it coming when I plunge the needle into her neck and depress the syringe.

She yelps.

Shhhh, I tell her.

'Please don't,' she whimpers. 'Amy, please. We were friends once.'

'There's nothing left for me,' I tell her as I toss the syringe into the passenger side of the car. 'You took it all away. Now, in a few minutes you'll be extremely drowsy, and I'd hate for you to hurt yourself. You'd better get into the car.'

I dig deeper into my jeans pocket and retrieve the key for the handcuffs. Emma's bottom lip is wobbling as I unlock my cuff, spin her around and cuff her other hand. The drugs are working quickly, she stumbles when I spin her.

Then I shove her into the backseat, headfirst, and slam the door shut. She'll roll around for a while. I would secure her, but I can't waste time. I'll stop after she passes out, tie her legs, and plug her into the seatbelt.

We're coming to join you, little one. Not long now.

Chapter Thirty

AIDEN

Maybe now I know what it's like, to have someone withdraw from you. Because when Mum called to tell us she wasn't coming to collect me, it punched me in the gut. I already overheard Grandma saying to Dad that I'm the priority, and we have to make sure I'm safe. 'If Emma is having a wobble, it's best that Aiden isn't with her.'

Then the concern turned to practicalities, like where I was going to sleep. I didn't have much of an opinion about this, but it caused an issue anyway. Grandad suggested I take one of the empty guest rooms. Dad told them I like the door left open and I can't do that in the public part of the building. He suggested that he take the empty room and I stay in his room. I tried to tell them I'd take the sofa, but in the end, Dad's idea won. I slept in his room with the door open and the creaking sounds of the old B&B filtering in.

When I woke, the sunlight was coming from a different angle. The sheets didn't smell like the detergent we use at home, instead they smelt floral, like Grandma's perfume. There are boots next to the wardrobe and a large, grey T-shirt slung over the back of a chair. I feel guilty for sweating on the

173

sheets and awkward as I make my way to the bathroom. I wish Mum was downstairs making toast. Gina at the table with her chubby hands banging the surface, her head bobbing around as she sings the theme song from her favourite TV show. Mum shushing her: 'You'll wake Denny up.' And her: 'What do you think I wanna do, stoo-pid' with that sassy little hand gesture she does because it makes people laugh.

I woke up slightly panicked, but with the sense that I'd slept the unmoving deep sleep of exhaustion. The kind of sleep I slept in the bunker at the end of a week of being afraid.

In the shower, I feel the walls of the cubicle closing in, and only spend a few minutes in there, hastily letting the water rinse away the sweat, before hurrying back to Dad's room to change. Then I make the bed, and sit for a moment, breathing deeply.

I pick up my phone from Dad's bedside table and notice a text from Mum. My fingers work fast, tapping in my pass-code, bringing up the full message.

I'm meeting Amy at 3 a.m. on the Wetherington Estate.
If I don't come home, try to track my phone.
I'm going to get Gina back. I love you.

I text back:

Mum? Are you OK??

And hurry down the stairs to the living area of the B&B. My chest feels like it's gripped by a vice, and that pressure builds and builds with every step. The pressure of knowing I have to speak, that I have to tell them about the message. I should shout it to save time, but I can't. Instead, I wander into the kitchen where Grandma is cooking bacon, and stand there,

174

my mouth opening and shutting. She's humming along to the radio. Grandad is flicking through the newspaper. I hear the sound of the television in the lounge and know Dad must be in there.

'Good morning, lovely,' Grandma says brightly. 'How would you like your bacon?

The words won't come out. I think I make a strange stuttering sound. Grandad looks up from his newspaper and frowns, he folds it and places it down on the table.

'Is everything all right?' he asks. He gets up from the chair and makes his way to me, where I continue to open and shut my mouth like a fish.

Both of them stand in front of me, staring, frowning, yet I still can't get the words out. My scalp is hot, sweat beginning to bead at the pores. I hold out my hand with the phone in it, begging with my eyes for them to take it from me. I clutch my chest and pull in a deep breath.

'Rob!' Grandma calls as she ushers me over to the tiny little table and sits me down in Grandad's original spot. 'I'll get you some water. Peter, will you read what he wants you to read?'

'I don't have my glasses,' Grandad says, patting the top pocket of his shirt.

It's too much. They aren't being urgent enough. Mum needs them and I can't tell them what I need them to do. I screw my eyes shut and place my head on the table. Did Mum go alone to meet Amy? Did she call the police? How did she find Amy? Is she in danger?

'Hurry up and find them!' Grandma snaps at Grandad.

'Everything all right?' Dad's voice now, he must have limped into the kitchen. I feel a hand on my back. It startles me, turns my body rigid. 'Take a deep breath, matey.'

'She's gone,' I groan. 'She went.'

'Who went, buddy?' Dad says calmly.

'Emma,' Grandad says. 'This message says she went to meet Amy last night.'

When I raise my head, Dad has moved away from me and is staring at the phone. 'Shit,' he says. 'You two call the police.

Aiden, come with me. We'll check the house and the Wetherington Estate.'

'I don't think that's wise,' Grandma says, her eyes moving towards me. 'He's upset.'

'No, I want to go.' I stand up on wobbling legs. At least if I go with Dad I'm doing something.

Grandma wrings her hands tightly, but she agrees.

'Call DCI Stevenson,' Dad says. 'Maybe he knows something about this. We don't know if Emma went alone or if she went with the police.' He glances at his watch and I know what he's thinking. It's after nine. If Mum got home safely, she would have called immediately to let us know. Or she would have at least texted me. If she had Gina with her, she'd want to tell us right away, she wouldn't leave it all night. Something bad has happened. That's why my body feels limp and unsteady.

My mind buzzes as I follow Dad out of the B&B. How did Mum get in contact with Amy? Was there another ransom note? If there was, it might explain why she wanted me to stay at Dad's.

We get into the car and leave without saying goodbye. There's no time for that. Dad drives quickly through the village, but not without caution. His movements and reactions aren't as fast as they used to be, and he knows that.

'Did she say anything to you?' he asks on the way.

'Nothing.'

'She didn't mention Amy contacting her?'

'No.'

He pulls over near to the house and mumbles, 'Her car is still here.'

The sight of it makes my heart skip a beat. Maybe I'm wrong. What if Mum drove home with Gina? Before Dad even has the handbrake on, I'm out of the car, pulling my keys from my coat pocket. They almost slip from my fingers, but I open the door; call out. Wait.

'Emma?' Dad shouts from behind me, limping into the house.

Silence.

I hurry into the lounge, then up the stairs and check her room, my room, Gina's small bedroom. Nothing. That excited beat of my heart fizzles away.

'She's not here,' I tell Dad as I meet him at the bottom of the stairs.

'Right.' He pulls his lips into a thin line. 'Then we go to the Wetherington Estate and look for her there.'

This is the longest amount of time I've spent apart from Mum since I came home from the bunker. We've never spent a night apart. A week away from Gina and now a night away from Mum. The more I dwell on it, the more I begin to panic. I feel myself slipping away from reality, desperate to go back to the silence. But I can't do that. They need me.

Out of the window, the green fields blur together. It's a short drive but we've been travelling along the narrow road that connects some of the estate, wondering how to approach this search.

'I've been thinking about why Amy would want to meet Emma here,' Dad says as he directs the car over a cattle grid. His voice reverberates a little. 'And I think I understand now. It all makes sense. Emma cutting her hair . . . the estate.' He sighs. 'For fuck's sake, Amy. For that?' He bangs the steering wheel with one hand.

'What do you mean?'

'There was a camping trip that ended up getting out of hand. A group held Amy down and cut off her hair. She was crying . . . it was pretty nasty.'

'So Amy made Mum cut her hair?'

He nods. 'Maybe that was some sort of signal between the two of them. I thought Emma was just acting strangely but this makes more sense. And I think I remember where it happened.' He pulls the car into a lay-by next to a stile. And then he sighs. 'I'm not going to be able to get over that.' He nods to the wooden step built into the wall.

'I'll go.' I unzip my seatbelt.

He grabs my forearm. 'It's not safe. We should wait for the police.'

I gaze out at the field. There's one old oak tree in the centre. It's the kind of picture that would make pretty postcard art, with sheep and stone walls and the edge of the woods encroaching from one side. A shiver runs down my body. What happened here?

After Dad hangs up his phone, he points to the tree. 'That's where they pinned Amy's hair.' His voice is slow and breathy. He sounds tired. 'It was so long ago. She seemed to get over it at the time.'

I'm quiet for a moment, and then the realisation hits me. Mum and Dad were there, and they didn't stop this event from happening. I thought they were good people. It feels strange to know they were part of something like this.

'Let me go to the tree and back,' I say eventually.

Dad sighs. 'All right. Stay where I can see you.'

I get out of the car and hop over the stile. The ground is still hard from the lack of rain, but there's a chill in the air for the first time in over a week. I pull my sleeves down over my hands for warmth. The sheep go from curious to terrified in a matter of moments, scattering through the grass, letting out worried little bleats. Before the bunker I would have chased them, laughing. But now I could never bear to frighten them any more than I just did.

As the sun tries its best to peek out from the cloud, I notice the glint of something metallic next to the oak tree. Stumbling on the uneven ground, I hurry towards the strange, alien object. Whatever it is, it isn't supposed to be in this field. Fields are for mud, buttercups and dandelions. Not metal.

I snatch up the phone first. It's Mum's, and when I press the power button, I see the display picture of our family. Me, Mum, Gina and Dad, grinning wildly. Gina had chosen it. She chose one with Dad in the photo because she wants Mum and Dad to be together. The sight of the phone makes my stomach lurch. I close my eyes and take a deep breath in the way my psychologist advises me to when I feel overwhelmed.

Closing my eyes makes me want to fade away into myself. I pull myself back.

The phone goes into my pocket. Then I kneel down to examine the other object nestled in the grass. I recognise it immediately as one of our kitchen knives. Mum brought this to protect herself, but she didn't use it. Maybe she didn't get a chance to use it. Amy stopped her, and then she took Mum with her, wherever she went.

Chapter Thirty-One

AIDEN

When Dad sees the knife he shakes his head, leans over the steering wheel and starts to cry. At the same time, a memory of Dad flashes into my mind. Him when he was young, with a can of beer in his hand, eyes glued to the television. There was some sort of football final on the TV and I think I had on a child's version of the kit. One of the players missed the goal they were supposed to score, and Dad's face crumpled in disappointment. He brushed a tear away from his eye and then looked at me. 'You didn't see that.' Then cleared his throat and carried on.

Men aren't supposed to cry but I don't really understand why. Hugh used to cry sometimes. Dad cried in the hospital when he heard me talk for the first time. He also cried when Mum was found not guilty of killing Jake. But I haven't cried for a long time and I don't know what to do or say to comfort him. Since Gina's been missing, I've seen Mum cry a lot and I always stand there staring, in a swirl of emotions, not knowing what to do about them.

Finally, he sits up, rubs his eyes, wipes his nose and

coughs. 'We need to get back to the house. The police want to speak to us.'

I nod, placing the knife in the glove box for safe keeping.

'There's no blood on it at least,' Dad says.

'I didn't notice any blood around the tree. It must mean she's still OK.' I rub my palms against my jeans as Dad starts the car. 'Do you think I should have left the knife where it was for the police to find?'

'I don't know.' Dad pulls out of the lay-by and begins to drive back towards the village.

'I brought her phone, too.'

'OK,' Dad says. 'Let's tell the police everything we've found.'

I know that we're both subdued as we make our way back to the B&B, even though I'm not good at noticing these changes in atmosphere. This time it hangs thickly over us.

'What else do you know about Amy?' I ask to break the silence, and at the same time try to follow a thread in my mind. A vague memory taking me back to the bunker. To Hugh.

'Well, she was picked on at school. But after the camping incident, she actually came out of her shell. She used to invite herself along to the pub, drink a lot, flirt with some of the lads. She liked me. A lot.' He shakes his head. He lowers his voice to little more than a whisper. 'I didn't tell anyone about it. I think I hurt her back then. But this . . . She must be so sick inside.' He hits the steering wheel in anger, and I decide not to ask any more questions. I'm not sure it's helping anyway.

There's a police car in the driveway of the B&B and Dad parks next to it. I make my way around to his side to help him with the walking stick. Dad leans on me, weighing less than I imagined. He seemed so big when I was little.

'I've got it,' he says as he positions his weight a little better and limps his way up to the house.

Grandma hurries out of the front door.

'Any news?'

Her slipper catches on a stone and she swears beneath her breath.

'We found some things in a field that belong to Emma,' Dad says, his voice straining. 'Her phone and a knife. We think Amy must have met her there and forced Emma to go with her.'

Grandma's eyes are wide, and her face is bloodless. She moves in jerky motions, full of anxious energy. 'The police are here.'

Dad nods.

'DCI Stevenson too. He seems angry.'

It should be a relief to know that the police are here, but I can't help thinking about how they leaked the ransom note information. Maybe Mum was right about not trusting them. I itch to message Faith, to talk to her about everything that's going on, but I can't right now.

'Chrissie, would you mind putting the kettle on?' Stevenson is saying to one of the PCs as we make our way into the lounge. With two coppers in uniform, DCI Stevenson and me and my family, the room is crammed with people. Stevenson turns to us, his expression tired. 'Rob. Aiden. Let's sit down shall we? There's a lot to go over.'

'All right,' Dad says, finding a spot on the sofa. I sit next to him. Grandad is already in his chair, and Grandma goes into the kitchen to help Chrissie the police officer.

'Emma contacted me yesterday,' Stevenson says, jumping straight in. 'She'd received a letter from Amy asking her to meet her on the Wetherington Estate by an oak tree.' The place I found the knife. 'The letter asked her to go alone without police or anyone else. But she was scared to go alone. She reached out and I arranged a team.' He sighs. 'Amy caught wind of this. She didn't show. We came back and I put a few officers on surveillance to make sure Amy didn't try anything.'

'Emma agreed to meet her later, without the police. Didn't she?' Dad leans forward and places his head in his hands.

'It seems so,' Stevenson admits. 'She must have slipped

out. Her car didn't move, so she obviously walked. When I checked on her this morning, there was no answer. And then your mum called to say she was missing.' He sighed. 'I wish she hadn't taken things into her own hands like this. But we're going to do what we can to get her back. Emma gave us access to her security camera app. We'll check that to confirm that she left of her own accord. There was someone monitoring it during the night, but they didn't see anything suspect at the time. If Emma decided to sneak out of the house, she made sure she wouldn't be seen.'

'She did go back,' I say. 'She sent me the message.'

'We're assuming it was her,' Stevenson replies gently. 'But that message could have been written by Amy, or Amy forced your mum to write it. But, for what it's worth, I think you're right. Emma went willingly to try and save her daughter.

'I guessed that the tree would be important to Amy,' Dad says. 'We went there this morning and we found Emma's phone. And a knife.'

Stevenson's eyebrows shoot up. 'What did you do with them?'

'We brought them back,' Dad admits.

Stevenson sighs, but then says, 'Well, we know who took her anyway. Forensics might not be that useful to us right now. What we need to figure out is where Amy might have taken Emma. Do you have any ideas? Either of you?'

I shake my head. Dad does the same.

'All right. I'll get a team out searching the area. We'll check Amy's old house again, though it seems unlikely that she left any clues. I'll have people on the roads and checking the woods.' He sighs again. 'If Emma had called me earlier, we might have been able to find Amy before all this happened.' When he stands, I notice that he does it slowly. I can see that he's worn out, and I can't help but wonder if he has the energy left in him to find them.

· · ·

They don't notice me sneak away from the room and disappear into the bathroom. At least no one watches me when I leave.

Sitting on the edge of the bath, I take my phone and load Instagram, going straight to my direct messages.

ME: She took Mum.
ME: I don't know what to do.

But Faith doesn't reply straight away. She's not online. I put the phone back in my pocket and leave, running the taps and flushing the toilet on my way out so as not to arouse suspicion. It seems stupid, but I do it anyway.

Back in the lounge, after several lengthy statements are taken, both Mum's and my phones given over, I get mine back once copies of her final message are taken, the knife is also handed to the police. Neither me nor Dad feel like we can sit around doing nothing. He calls around Mum's friends first. And then he calls Amy's friends. Only a phone call from Josie Barratt provides interesting information. Mum asked her to search through Hugh's papers and see if there was anything else suspicious that may have been overlooked during the first investigation.

'Your mum thought Hugh was connected somehow. What do you think?' Dad asks.

With his eyes staring at me, the expectancy on his face and the people in the room, my throat feels clogged. I wrap my arms around my body, wanting nothing less than to talk about this. But it might help Mum and Gina.

'I think it's likely,' I reply. Again, my mind drifts back to a throwaway comment I heard Hugh say in the bunker, about wishing there was another place, somewhere closer. I feel like it's an important memory that I've buried somewhere deep in my subconscious, but I can't seem to access it no matter how hard I try. As I got older, I knew that Hugh wanted a replacement for me; I remember that much. I think he might have told me part of his plan to do it. But it's all entwined with the things I've made myself forget. But if Hugh wanted a replacement, did that mean he wanted a new location, too?

'Stevenson.' Dad stands and nods over to the detective, who is at the back of the room speaking with the other PC who isn't Chrissie. I've already forgotten his name. 'We're going to Josie Barratt's house. We think there's a connection between what's going on with Amy and Hugh Barratt's past.'

'I'll come with you,' he says.

On the way out of the door, I check my phone for a reply from Faith, but there's nothing. She hasn't seen my message. In the back of the car I keep refreshing the app but there's still no reply. I have to remind myself that there are times when Faith doesn't reply for several hours. She once said the internet connection is patchy where she lives.

When we arrive at Josie's place, I realise that I've painted this house many times. Not as often as the bunker, or Mum's childhood home, but still many times. Every now and then the memories resurface, and I get to view them with the benefit of hindsight. The happy evenings with the adults having dinner together. Sometimes Hugh or Josie would read a story. Hugh told a lot of jokes, especially to me.

I trusted all of them completely, because why wouldn't I? And this house was a place of happiness for me. I'd actually ask to come here so that I could spend time with Uncle Hugh and Aunty Josie.

This is the first time I've been here since the bunker and I don't know what this house is anymore. It's beautiful. As buildings go, I've had limited experience, but I know it's expensive, clean, big and fancy. It has a doorbell that sounds like a real bell, and a large door with a handle in the centre.

Josie's eyes are red-rimmed and flaky. She tucks a strand of hair behind her ears as she leads us through to the kitchen.

'I can't believe this is happening,' she says, for the second time. 'I thought we were safe. That it was over. First Gina . . .' After speaking, she glances guiltily at me and smiles. It's an apologetic smile. I remind her of what her husband did, and that isn't comfortable for either of us. 'This village is . . . well, it's rotten.' She wipes her face, sniffs loudly. I watch her. Is this genuine? Mum loves Josie like a sister but I don't know if I feel the same way. She was married to Hugh for years; how did he not rub off on her like he did on everyone else? Amy. Jake. Hugh was friends with both. I think he fed their evil.

But Josie is immune?

'Would anyone like a drink?' She hovers near the kettle, half-heartedly gesturing to it.

'We don't want to take up too much of your time,' Stevenson says with a smile. I get the sense that he's smoothing over some awkwardness. Josie doesn't want us here.

She doesn't offer us a seat either at the dining table or through in the living room. Dad leans against the wall. Stevenson stands up straight, his notebook out ready to jot down information. I cross my arms and watch her with interest.

'You mentioned on the phone that Emma was interested in learning more about Hugh's finances. What do you think she suspected?' Stevenson taps a pen on top of his notebook.

'That he had a plan for a second kidnapping once Aiden turned sixteen,' Josie says, her finger tracing a line along the kitchen counter.

The words send a shiver down my spine. *Gina is the second kidnapping.* But Hugh is dead so what's the point?

'I searched through his paperwork, but I don't know what I'm looking for,' she says.

'Would you be willing to turn over Hugh's documents to the police?' Stevenson asks. 'Hugh also had an office in London that he shared with his brother. Is that correct?'

'Yes,' Josie admits. 'There could be important paperwork there too.'

'Perhaps I could send a team there. We have forensics who are experts in finances. If there's anything important hidden in Hugh's papers, then I'm sure they'll find it.'

'I don't know what it could be,' Josie says. 'I inherited everything. Surely I would have noticed any hidden properties.'

'Another bunker?' Stevenson asks.

The word is a punch to the gut. *Another*. The room fades away and I'm in my cage, sat on the floor at Hugh's feet. He's stroking my hair. *It would be so much more convenient.* He isn't talking to me in particular, more to himself.

'Yes.' Josie folds her arms across her body. Stares at the tiled floor. 'A second bunker.'

Chapter Thirty-Two

EMMA

I'm in water. The coldness of it seeps through my clothes, my flesh, my ligaments and into my bones. My eyes flutter open and I expect to choke on the freezing cold liquid, but I'm surprised to find that I'm dry. There is no water. The room is dark. Confused, my gaze drifts down to my arms. Someone has removed my jacket. I'm lying on stone. I gasp, pull myself up to a sitting position and allow my eyes to adjust to the darkness.

It all comes flooding back. The panic as the people in the studio hurried out of the building. The fire alarm blaring. Finding Walnut on the stairs. The week of sheer pain, of missing her. Amy's games with the letters. The tree. The hair.

I get to my feet and a blinding light comes on overhead. I shield my eyes from it and take a few staggering steps back, coming into contact with cold metal. When I turn around to inspect the barrier, I find metal bars in front of me. I'm in a cage, looking out at an underground room.

'Gina,' I whisper.

Amy drugged me and pushed me into a car, but before then she said I would be reunited with my daughter. *Gina*. My body spins around. My eyes lock on the tiny mattress in the corner of the cage, to the tiny body tucked into a duvet, honey-hued hair spilling over the pillow.

I lunge forward and drop to my knees, not even feeling the hard stone floor beneath me. Trembling hands reach greedily for the covers and yank them away. My hand flies up to my face. I fall onto my backside and crawl away from the thing in the bed.

There are footsteps coming down a set of steps I can't see. She walks into the room and my head snaps towards her.

'You found her,' Amy says. She walks over to the bars and gently caresses them. 'My baby.'

'No,' I whisper.

Amy doesn't even notice me speak; she just stares at the thing in the corner. 'I wanted you both to meet. It's something I've wanted for a very long time. Emma, why don't you say hello to my baby daughter. Say hello to Lily.'

I shake my head. 'You lied to me.'

'Yes,' Amy says. 'I did. I'm not sure what you expected.'

Finally, I allow my eyes to trail back to the mattress in the corner of the cage. The duvet is rumpled up on the floor from where I threw it back, uncovering the child beneath. But it isn't a child, not a living, breathing child anyway. Instead, an incredibly lifelike doll lays on the crumpled bedding. Her face is perfect porcelain. Her hair is fine and downy. Her eyes are blue, staring up at the bars above. But she is not alive, and she is not Gina.

'Where is my daughter?' The back of my throat is thick with the taste of bile and my head throbs from whatever drug she gave me. But now that the initial shock of finding the doll is beginning to wear off, I can at least start to concentrate on what counts: finding Gina.

Amy backs away from the bars. 'Say hello to Lily and perhaps I'll tell you.' She smiles, revealing slightly crooked teeth. They are darker than I remembered. Has she been living here? Wherever this is.

I take another quick look around me and a cold chill spreads over my skin. We're below ground, in some sort of vault or crypt. The place reminds me of the crypts below York Minster that gave me nightmares when I was a child. This room, or crypt, is much smaller than the one in the cathedral, but still has the high, vaulted ceilings. The floor is dusty. There are cobwebs in the corners, plenty of shadows.

A few electric lanterns have been set up around the place, along with some candles, but the bright light comes from a portable spotlight, the kind builders might use on an outside job.

'Well?' Amy prompts.

'Hello, Lily,' I say.

'Make sure she's comfortable then.' Amy nods towards the doll.

I can barely bring myself to do this, to play pretend with her. But I get back on my feet, walk across to the mattress and tuck the doll into the blanket.

When I walk across to the bars, Amy is smiling.

'What makes you think I know where Gina is?' she says.

My stomach drops. A heavy stone hitting the bottom of the ocean. I can do nothing but gape at her. 'What?'

Amy just laughs and turns away.

I grab the bars, pressing my face between them. 'You're lying! You know where she is. You had her hair. That was her hair, I'm sure of it.' I know the touch of my daughter's hair; I know the smell of it. Surely I wasn't wrong. 'Come back, Amy! Tell me!'

Her footsteps begin to climb up the stairs. In desperation, I grab the doll and pull her closer to the cage bars.

'Tell me where she is, or I'll smash Lily into pieces.'

The sound of the footsteps suddenly stops, then I hear them descend. Her face comes back into view, wan and sickly.

'I mean it,' I say. 'I'll do it.'

She shrugs. 'It's just a doll, Emma. I can buy another one.' Her laughter echoes back up the steps, and I'm left in the cage with a doll for a daughter.

. . .

She doesn't come back, no matter how much I scream and shout. She doesn't come back and I'm left to examine my surroundings alone. These are the same sort of bars that I remember from the bunker. Did Hugh put this cage here? How could the police miss this second location? There was supposed to be an investigation after Aiden was found, but because Aiden didn't remember much, and Josie didn't know anything, it seems as though they missed this.

But maybe Josie will find something now. She promised to check his finances again. Maybe it'll lead the police to wherever I am.

I take a walk around the cage. Just like in Aiden's bunker, there is a small bed, the same place I found Lily. But there isn't a toilet or sink. Perhaps he hadn't got around to the plumbing or electricity yet. There's no generator keeping the place going. Instead, there are several large plastic bottles of water and a bucket in the corner. There are stuffed toys lining the cage. I pick up a red dragon and press it to my face. All I smell is the same damp air I'm breathing in.

Aside from the toys, there's a rug and a beanbag chair. That's it.

I sink to the floor. What do I do now? How do I get out?

When I close my eyes, I'm back in the flat in Manchester. Making breakfast with Aiden at the table or playing with Gina in the park. Or she's helping me out in the art studio, paint on her nose.

Stop.

Wishful thinking is going to get me nowhere.

Because of the high ceiling, this cage goes over my head and joins the wall behind me. The last cage Hugh built was floor to ceiling. I try to hook my feet between the bars and push myself up so that I can examine the upper section. Everything is welded together. But how long ago was this made? Is it secure? Will it hold me?

I soon find that I don't have the upper body strength to lift myself up, so I drop to my knees and check the bottom of the cage. Could I lift it? It's doubtful, but I try anyway. No. It won't budge.

Moving the doll from the bed, I sit down and try to stop the increasingly terrifying thoughts from taking over. I've had claustrophobic nightmares for years, and now I'm living them. Not even deep breaths can keep my mind from spinning, but I have to think.

My eyes drift to the porcelain doll. *Lily.* There has to be a story behind this doll. Why does Amy have it? And why is it here? That's something I can use.

I track all the events leading to this moment, from the most recent, to the furthest back in time. Firstly, whose hair was in the note that the teenage boy gave to me on the street? I'd felt that gut punch of motherly instinct when I'd touched that hair. Was I wrong? Or does Amy have Gina and is withholding her from me? I don't know what to think anymore.

The sound of echoing footsteps and an opening door infiltrates the quiet. I instinctively move closer to the bars to wrap my fingers around the metal.

The stairs are too far away from the cage for me to see her descend, but a few moments later she turns a corner and is visible. She carries a tray containing some fruit, chocolate and what appears to be cooked meat with vegetables.

'Rabbit again, Lily. Some for you too, Emma.'

I don't say a word.

'Don't eat it if you don't want to.' She shrugs and sets the tray down. 'It probably doesn't matter.'

I don't like the sound of that.

'Away from the bars, please Emma.' Her eyes remain fixed on mine until I do what she says.

I take three steps away and watch as Amy lifts the small bowls from the tray and pushes them through the bars of the cage. Could I drop to my knees, lunge forward, grab her arm and pull her close to the bars? I wait, ready for the next set of bowls, but when I drop forward, she moves away.

'Stay still or you won't eat, Emma,' she says. 'Don't you want to keep your strength up?'

I remain in my crouch, watching her, waiting for her to move first. She does. She takes one step. I launch myself at the bars, right arm stretching through, fingers groping wildly at thin air. She laughs. She's two steps out of reach.

'You're just making it harder on yourself,' she says, lifting one eyebrow.

'Why did you bring me here?' I say, dropping my arm but remaining close to the cage.

'Three steps back. Unless you want to starve.'

She's enjoying this, the power. Is that because she's felt powerless her entire life? She was always so easily led. She needed to be, most of the time. That's why she was never respected, why she became Hugh's pet. But now it makes sense that she trained to be a teacher, because every day between 8 and 3, she got to wield a little bit of power over vulnerable human beings. I'm beginning to understand her, and maybe I can use that. Obediently, I take three small steps back.

Amy tosses the fruit through the cage, not caring if it bruises on the hard floor. Then she slides the last bowl through, snapping her body into standing position and stepping swiftly away. The fact that she moved so quickly tells me that she's worried about a physical confrontation. I suppose we are quite evenly matched.

'Go on.' She nods to the food on the floor of the cage.

I bend down, pick up the food. 'Where am I?'

She shrugs.

'It's a church, isn't it?' I say.

'A chapel.' She lowers herself to the floor and sits cross-legged. Her posture is straight, but relaxed. Everything has gone according to her plan and now she is content. Nothing I or DCI Stevenson or DI Khatri or Aiden or Rob or anyone else has done has made any kind of difference.

'Hugh made this?'

She nods. 'It isn't quite finished. There's supposed to be more to it. A working toilet. A sink. He was going to build a fence around the entire building to make sure no one came inside.'

'This is where Aiden's replacement was supposed to come.'

193

'Not exactly,' Amy replies. 'Hugh was going to move the child around to make it more convenient for him.'

'Why would he need that?'

'So that he could be closer to London when he needed to be.'

'And you've kept it waiting for me.'

'Yes.'

'Tell me where Gina is, Amy. I know you have her. Is she upstairs? Is she in the chapel? Please tell me she's safe. Let me see her. Whatever happened between us, please. You know my family doesn't deserve this.'

Amy's eyes flicker. 'That's enough.'

'Your aunt and uncle are dead. You can move on now. You're not the victim anymore.'

She scoffs. 'I was never a victim.'

I shake my head. 'I saw your house. I heard what your neighbour said about your uncle and how he yelled at you. I saw your photo album and I saw your mother. I know that you were good once. I saw it. Why else do you think I invited you camping that time?'

'To ridicule me!'

'Is that what you think? No, Amy, no. That's not why. They were off their faces on pills. I don't think even they planned to cut your hair.'

'It wasn't just that,' Amy says. 'They shat in my tent. A month later, the girl who cut my hair beat me up and stole my necklace. When I went home, my uncle hit me for losing it. He hit me . . .' she trails off. 'There is so much more to all this than you could imagine. You have no idea what I've been through in my life, so be quiet.'

'You can tell me, you know. Here is your audience, Amy.' I gesture to the cage. 'Tell me.'

She just smirks. 'Not yet.'

I reach forward and wrap my fingers around the bars. 'Listen to me. You're not that girl from school anymore,' I say. 'You can be better than this. Better than those bullies. Let me go to my daughter. Please. I'll do anything. Tell me where she is!'

She shakes her head. 'That's not the plan.'

'What plan? Hugh is gone. You're in control now. You can change the plan whenever you like.'

She doesn't say another word. Instead she stands up and she walks out, ignoring me as I rattle the cage in desperation.

Chapter Thirty-Three

AIDEN

As we emerge from Josie and Hugh's house – I continue to call it Hugh's house in my mind because I can't think of it any other way – the midday sun warms my skin. I forgot to put on the high SPF cream Mum buys for me. My skin is still delicate, so I hurry to the car and get in the backseat, watching Dad and DCI Stevenson amble down the drive.

The first thing I do is check my phone. Finally, a reply.

FAITH: What?? Are you OK?
  FAITH: Aiden, I'm so worried about you. Are you OK?

I quickly type back: I'm fine.

'That must have been hard for you, mate,' Dad says, pulling me from my thoughts. DCI Stevenson gets in the driver's seat and starts the car.

I'm not sure what to say, and I don't know how to say it, so I just nod, before looking back at my screen.

FAITH: I wish there was something I could do. I wish I could comfort you at least.

'Do you think it's possible?' Dad's eyes reach mine through the rear-view mirror. 'Did he ever . . . ever mention a second bunker to you?'

My heart is hammering. Between Dad's sad eyes in the mirror and Faith's sad messages, I feel like I need to console both of them somehow. I lean forward, put my head in my hands, pull at my hair with my fingers. Someone reaches back and touches me, but I move away from them, I shrink back. The car feels too small and I want to open the door and run away, but I force myself to stay. I lift my head and the car begins to move. Outside, the sun goes behind a cloud and my skin begins to cool down.

Once I'm composed again, I reply. 'It's possible. He once mentioned that he wished I was halfway between London and Bishoptown. Hugh would travel back up to Bishoptown in the middle of business trips in London.'

Dad roars, punches the dashboard, the glovebox pops open. DCI Stevenson calmly reaches across and closes it.

'Well, perhaps he bought some sort of property. A house, a piece of land, whatever it might be, he had to spend money on it. There'll be a paper trail and this time we'll know what we're looking for.'

'But this isn't Hugh is it?' Dad says. 'It's Amy. What if we're wrong?'

'She's finishing what he started,' Stevenson says. 'And she's punishing the person who brought it all down in the first place.'

'Emma?'

'Yes,' he replies. 'Or Aiden. Perhaps both.'

But I'm only half listening. Instead, I feel the vibration alert on my phone, and I open up my messages.

ME: I wish you could as well.
    FAITH: You know I'm thinking of you, don't you?
    ME: Yeah, I know. Thank U.
    FAITH: You mean the world to me.
    FAITH: I mean it.
    ME: You mean so much to me too.

I pause, my skin on fire, my fingers hover above the screen. What can I say to convey how she has made me feel these past months?

ME: You help me process the world.
    FAITH: I love you so much.
    ME: I love you too.

DCI Stevenson spends a lot of time on the phone talking to various team members. Every now and then I see him take out a packet of chewable indigestion tablets and take two. At other times he sits and stares into space. We're usually crowded into the B&B, but right now we're sitting outside in the little garden behind it. Perched on the wrought iron garden furniture.

The sun is intermittent, often masked by clouds. Shadows come and go along the lawn. Grandma makes tea or delivers soft drinks. They've asked their B&B customers to go home so that they can concentrate on the disappearance of Mum and Gina.

I'm quizzed a lot. Do I remember what Hugh said exactly? Did he mention any specific locations? Was I supposed to move there? Was he going to keep both me and a second child? Did he mention finding a second child?

But my answers aren't detailed. The truth is, I remember some of what he said, but I tuned a lot of it out because the conversation was scaring me. All I know, and all I tell them, is that I believe he was looking for somewhere convenient for him.

Bringing back the memories makes my stomach churn and my hands shake. I just want it to be over.

DCI Stevenson wipes sweat from his brow and sits back on the chair. For the past fifteen minutes he has been pacing the length of the lawn, talking on his phone again. 'We have a warrant for Hugh's offices. We have officers checking maps for world war two bunkers. We have officers checking the woods and the surrounding area. We're going to find them.'

'I don't think I can sit here and wait,' Dad says. He stretches out one leg as though it's aching, and then flexes his fingers.

'You've done too much already,' Grandma warns. 'You need rest.'

'No. No I can't.' He stands, takes a few paces. I can tell he doesn't know what to do with himself. He turns to DCI Stevenson. 'Where can I check? Where can I go?'

'It's best that you let us handle it, Rob,' Stevenson says, not unkindly. 'I swear we're pulling all of our resources. We're going to find them.'

I slip away from the group outside and head into the lounge, where I find the laptop resting against the sofa. I open it and begin to search through as much as I can. Mum's disappearance has made several news sites so far. There's disbelief in the comments and some anger about the police. Some say that the media coverage has caused Mum to commit suicide. In a fit of anger, I begin to reply back to these comments. Vile language spews from my fingertips. I wish them death. I wish them pain. And then, I delete them all.

What happened to Hugh that made him the man he was? No one seems to know his background. I pull my phone out of my jeans pocket and think for a moment. After scrolling through my contacts, I find Josie's number. I keep thinking of the time she spent with Hugh, sleeping next to him, making him food. We're the two people outside of his parents who know him the best. I tap the call icon. She answers with a curt hello and I let her know who it is.

'Oh,' she says, exhaling sharply, 'I thought it was going to be one of those cold calls, you know. How are you holding up? Any news about Emma and Ginny?'

'No.'

'That's . . . that's a shame. I just can't believe this is happening to your family again. I'm so sorry.' There's a hurried, anxious tone to her voice. From what little memory I have of her from when I was a child, I remembered her laughing a lot and making bad jokes. But she hasn't been like that since Hugh died.

'I wanted to talk to you about Hugh.'

'Oh, OK.' Again, anxious − like the awkward conversation in her kitchen − acting as though she would rather do anything other than talk about Hugh.

I take a moment; words are still difficult to find when I'm stressed. 'I . . . I want to say something.'

'OK, honey,' her voice cracks.

'He was as evil as anyone can be. But he wasn't always a monster to me. He talked to me, taught me to read and write, gave me gifts and sometimes I miss him. I know that sounds sick, but I do, and it's OK if you miss him too.'

I can hear her crying on the end of the phone. But for me the tears won't come. I'm empty.

'We shouldn't feel guilty for that. Should we? That's what Dr Anderton says, anyway. He was the abuser. The predator.'

'Yes,' she whispers.

'But we know him better than anyone, don't we? We've spent the most time with him.'

'Yes.'

'We need to figure out what he was planning before he died, because Amy is following through with it.'

'OK,' she says, voice still croaking slightly.

'We can do that together, can't we? Because his darkness has rubbed off on us both.'

Breathy now. 'Yes.'

I let out a long, slow sigh. Hugh's face comes into my mind, the way it looked before he begged me to kill him. There was some humanity left inside him. Whether he felt guilt is something I often think about. At times I think he did, other days I think not. On those days, the memory of his blood on the concrete floor brings me nothing but comfort.

'He was extremely thorough with his business,' she says. 'He researched and investigated as much as he could, not because he wanted to go by the book, but because he wanted to figure out where he could break the rules and get away with it. What's in it for me if I do it this way? That was the question he often asked himself. What will I get in return?'

'Maybe that was how he saw his relationship with Amy. By being with her, he knew he had someone willing to give him an alibi at a moment's notice. A woman with access to young children who knew how to put them at ease.'

The words hang heavy between us.

'Yes,' she says. 'I'm sorry, I haven't quite come to terms with it yet.'

I say nothing because I can't relate. I've had no major relationships to compare to her marriage. I suppose it would be like finding out Mum was secretly a monster.

'If he wanted to make improvements to the way he kidnapped me, what would he do?' I ask, half to myself and half to Josie. 'How would a different bunker help him achieve that?'

'Hugh would want convenience,' she says.

'Right.' I remember the throwaway comment Hugh made one day in the bunker: *Sometimes I wish there was somewhere in between there and here. Halfway.* It sparks another conversation between me and Hugh that I'd forgotten about. One that's important. 'Thanks, Jo, that's so helpful.'

'It is?' she says.

I say goodbye and hang up. I need to speak to Dad.

Chapter Thirty-Four

AMY

It isn't exactly what Hugh imagined it would be. I unroll the plans along the church floor next to the first row of pews. The stretch of thin paper reveals several diagrams drawn by him, along with a page of notes.

The cage had been fitted before I started squatting here. There was supposed to be a toilet and a sink, and a security camera so he could monitor the place at all times on his phone. I managed to set up battery powered nanny cams, but they aren't ideal. He was also going to make the chapel more comfortable and put a lock on the door to the crypt. I've fitted the lock, but the door is old and crumbling. It wouldn't be much use for keeping people out. His plans are deviously clever. I felt privileged to be brought into his secret world. The morality of it never bothered me. The powerful rule the weak. That's the way of the world. Hugh was the most powerful man I ever knew, and he loved me. That was what I cared about.

He bought the chapel from the owner of the estate with cash. Literal cash. In a briefcase, off the record. He even let the estate owner keep the deeds as long as he could do whatever he wanted with it.

There was a risk involved. This place is more known, and more visible, than the bunker. But as long as he kept it in its run-down state, he figured that no one would pay much interest. The chapel would soon be another abandoned renovation project lost to the recession.

I make my way out into the woods at sunrise. There was a downpour overnight, and the rain hasn't quite finished. I stand on the stone steps outside the church, naked, letting the rain wash me clean. At my feet there are green vines snaking up from the forest floor. Since it was left unused, nature has begun to take hold. Soon nature's roots will push the bricks out of their way and the walls will begin to crumble. Power often changes hands, but it always wins over the weak.

I wonder whether the rich family who used to own this building allowed any of the locals to attend their services. This place would have been a sanctuary long ago. But someone failed to take care of it and the woods grew wilder and more unkempt, until it stopped being a sanctuary and someone turned it into a prison.

In this holy place, I can't help but wonder about souls and whether mine exists. I didn't stop believing in God until I was in my late teens. Mum wasn't devout, but she talked about God sometimes. *He's watching*, she'd say. *You have to be good. He loves you.* When I mentioned this to my aunty, she said that it was the drugs.

The rain is beginning to make me cold. Back inside the building, I wrap myself in an old towel until I'm dry, and then dress. I have dry cereal to offer the captive. It isn't much, but it'll do. I hope Emma is being sensible.

Nerves prickle at the base of my belly. I don't like the fact that Emma has been in my house, seen the attic and the photographs. The attic was the place I went when I'd been bad. Sometimes Aunty Kim would come up and talk to me, but most of the time I was alone. No, I wasn't scared, the room was comforting for me. I liked being constrained, knowing that this . . . these few feet . . .

were the limit to my movements. I liked being told that I couldn't leave. Why, I don't know, but I did. Which means Emma's presumptions about who I am and why I do what I do are all wrong. I'm not damaged. This is who I was destined to be.

The problem is, who I am is unique. So unique that I think I'll always be alone.

Perhaps things would be different if I'd kept you, Lily. I would have raised a child infinitely better than Aiden. If I'd had a child, I wouldn't have to be alone. That child would have been unshaped clay for me to mould. A part of me.

I put the cereal on a tray and begin my walk down to the crypt. At the door, I place the tray on the step and unlock the padlock. The door is stiff and makes a scraping sound that sets my teeth on edge. Below I can see the battery lanterns I set up. It keeps the room illuminated with a low glow.

Emma is awake and sitting up on the mattress, with her legs crossed as though she's about to meditate or begin her yoga class. There's a faint sheen of sweat along her forehead. Lily lies next to her. I thought I would feel more about Emma sharing the cell with Lily, but I don't. Now that Emma is here, Lily is just a doll again.

'Let me go.' Emma's eyes burn bright. Hatred shimmers through them like water on colourful marbles.

'I brought you breakfast.' Slowly, I bend down, lean back on my haunches, and slide the bowl through. Emma eyes the cereal with distaste, but she still lifts it and begins picking through the cornflakes. I sit down on the cold stones and cross my legs.

'Are you trying to keep me weak?' she asks, lifting a cornflake.

I shrug. 'Supplies are low, that's all.'

Emma is quiet for a moment, her hard glare fixed on me. Then she says, 'I should've killed you.'

'Murdered,' I correct. 'I was defenceless. If you'd killed me, it would have been murder, wouldn't it? We weren't on a battlefield. I hadn't broken into your house or attacked you. If you'd killed me in that house with that knife, it would have been cold-blooded murder.'

She sighs sadly, 'I don't care anymore.' She sets the bowl down on the mattress and gestures to the cage with one hand. 'So this is it? This is what your life has been leading up to. This is the grand plan that Hugh started and you're finishing. What a sad little life you lead. I wouldn't be you.'

'What if it let you out of the cage?'

She turns away. 'Is all of this about the camping trip? I already said I was sorry about that.'

'No.'

'Is it about Hugh? Did you love him?'

'Yes, I loved him. And he was the only person in the world who loved me.'

'I don't believe you. I think you're incapable of love.' She stares me down. Judgemental. Hateful.

'And I suppose you know everything there is to know about love.' My voice sounds as hard as her eyes, letting her know she's got to me. I think I hate her as much as she hates me.

'I know more than you. I'm a mother.'

I taste her words, chew them up in disgust. How dare she? I begin to stand, to get away from her.

'Wait,' Emma calls out. 'Tell me where Gina is. Wherever she is, please let her go. I know that you hate me. Keep me here. Torture me. Kill me. I don't care. Just tell me my daughter is safe.'

I sit down and cup my chin in my hands, watching her, wild-eyed and desperate. That's the love, I think. The famous motherly love that I never got to experience. The one that so many women love to shove in the faces of the childless. So different from any other kinds of love. Fatherly love. Sisterly love. Romantic love. Platonic love.

'Amy, listen to me. You're not Hugh. You're better than him. You have more humanity in you, I know you do. And I know that you don't want Gina to suffer. Please, Amy.'

I watch her, begging me, and I can't help but blurt out the words I've been holding in all these years. 'I had a child once.'

She falters from her begging, mouth opening and closing, not knowing how to respond. 'You did?'

'Rob's child.' There it is, the secret I've kept hidden all this time. Like acid it had burned away at me, as I watched Emma live the life I'd always wanted.

Emma's head tilts from one side to the other. 'No, that's not –'

'It is. It's true.'

Her hands grip hold of the mattress. 'This is another delusion, isn't it?'

'No,' I say simply. 'I was pregnant with his child, but he didn't want me to keep it. He loved you. He wanted you, not me.'

She's just as flabbergasted as before, her jaw working. A glaze covers her eyes, dulling the intensity of them. I think for a moment that she's about to cry.

'What? What happened?' she asks.

'We went to the clinic together.' I pull in a deep breath. 'I bled for days. Couldn't tell anyone though. Not my aunt or uncle. I had to pretend I had period pain, when it was nothing short of agony. My uncle was so disgusted with me that he made me sleep in the attic for three days. It was during those three days that Lily died.'

Emma's head turns to the doll on the mattress. She whispers my daughter's name under her breath. 'Lily.'

'That's right,' I say. 'I named her because I wanted to keep her, but I was so in love with him. Have you ever been so disappointed in someone that one event brings everything you thought you knew shattering down?'

'Yes,' she says.

I nod. 'Yes, you do. You experienced that with Jake, didn't you? Well, I had that moment with your boyfriend. Sorry. I thought he'd leave you for me, but instead he begged me not to keep the baby because of how much he loved you. I was the one with the baby, but he wanted you.'

Her eyes close for a moment. Then she opens them again. When she speaks, her voice wobbles with emotion. 'I'm sorry you had to go through that. I'm sorry you lost Lily and were alone at the time.'

'I'm sure you are.' And yet I don't care how sorry she is. Whether she means it or not is inconsequential.

'You don't get it though, Amy. We didn't do anything wrong. He did.'

I shrug. 'Everything I do to you has the added bonus of hurting him.'

She's silent for a moment, letting it all sink in. I consider leaving the cellar, but she begins to talk again.

'Tell me how it happened,' she says. 'You and Rob, I mean.'

'Well,' I start. 'I loved him from afar, but you knew that. I wanted him to be with me and I wanted more for him. You were away with your parents. A family visit or a weekend away, something like that. I went to the pub with the group as usual. Rob and I got very drunk and we had sex.'

Her face clouds. It has a grey tinge to it. 'Where?'

'The woods.'

She screws her eyes up tight.

'And then in his car the next night.'

She turns her face away from me.

'After I went through all of that . . . After losing Lily, you ended up pregnant with Aiden. But Rob didn't march you to the clinic, did he?'

'You went through a horrible thing and Rob was cruel to you,' she says. 'But none of this excuses the evil things you've done to my family.'

'No,' I reply. 'I suppose I just like doing this kind of thing.'

Emma closes her eyes sadly. There are tears running down her cheeks. 'I thought you were like this because of Hugh. Because he groomed you.'

I consider the shadow cast by him. Almost as powerful as the man himself. Would I have done any of this if I hadn't met Hugh? Rob had been an infatuation, but Hugh understood me. 'I think I would have killed you eventually,' I say honestly. 'The truth is, we can't both live, can we?'

'No,' Emma says.

'The hatred has grown bigger than both of us. It's real now. Living.'

She nods her head up and down, tears still wet on her skin. 'But I think I could forgive you, if you let me find my daughter.'

I just shrug. 'I don't think you would. I think you'd still try to kill me.' I pause, pull at the dry skin on my lip, and then say, 'Unless we both die.'

Chapter Thirty-Five

EMMA

The part that surprises me about all this, is that I believe her. Rob was my first love, Aiden's father, and a person I've adored for many years, but he was flawed then and I'm sure he still is now. While I was writing silly, childish love letters to him from France, he was screwing a girl in the woods. It's been twenty years and I have other things to worry about, but it still stings.

The thought of him pressuring Amy to have the abortion makes my stomach churn. God knows he didn't react well when I showed him that fateful plastic stick with two blue lines. He'd acted like his life was going to end until I talked him around. But after that he'd supported me. I pick at the dry cereal and wash it down with some water. Even though I believe her, the things she said don't marry up with the Rob I thought I knew. We all make mistakes when we're young. We're half-formed, often selfish and usually stupid, but it was still a terrible thing to do. It hits me then that the idea of the teenage boyfriend I thought I knew, and the reality of that person, are two completely different things. If I get out of here, I'm not sure I'll be able to look at him in the same way, but perhaps that's OK.

I redirect my thoughts to what matters: getting out of this place.

While I'm chewing on the cereal, it dawns on me that Amy must shop somewhere to buy these supplies. That means she has interactions with other people. Her face will be all over the television and the newspapers by now. Surely someone will recognise her and arrest her.

But what would happen to Gina if Amy was arrested? My thoughts keep drifting back to that lock of hair inside the envelope. I was so sure that was Gina's hair, which means Amy must know where Gina is. Could Gina be up there, wherever the stairs go? No, surely I would have heard her voice. If Gina isn't here, then she must be with someone else? But who?

There's a possibility that even if the police find Amy, she might never tell them where I am, leaving me to starve to death inside this cage. The thought makes my skin itch. It creates the illusion that the bars are moving, coming closer to me.

Aiden and Rob will be searching for me. Josie will be helping them, and she might have found something about Hugh's plans. Aiden and I had discussed the idea of a second bunker. Perhaps he might remember something important if Josie doesn't uncover a clue in Hugh's finances. They'll have the help of DCI Stevenson, who I know is a good detective. Even more than just being a good detective, I know he cares. Maybe even Khatri is helping in some way. There's hope, there has to be.

Do the locals know someone is living in this chapel? I know Amy told me it was part of the forestry, but how deep into the woods are we? This kind of building must be rare, and you'd imagine that would mean local people are aware of it. Maybe walkers come out here to explore it. Unless it's on private land. That was how Hugh came to be in possession of the bunker. Perhaps I'm wrong and I'm in an industrial building in a city. An abandoned factory on some sort of estate. There's no proof that Amy is telling me the truth, she could be spinning any sort of lie. On and on my thoughts spiral.

As the day goes on, each breath I take brings a wave of fresh panic. Last night I slept for an hour, maybe two, but each time my claustrophobic nightmares came back to me. I dreamt I was buried alive, and then I woke and realised my nightmare had come true.

If Gina was here with me, she'd make up funny games to keep us occupied – walking like a penguin around the cage, jumping up and down on the mattress, singing her favourite Disney songs – but all I can do is think about my conversation with Amy. I'd never seen her so at ease. She'd sat calmly and told me her motivations.

No, I won't allow myself to fall into this darkness; I grasp hold of one of the fleeting feelings of hope and refuse to let go. I force myself to think about my captor. Amy answered nearly all of my questions, telling me about her enjoyment of power and the way she likes to control people. No matter what she says, I don't believe she was born a psychopath, like Hugh, but her trauma has whittled away her sense of self until she became someone easily moulded by a psychopath like Hugh. Her tough childhood. The bullying. The abortion. Watching me live the life she longed for, with my loving parents and my strong relationship with Rob. The little girl abandoned by her mother, hurt by her guardians and bullied by her peers wanted nothing more than a family. But Hugh twisted that longing and turned it into an aching to inflict pain and revenge.

She's right about one thing. We hate each other so much that either she will kill me, or I will kill her. I don't intend to die.

Unless we both die. That's what she said.

My blood turns to ice.

I look at the doll in the corner of the cage. I'd put it there out of the way, so I didn't have to see it. But now I walk over to the doll, lift it and smash it on the cold, stone floor. Its face splits apart into shards of sharp porcelain. Amy made a huge mistake leaving this doll in the cage with me. Just as I hear footsteps running down the steps, I pick up the largest, sharpest shard of porcelain and tuck it into my jeans pocket.

Chapter Thirty-Six

AIDEN

Early Tuesday morning, I wake up and without Mum, without waking in my own bed, the world is different again. It keeps changing and all I can do is adapt to it. But that isn't something that comes naturally to me. Not after ten years in the same place, with the same person. It takes me a moment to calm my breathing and heart before I get out of bed. *Words can heal.* Dr Anderton says this to me a lot. *When you feel that the silence is taking hold again, remember that words heal.*

The first thing I do is message Faith.

ME: Are you up?
    FAITH: Morning! How are you feeling?
    ME: Like I have no control over anything.
    FAITH: That's not true.
    FAITH: You have more control than you realise.

. . .

I'm not sure what she means by that. But I decided to get a quick shower and come back to my messages later. When I go back to my phone, she's sent another.

FAITH: I think it's time for us to meet.
    FAITH: I have so much I want to say to you.
    ME: It's not a good time. Mum's still missing. And Gina.
    FAITH: I know. But I can help you.
    FAITH: I mean, I can help comfort you. I want to hold your hand and tell you everything is going to be OK.

I close my eyes and lean back on the bed. What did I expect? We couldn't stay messaging each other forever. We had to meet eventually. But the thought of it makes every muscle in my body tense up.

ME: Let me think about it. Give me a day or two.

She replies to tell me that's fine, and I head downstairs for breakfast. I find Grandma sitting in the doorway between the kitchen and the garden, a cigarette in her mouth. She turns to me and hastily smashes the cigarette into the concrete step below the door. Her other hand is wrapped around a mug. Her smile, I think, is a guilty one.

'Don't tell Grandad.'

'OK,' I reply, but I'm not sure why I shouldn't tell him. Isn't she allowed to smoke? I thought grown-ups made their own decisions. And then I realise that I'm thinking of myself as a child again. An adult should understand why people do what they do. And an adult should be able to make their own choices, like meeting up with Faith would be my choice.

'Want some breakfast?'

I shake my head. 'I'm not hungry.'

I sit with her for a while as the birds sing in the tree at the bottom of the lawn. The world provides a few moments of peace.

On the phone with Josie, I realised that I remembered Hugh talking about his plans to build a second bunker for a replacement, just as we'd been speculating. It was that memory I kept trying to pull at, and now it was coming loose. But there was more. I felt like Hugh had given me something important while I was there. Some sort of diagram. Dad and I are planning to go back to the flat in Manchester to see if we can find it. I kept some of my art from the bunker.

But first we need to speak to DCI Stevenson, who pulls up at the house around nine.

'I've organised an interview with the builder who converted the first bunker,' he tells us.

Dad, who is awake and dressed now, insists that we go with him. But DCI Stevenson is just as insistent that this is police work. We shouldn't be involved.

'I've been letting you into this investigation much more than I would any other family,' he says. 'Too much, probably. But this could cross the line.'

'It's informal though, isn't it?' Dad says.

'Well –' DCI Stevenson starts.

'I'd like to meet him,' I say. I want to see the man who built my old home. I want to look him in the eye. I want to know if he knew what he was building.

Stevenson sighs. No one can say no to the boy from the bunker. 'I do the talking.'

We meet him at his current job, and even I can tell that he's defensive from the beginning. He keeps his arms folded tightly across his chest. There's a smattering of stubble across his chin, around the same length as the hair on his head. He wears cargo shorts covered in dust and paint, and a grey polo neck on top, ripped at the pocket.

'This is Aiden Price.' DCI Stevenson gestures to me. 'The boy who lived in the bunker you made.'

But the man had already recognised me, I knew that from

the expression on his face. It's one I see people make all the time when I walk down the street. First, it's confusion, because they know me from somewhere, but they can't figure out where. Then they either turn red, or stare at their feet. I often wonder if they feel ashamed for following my story, for knowing all about my trauma, about the grisly details.

This man, however, continues to look me in the eye. He keeps his back straight, face twisted into a grimace. He seems angry.

'I suppose you brought him here to make me feel guilty, did you? I did a job. I didn't know what it was for. Hugh told me it was going to be converted into some sort of fancy overnight experience for people who like camping.'

'And you weren't suspicious about that?' Stevenson asks, as calm and measured as always.

'Why should I be?' He shuffles his feet, wrinkles his brow.

'Did Hugh ever mention a second project?' Stevenson asks.

I ball my hands into fists. Seeing this man, the one who built my old home, makes all the injustice come flooding back. This terrible thing happened to me. It happened in my village, in the place I live, not in some country separated from us by an ocean. It happened to my family, my mother, my sister. Dad places a hand on my shoulder, and I realise that my breathing is loud, coming out between gritted teeth. The man seems concerned for the first time. Does he think I'm going to attack him?

'I'm not sure I like the idea of him knowing my name.' He gestures to me.

'Aiden doesn't know your name,' Stevenson says. 'Or where you live.'

'He knows my face.'

'Yes,' Stevenson admits. 'He does.'

That rests for a moment. Then the man says, 'No. He never asked me back for anything else. But he had plenty of contacts in the business. I knew a few of them.'

'Could you get a list to me?' Stevenson asks.

'Give me a minute.'

He comes back with a piece of paper with various male names written on it. DCI Stevenson thanks him and we leave, but I can't help looking back one more time. It takes a village to raise a child, but in some ways, it also takes a village to help a monster.

Stevenson drops us off at the B&B before heading back to the station. They have some leads to check. A car on CCTV that could be Amy's. Various eye-witness testimonies. One teenage boy says that a woman around Amy's age gave him a note to pass on to a woman who matched Mum's description. He even described her car.

The monotonous, relentless stretching of time makes my skin constantly itch, and I can't make it stop. I can't sit in a chair for longer than ten minutes. Before we head to Manchester, Dad drives me to Mum's house, and we search through her things. The police have already done this and found nothing important, but we do it again.

Nothing.

It's late afternoon when Dad parks the car in Mum's usual parking spot below the Manchester apartment. Inside, everything is as we left it, not particularly tidy, old food in the fridge. Dad offers to clear out the fridge while I find what I came for.

I leave him with a bin bag as I head to the back of the flat. Inside my old bedroom, I drop to my knees and reach under the bed for a box. There's nothing particularly precious inside; a bunch of drawings, mostly done with crayon. Some paintings that gradually progress as I get older. A few stuffed toys that Hugh gave me. I used to sleep with them, but I don't anymore. I know that isn't what a twenty-year-old man should do. Not that I feel like a man. Books, too. He brought me lots of books and convinced himself that if he was teaching me to read then he was taking care of me.

Scattering the drawings and paintings around the floor, I allow my eyes to roam from left to right, examining each one as closely as I can. Most of them are based on the imaginary places I created with Mum before I was kidnapped. Seeing them makes me long for a pen and paper. I don't even know what I could create, but it would be something. It would be a release, to let out the building emotions, because every day a new feeling fights its way through the barrier.

One by one, I turn the drawings over. Hugh often brought me papers from his office. Discarded plans. Old letterhead. Pages from his notebooks. I turn them over and I kick myself for not thinking about this sooner. Well over a week has gone by since Gina was taken, and I never thought about the old papers he gave me to scribble on? I never considered them as important business papers. They were bits of scrap paper, nothing more. But since talking to Josie, I've considered them in a different light.

There was the day he mentioned the second bunker, when I sat at his feet, drawing. He'd brought me more paper to draw on that day and then rambled on about why they were worthless. They were discarded plans. Discarded, but related to the bunker. I snatch up all the bits of paper and hold them to my chest.

Back in the kitchen, Dad is staring at my phone. I'd left it on the counter while I went into my bedroom.

'Who's Faith?' he asks.

A weight drops in my stomach. I glance down at my feet. There are no words coming to my rescue, I simply stand there like an idiot.

'Aiden? Tell me who she is.'

'You . . . you shouldn't look at people's phones,' I say.

'I saw the notification on the screen,' he replies. 'I saw someone called Faith asking if you were going to meet her.' He limps towards me. 'Aiden, what are you doing, mate? You're talking to a random person on Instagram about Gina and your mum's disappearance. Don't you know how bad that is?'

Heat floods my face. I can't meet his gaze.

'Did you ever stop and consider the fact that Faith might be Amy?'

The papers fall from my arms. 'What? No. That's not possible.'

He holds the phone aloft. 'Are you sure about that? Do you know for certain who this woman is? The profile is anonymous. There's no photograph. None of her posts are personal. The people she's 'friends' with don't even seem real.'

I hold out my hand to take the phone, but he snatches it away.

'I put her name through Google and nothing came up. Nothing at all. Do you know how weird that is?'

I just shake my head.

'Of course you don't, because you don't know how the world works. You don't know that people can be groomed online. You're being catfished, Aiden. This person does not exist.' As he continues talking, his face grows red.

I lift my arms in confusion. 'What's catfish?'

He sighs. 'It's when someone online pretends to be someone else. Grown men pretend to be young women to get people to talk to them. They usually scam them out of money.'

'Faith has never asked me for money!'

'It doesn't matter, mate. They could be after information. It could be Amy for God's sake!'

'No. She's not Amy.'

'You don't know that!'

'Give me my phone.' I reach out and try to snatch the phone, but he yanks it away. I could take it by force, but I don't.

'I'm handing this over to the police,' he says. 'They need to see this.' He glances at the papers in my hands, seeing the crayon, the scrawled pencil. 'Are they from the bunker?'

I nod.

'Pick them up. Let's go.'

Chapter Thirty-Seven

AMY

I won't allow her the space she thinks she deserves. Worming her way underneath my skin, putting ideas in my head, making me feel sorry for her. I won't allow it.

She won't paint me as the victim. No, I'm not that, never that. I've known pain and suffering. Loneliness and spite. None of those things have made me who I am. I'm stronger than that. She won't explain it all away by telling me what I already know. Uncle slapped and kicked. Aunty fussed and smothered. Students teased and bullied. Boys fucked and left. Mum abandoned. None of those things are me. I'm independent, above it all. I'm me because I choose to be me, not because of Hugh.

'What have you done?' I stare at the broken shards of my precious doll.

She's killed my child twice now. First Lily had to die so that Emma wouldn't find out, and now she's brutally smashed the doll against the floor. I ball my hands into fists, digging the nails into my palms, trying not to look at Lily's broken pieces.

'I couldn't stand it staring at me any longer,' she says.

I see that she's agitated and close to the bars. Her brown

eyes are open wide, dashing back and forth from me to the walls, to the steps, to the vaulted ceilings. Was it a mistake to give her food? Something has energised her, but I'm not sure what.

While Emma prowls the cage, I go back upstairs and remove the tin box from behind the altar. Inside there's a needle and two vials. I fill the syringe with the sedative and then return to the cellar. There's no way I can go into the cage with Emma like this.

'Step closer to the bars,' I say.

Emma sees the needle straight away. She shakes her head.

'If you want your doll, you need to come inside and get her.'

She thinks she has the upper hand. Her stance is proud because Emma believes she's managed to get into my head. But what she doesn't realise is that I knew this might happen and I'd steeled myself for it. *The doll is not Lily*, I think to myself. Lily made the point I wanted to make and now her purpose has been fulfilled.

For the first time since I put this plan into action, my heart thuds against my ribs. If I go in there with her awake, she could overpower me. But I need to collect the shards of porcelain. Any one of them could be a weapon. Unless I starve her out. I could collect Lily's remains after Emma has died.

I put the needle down and take a step back. 'Fine. I can take Lily after you're dead.'

A bead of sweat runs down Emma's right temple. She hurries towards the bars. 'Are you sure about that? I'll grind up all the pieces into the stones. This is your *child*, Amy!'

I suppress a shudder at her words, refusing to allow her any small victory. She must not know that I care. 'She's just a doll.'

'Is she? Isn't she the symbol of everything I took from you?'

I can't help myself, I move closer, running on anger now. 'Be quiet and die, Emma.'

Her hand dashes out between the bars, so fast I barely

register the movement. Her left hand grasps my arm before her right hand makes a slashing motion. Heat spreads over my skin. Blood seeps from the wound.

'Tell me where my daughter is!' she demands.

As I cry out in pain, I manage to move my right hand through the bars and jab the needle into her shoulder. At the same time, Emma slashes the sharp porcelain at my face. I lean away from her, finally yanking my arm out of her grip and staggering away from the bars, shocked by the sudden agonising, throbbing cut. Emma pulls the needle out of her shoulder and stares at it. I'd managed to depress the plunger and the sedative will be working through her bloodstream now. I won.

While the sedative starts to work, I go back upstairs into the chapel to dress my wound. It's not deep, but the skin is ragged and torn from the uneven edge of the porcelain. There's the sound of voices outside the church. A dog barks but I'm not afraid. My car is hidden beneath branches on the old driveway to the long-abandoned estate. My vegetable patch is far enough away from the usual walking path to not be noticed. Their voices aren't too close to the chapel.

It amuses me that a wanderer could come in and find the cage, the woman in it, the other woman upstairs with a bloody arm. I take a bandage out of the tin and start to wrap it around my cut.

Of course, there have been times when so-called explorers have come into the church to take photographs for their blogs. When that happens, I hide in the crypts and throw a tennis ball at the ceiling. The noises scare them away within ten minutes or so. Once someone stared through a broken window and saw me. I hissed at them and they screamed. I thought they would tell someone, and a social worker or police officer would turn up to check on my safety. It seems no one cared because it never happened.

Most people are too afraid to step into an abandoned building. There's no safety guarantee. No building code or safety officer telling them everything will be OK. People need that reassurance. We live on a spinning rock with billions of people and almost all of them are following the rules because they're too scared by the alternative. I used to be one of those people. Hugh showed me another way.

Next to the bandage inside the tin box is a cardboard packet of pills. I reorder them, count the number of pills and nod my head. These are important. I've been saving these for a special occasion. I take a deep breath, knowing that soon all of this will be over.

The barking fades away as the walkers move on. I had wondered if the dog might run into one of my traps, but there's no yelp. The animal gets to live another day.

I don't stand up and I don't leave the chapel, I just sit here, watching the sun come in through the tall windows. Mum's voice pops into my mind as she talks about God, about heaven, about hell. For the first time in a while, I wonder whether any of those things exist. My mum is dead now. I got a phone call long ago about it. She died doing what she loved, taking drugs. I didn't attend the funeral. Perhaps there'll be another way for us to see each other again. We'd both be in hell.

On the nanny cam, I watch Emma collapse. I begin to descend the steps to the cellar now that she's finally asleep.

Chapter Thirty-Eight

AIDEN

While Dad's on the phone with DCI Stevenson, I log into my Instagram account on Grandad's computer. It's there that I see the latest messages from Faith.

FAITH: Will you meet me in York? There's a park I like. It's pretty, you'll love it too.

ME: I don't know. Dad thinks you're catfishing me.

She starts typing. Then stops. Then starts again. Finally, a message comes through.

FAITH: You told your dad about me?

ME: He found my phone.

FAITH: Don't listen to him. He doesn't know me. He won't understand *us*.

ME: I know.

FAITH: Will you meet me?

ME: Yes. But not at the park. I want it to be private. Where do you live?

My eyes scan the screen, waiting for what feels like an eternity while the same grey text pops up over and over. *Faith is typing… Faith is typing…* She must keep deleting her answer and typing it again. Finally, her response comes through. *That's even more perfect.*

She gives me an address and a time. I print it out, fold it up and put it in my pocket.

When I go downstairs, no one suspects a thing. Dad is in the kitchen talking to Grandma and Grandad. My phone is on the pile of papers next to the sofa. While they're distracted, I quickly snatch up my phone and erase the notifications of Faith's most recent messages before replacing it.

'Is this true, Aiden?' Grandma comes into the living room, her fingers worrying at the sleeves of her cardigan.

'Yes,' I say simply.

'Oh, hun. You can't talk to strangers like that.' She turns to Dad as he enters the room. 'You can't blame him, Rob. He doesn't understand the way the world works.'

I ignore them as they bicker, pick up the drawings from the bunker and take them to the dining table. There I spread them all out. A timeline of my life emerges as I move the drawings around the surface of Grandma's mahogany table. Development through pencil that begins with scribbles and ends with portraits. There are bad line drawings of Mum and Dad when I was six. The house I grew up in. Then, the naked bulbs inside the bunker, cage bars, my bed. After ten, I started copying pictures from textbooks, sketching lions and tigers, or mountains and forests. I used the places Mum and I imagined before I was taken. I even drew Hugh. I remember him sitting and posing for me.

As I turn some of the pictures over, Grandad leans in.

'There are some plans here.' He picks up a page and examines it. 'For a room, is it? I can't make it out.'

Dad and Grandma come closer.

'That's the one I remember him giving me after he'd been talking about the second bunker.' I'd drawn a self-portrait that day. Thin face, straggly hair, deep-set eyes. 'He said something about how it wasn't working, and he had to start again.'

'We should take these to the police,' Grandad says. 'They might need to get an expert to look at them.' Grandad peers at the blue lines on the thin paper. Every time he moves the paper, my sketch shows through on the other side. 'The shape of it reminds me of a church. Don't you think?'

'Yes.' Grandma adjusts her glasses. 'I think so too.'

'Churches have plenty of underground space. They usually have some sort of crypt or vault. But they aren't exactly inconspicuous,' he says. And then he sighs. 'Aiden, are you sure that Amy is linked to this second bunker idea.'

'I . . . I don't know.' And it's true. I don't know anymore. Nothing makes sense.

Grandad glances at me and then at Dad. 'I didn't want to say this before, but I can't say nothing.'

'Just say it, Peter,' Grandma insists.

'Why would a young woman want to keep a child in a bunker?' he says. 'Hugh took a great risk because . . .' Grandad's face pales but he carries on. 'Because of who he was. Amy isn't Hugh, is she? So what made Emma so sure it was her?'

'Mum thinks it's revenge,' I say.

'She doesn't need to use this,' Grandad slaps the paper with the back of his hand, 'to get revenge. Kidnapping a child is revenge. Taking Emma is revenge.'

'You think this is a waste of time?' I say. I snatch the pages up. 'You think I'm stupid.'

Grandad watches sadly as I roll the pages up. 'No, I don't think that.'

'You do. You all think I'm an idiot who doesn't understand the world. You think I'm obsessed with this, don't you? You think I can't stop thinking about Hugh.'

'Mate.' Dad places a hand on my shoulder.

I pull away from him. 'Fuck off.'

Dad's eyes widen. 'Hey.'

'Aiden, sweetheart,' Grandma starts.

But I turn around and walk out of the house with my papers from the bunker.

At Mum's house I charge up Mum's laptop, spread the papers across the kitchen table and busy myself by tidying the kitchen. Because the house is so quiet, I put the radio on just so I can hear voices again. That's when I realise how much I'm starting to change. I *want* to hear the sound of voices.

While poking around on Mum's laptop, I come across a few emails from private detectives. Most are emailing to tell her that they haven't been able to find anything, or they can't take on the work, but there is one that catches my eye. It came through the day Mum disappeared.

Hi Emma,

I had a stroke of luck. While putting out some feelers, I came across a friend of a friend who reported to the police that they may have seen Amy Perry in the background of their photograph. Could you take a look at the image and let me know if this is Amy?

I open the attachment and pull in a deep breath. The picture is blurry, but I can just make her out. Amy Perry, a baseball cap trying to conceal her features, pushing a trolley in a supermarket. There's no date or location, but it must be recent. It has to be. Why else would she be wearing a hat inside a shop?

My fingers hit all the wrong keys as I hurry to send a reply back to the investigator using Mum's email account. I have to explain who I am, because obviously Mum is currently missing. When I'm done, I sit there anxiously tapping my fingernails on the table for the fifteen minutes it takes to get a reply.

The investigator confirms that he sent the photograph to the police and goes on to tell me that the young woman who sent the photo to him took it in the Midlands, which is pretty much halfway between London and York. The girl is a backing singer in a local band on tour around the area, which means she doesn't remember which town they were in at the time. He knows that the shop is a Co-op, but that's it.

I zoom in and zoom out. There's water and chocolate in the trolley she's pushing. There's something else, too. My heart sinks. A red toy dragon.

After replying back to the investigator to thank him, I hurry upstairs and rummage through Mum's boxes of things for a camera. Without my phone, I can't take snaps of anything. Finally, I find an old digital camera that needs charging. It takes another twenty minutes to find the right charger, and an hour to charge it. Meanwhile, I keep staring at the plans on the table. Every now and then the landline rings. Dad, probably. I ignore it.

After the camera's charged, I take photos of every single plan, upload them to the laptop, and send everything to Josie. If anyone can help us track Hugh's final plan, it's her.

Then I check the time. I don't know where it went; it's 2 a.m. now. So as not to get an unexpected visit from Dad, I send him an email to say I'm fine, that I'm staying at Mum's house, and that I'll see him tomorrow. Then I get into bed to get a few hours' sleep.

The next morning, before sunrise, I get up, walk to the bus stop and wait. Once on the bus, I unfold the piece of paper and check the address again. Leaving Mum's house early was crucial, because I knew I had to work fast before Dad checked up on me, which I know he will. I had planned to sneak away from Dad's after dark, but the argument meant I didn't have to do that in the end.

I watch the sunrise as the journey continues. I wish I had my phone. Without it I feel unarmed and vulnerable.

This is my first time alone on a bus. I hadn't known how much it would cost, but luckily Mum left her bank card behind before she met Amy, so I used the scanner to pay, saying nothing to the bus driver before I found a seat at the back. I checked how many stops the bus would take online and now I watch and count to make sure I get off at the right one.

It's the twelfth stop, forty minutes away from Bishoptown. I press the bell, say thank you, and step onto the pavement. This is the part I'm most worried about, but I wrote down the directions carefully. The air is still cool at this time in the morning. It doesn't smell like Rough Valley woods here. There are brick-fronted houses everywhere, but as I walk, as I follow my own directions, the roads become lanes. The houses become sparser. It reminds me of the outer areas of Bishoptown.

Finally, I come to a detached house fronted by a gate. I press the buzzer on the gate post and it opens to allow me in.

Chapter Thirty-Nine

EMMA

It soon becomes exhausting trying to stay positive, especially considering the groggy feeling of being drugged. There are no time references here. I can't peer out of a window and see if it's morning or afternoon. I talk to myself until Amy brings me food and then I fall asleep again.

I don't know how long she left me here alone, but I know she came in the cage to take away the porcelain shiv. What she didn't realise was that I'd snapped my original piece in two, stashing one inside my mattress. Then, while she'd been upstairs, I'd kept my body angled to obscure my actions and retrieved that small, but sharp, final piece, sliding it gently into my pocket.

When Amy comes down the stairs carrying another tray of dry cereal, I assume that it's the next morning again. Would that make it Wednesday? She places the tray down and goes away again. She won't engage with me. Not after I sliced her arm. I see the bandage, the way she holds it, like it still hurts. There's the faintest scarlet shadow signalling the blood seeping through the fabric.

I feel disgusting. My hair is greasy and limp, my clothes

are stale. I've splashed cold water on my body, but that's about it. The vault stinks because there's no flushing toilet. If Amy wanted to degrade me, she has. She's turned me into an animal, dehumanised me, taken away all the civilities of modern life.

I move closer to the bars. When she emerges again, I have my fingers wrapped around the metal.

'Where's my daughter?' I say. It has become my catch-phrase. It's the first thing I say to her whenever she comes to feed me.

This time she has three litre bottles of water in her arms.

'Move back.'

I take one step away.

'More,' she says.

Another step. A small one.

She holds her arms out as she pushes the water bottle into the cage. As I watch her, hot anger flushes all along my skin. Neck, face, arms. I'm hot all over, but I'm composed. What she doesn't know is that inside I'm coiled up tight.

When she reaches out with the third bottle, I'm faster. My arm comes out and grasps hers. She gasps, tries to pull back, but I dig my fingers into her flesh. I come closer and get my other hand around her arm. She fights me, yanking away, pulling me into the bars, but I won't let go. Sweat rolls down my scalp. I won't let go.

I pull the weapon from my pocket. Amy starts shouting, *get off, get off, get off!* She produces something from *her* pocket.

But this time I'm quicker, I knock it from her hand. The metal clatters as it hits the stone floor. Both of us stare at the needle, watching as it bounces into the cage. She tries to move first, but I press my fingers into her wound. With my nails digging in, refusing to let go, I bend down to snatch the syringe, but I can't reach.

She pulls back, shoving me face first into the metal. My cheekbone hits it hard and pain explodes there, but I only dig my nails deeper, gritting my teeth, watching her howl. This time, when I bend down to snatch the needle, I reach. She tries to block me when I lift it towards her. It's awkward, but I stab her, managing to plunge the metal into her forearm.

The needle remains there, wobbling back and forth, as she finally wrenches free from my grip. I try to keep hold of her for longer, but she woozily staggers away from me.

'No!' I scream, watching as she steps back out of my reach.

'What are you going to achieve, Emma?' Amy says, her voice slurring, the sedative kicking in already. 'You'll never get out.'

I hate her so much.

Her eyes begin to droop, but she continues to talk. 'I won't be out for too long. You'll still be there when I come back.'

'You don't know that,' I say. I wipe sweat from my forehead and watch as Amy loses consciousness, dropping hard onto the stones below her feet.

Chapter Forty

AIDEN

This isn't where I pictured Faith living. I assumed she was like me, and that she came from a modest home, not a mini mansion. There are two stone lions, one on each gatepost, staring at me with cavernous mouths and sharp teeth as I walk through the gates onto the slate-grey driveway.

This is a place cut off from the world. A place to hide away. Does Faith live here alone? She never mentioned family to me, but she's my age, so how else could she live here? Her parents must live here, too.

And then it strikes me. Faith never told me how old she is. She never mentioned her family, her house, her age, or anything like that. My dad's words play on a loop in my mind: *How do you know Faith isn't Amy?* I gaze up at the house. Could this place be connected to Hugh? A second home he hid away for his girlfriend, Amy? There's only one way to find out. This is why I came in the first place, to get answers.

I press the doorbell next to the wide, blue-painted door. From a distance, the door has a feel of grandeur to it, with panelled wood and the stone steps beneath. But when you come close to the place you begin to notice the disrepair. The paint is peeling. I press my fingers against the stone-clad exterior of the house and some dust crumbles down. This is a beautiful house, but it's neglected.

The longer I wait by the peeling blue paint, the harder my heart thuds. Just as I lift my fingers to press the button again, I hear a key scraping the lock. The handle turns and the door opens.

A woman stands in the doorway. She seems frazzled. Her greying hair is damp and stuck to her forehead. She has a full face of make-up on, but it isn't precisely applied like my Grandma's, it's smudged at the corners of her eyes and lips. When she smiles, I see more of it on her teeth. She wears a long, cream dress that fits too snugly around her soft abdomen. I'm not the best at estimating ages, but I would place her at around fifty years old.

'Can I speak to Faith, please?' I ask.

The woman's chest rises and falls quite quickly, as though she has been hurrying from one side of the house to the other. She's breathless when she answers. 'Come in.'

There's something about this woman's appearance that makes me want to turn around and run away. The strange, formal dress, the sweaty hair and smudged make-up. None of it seems normal. But I need answers. I need to stay. I step over the threshold and into the house.

'You're early. I didn't have time to finish getting ready.'

I don't understand, because she already seems far too dressed up for a Wednesday morning. She beckons me further into the hall and then slams the door shut. An old-fashioned key appears between her fingers and she locks the door behind me. The sound of that door slamming, the scrape of the key, it's all too familiar. My skin feels hot all over.

She stands facing me with her back pressed against the front door. Her mouth stretches into a smile and her eyes water with tears. She says my name as though it's a caress on the wind. *Aiden*.

My heart sinks. A weight hits the bottom of my stomach. I stumble backwards, following the corridor into a larger foyer, a winding staircase with an old wooden bannister, black and white tiles on the floor. She can't be. That's not . . .

'Aiden, it's so good to meet you at last.' The more she speaks, the more I realise that she's speaking in a slightly high-pitched voice, as though trying to make herself sound younger. It sends a chill running down my spine. 'I didn't reveal myself to you when we met.'

As I'm backing away, I frown, no idea what she's talking about. I haven't met this woman. This *woman* cannot be Faith. She can't be. Part of me had wondered if Dad was right about Amy, but I never pictured *this*. It's not possible.

'Where's Faith?'

She stands with both hands behind her back, head tilted to the side. Her eyebrows pull together. Every expression is exaggerated, like she's an old movie star in a black and white film. '*I* am Faith. Don't you see? Don't you understand? I've waited so long for this moment. It's finally just us.'

I turn around and hurry through the house, searching for a back exit. A bead of sweat works its way down my temple. I find the kitchen and follow it through to what appears to be a utility room. The glass panelled door is locked.

'Aiden, where are you going? I thought we were going to talk?'

There's the swish-swish of her skirt every time she moves. The bare feet padding along the tiles, slapping slightly. Every sound makes me feel even sicker than the last. I turn around and make my way back into the kitchen, noticing the faded paint, the mis-matched dining chairs around the dirty table, the cracks in the plaster.

She appears in the doorway and leans against the wood. 'This isn't how I wanted this to happen. This is all because of your parents. They've been feeding you poison, Aiden. It's not your fault. You've been abused by everyone in your life.'

When her arms outstretch towards me, all I can do is duck around her and move away.

'Stop this,' I say.

Her outstretched hands ball into tight fists.

'You don't recognise me, do you?' she says. 'We met once. We took a photograph together.'

'What?'

'See.' She holds up her phone, the picture of us both is her background picture.

'You were the woman in the pub,' I say, barely conscious of my lips moving.

'That's right,' she says. 'It took every bit of willpower not to ruin the surprise and tell you that we'd been chatting for months. But even though I didn't say anything, I could tell you liked me. You sent me a signal that day, don't you know that? The way you looked at me made me think you knew who I was, that we had a connection, even if you didn't say it. Oh, Aiden, I've been waiting all this time to show you who I am.' She frowns. 'But you don't like it. Do you?'

'I thought you were my age,' I say.

Faith shakes her head violently, agitating her damp curls. She continues to stare at her phone while she replies. 'Age is just a number. I'm not like them, the mothers, grandmothers. I'm young at heart. You'd understand this if you hadn't been poisoned by your family.'

'Why do you keep saying that?'

She directs her attention to me. 'Because it's true. Emma doesn't deserve you. She's a mean, foul-mouthed, violent little woman who allowed *two* of her children to be kidnapped.' She snorts. 'She scowls in every photograph. She *never* looks grateful. And then there's that army idiot of a father you have. He's even worse. He left your mother as soon as the opportunity arose.'

I stand there aghast at the vitriol spewing from her mouth. Mum always tried to shield me from the nastiest comments about us online, but I saw many of them. Faith is simply saying the exact same things that people say in the comments section of the MailOnline. It's as though she's internalised it all.

'What makes you think you know my family? What makes you think you know me?'

She moves closer. 'I do know you, Aiden.'

236

My face flushes red, because it's true.

She starts to move around the kitchen, picking up a kettle and filling it with water. I notice the black mildew around the spout of the kettle, the thick layer of greasy dust on the lid.

'How long have you lived here alone?' I ask, watching her every move.

'Since my daddy died,' she says. 'Mother died first, a long time ago. I was ten. Daddy died last year. Slipped away in his sleep in the bed upstairs.' From somewhere in the house there's a thump, and Faith goes very still, but as she continues, she forces cheer into her voice. 'Perhaps that's him.' She shakes her head. 'It'll be something falling over or old pipes. This house is so old.'

'Don't you get lonely living here alone?'

She moves closer to me and I back away until I'm pressed up against the table.

'Yes,' she breathes. 'All the time.'

'That's why you talk to strangers on the internet.'

Faith appears confused by that statement. Her mouth opens and closes twice before she answers. 'You're not a stranger.'

'I was once,' I say. 'Until you messaged me.'

'No,' she says. 'I knew you even then. I read everything about you. I knew that sunlight could hurt your skin. That you wear sunglasses to help your eyesight. You were in the bunker for three thousand, five hundred and eighty-nine days. You're the most talented painter in the world. Your mother gave up on you and wrote you off as another dead child.' When the kettle boils, she snatches it up and sloshes hot water onto teabags in her grimy mugs. 'Another dead child.'

'Faith,' I say carefully. 'What do you want?'

With shaking hands, she carries the two mugs over to the table and places them down. 'I want us to be a family. Me. You. Gina. The three of us.'

Chapter Forty-One

EMMA

Amy drops down hard, hitting her head and jolting her body. The violence of it shocks me. For a moment I can barely move, simply stare at her as a thin trickle of blood runs from the back of her head. *Fuck*. That was more extreme than I intended it to be. She's supposed to slip into unconsciousness so that I can try and get to her keys. I examine her body. Her eyes are closed, but it's hard to figure out if she's breathing. Then I try to calculate how long her drugs are effective. The last time she injected me, how long did I sleep? The truth is I can't remember. That means I need to work fast if I'm going to use this moment. To do that, I begin to run through all the things I know about where I am and what Amy is doing to keep me here.

There's a door at the top of the stairs that I believe she locks. If that door needs to be unlocked every time she comes to feed me, then she may have all of her keys together, probably in a pocket.

I reach through the bars to see if I can grab Amy's extended leg. My fingers grope against the stone flags, but I

238

can't quite reach her. Ramming my shoulder right against the metal, I try with the other arm.

Frustrated, I sit back and look at her. What if I killed her? It's hard to tell whether she's breathing from this angle. What if the blow to her head killed her? I crawl towards the bars and press my face between them. Is she breathing? She hasn't moved since the moment she dropped to the stone floor. Her body lies lifeless on the ground.

If she's dead, and I can't reach the keys, then I will starve to death in this chapel.

The thought makes my chest tighten.

Telling myself that death by starvation isn't an option, I manoeuvre my body so that I can get both legs through the bar of the cage. Grunting from the exertion, I twist and hook my legs around Amy's ankle, trying to drag her towards me. Both of my feet end up in the pool of her warm blood. If she's still bleeding, perhaps that means she's still alive. It's when the blood goes cold I should worry.

Slowly, slowly, I start to drag her closer to the bars. But my muscles have weakened from lack of food and movement since being trapped. It becomes unbearably hot in the vault and I have to take a break and wipe sweat from my forehead. During my break I assess what I have in the bunker. There's a small stash of food: chocolate and a packet of beef jerky. Barely enough for two days. I have four and a half litres of water to ration, but in this heat, it would be hard to stretch this to five, maybe six days. I could try if I have to, but the best solution is getting access to the keys.

After stripping away some of my filthy clothes, I go back to my task of dragging Amy's body closer to the bars. Now I can grab hold of her leg with my hands and pull her even closer. She doesn't even register the bumpy movement along the stone. A red smear coats the floor behind her.

My heart pounds as I slip my fingers into her jeans pocket. The fabric is tight against her hip. Amy is skinny now. She's more muscular. With her face at rest she's far prettier than ever before. My fingers reach metal and a sense of relief washes over me. This is it. This is my escape.

I stand, staring at the keys in the palm of my hand. And then I get to work. The lock is on the outside of the cage, which means I have to move my hands at a strange angle to insert the key. There are four on the ring. One appears to be a car key. I try the longest key first. I turn it both ways. Nothing happens. Then the second key. Again, nothing happens. I pull in a deep breath, say a prayer and try the last key.

Nothing happens.

Chapter Forty-Two

AIDEN

'You took Gina.'

She simply stares at me with wide eyes. I check my knowledge of emotions. Wide eyes mean surprise. Shock. Confusion.

'I didn't take her,' Faith says. 'I wouldn't.'

'Then why did you say her name?'

'Because we can all be together. Like a family.' She reaches across and takes my hand.

Every part of me wants to wrench it away from her. The feeling of her warm flesh on mine makes my stomach heave with disgust. But I decide that if I want to know the truth, I have to pretend to be interested in her like she's interested, no, *obsessed*, with me.

'Does that mean you know where she is?' I ask.

Faith squeezes my hand, which makes my abdomen clench.

'Tell me, Faith. We need to be honest with each other.'

She sighs. 'This isn't going how I wanted it to go.'

'How did you want it to go?'

'Well,' she says, and gives a derisive snort, 'I thought you'd be more interested in getting to know me, but you clearly care more for that brat of a sister.'

Above us, there's a thump. A flush of heat spreads over my skin as adrenaline and anger surge through me. I squeeze her hand right back. But it isn't a friendly or romantic squeeze. No, it's a squeeze that makes her gasp. She tries to pull away, but I keep her trapped in my grasp.

Through gritted teeth, I ask, 'Is my sister upstairs in your house? Is she here?'

'Stop it!' she yells.

I let go, disgusted at the pain on her face, disgusted at myself, but at the same time utterly focused on what I have to do. While Faith rubs her sore hand, I run out of the kitchen, back through the hallway and up the stairs in the foyer. Feet flying, stairs disappearing beneath them, thighs burning, lungs sucking deep. There's a cry, but it isn't a child's cry, it's the sound of an adult having a tantrum. I've heard that sound before, I know it well. It's like Hugh, calling me ungrateful, telling me I'm worthless. Dark, dangerous people with a spoiled child's soul.

'Ginny!' I cry. 'Ginny where are you!'

Faith is chasing me, her flat bare feet slapping up the stairs as I reach the next floor. I work quickly, opening and closing all the doors along the corridor, calling for Gina. The lack of mobile phone makes this even harder. Somehow, I'm going to have to get her out of here and explain it all to the police later.

'Aiden!' Faith shouts, blocking out any chance of me hearing my baby sister. She won't stop screaming my name at the top of her lungs. I hear the tears in her voice. I hear the manic edge of it all.

The first two rooms are bedrooms that don't appear to have been cleaned or redecorated for at least twenty years. Next is obviously Faith's room. I stand in the doorway, transfixed by what I'm seeing. There are stacks of newspapers all over the floor. Scissors lie on the bedside table. I'm about to snatch them up when I see the cuttings spread out over the bed. *Aiden's sister goes missing. Bunker Mum loses second child to abductor. Boy from the bunker looks innocent, but is he? Lost girl. Bunker sister. The dark secrets of the Price family. What is Emma Price hiding from the police?* On and on they go, blaming us.

The extent of Faith's obsession hits me full on. I feel like such an idiot. Why did I send all that personal information to her? To a stranger? Dad was right about her all along. What if she's the kidnapper? I remember the video footage of Gina being carried out by a woman. Could it have been Faith? Wearing a wig, perhaps?

'They don't know you like I do.'

The sound of her voice makes me start. As I turn around, I grab the scissors and hold them out between us.

She glances at them. 'You wouldn't hurt me. You love me.' She makes it sound like a fact. The Earth is round. You love me. There is oxygen in the air. We belong together.

'Tell me what happened,' I say. 'Tell me everything. Who are you?'

'You know who I am. I'm Faith. I'm your best friend. You told me that once.'

'Yeah, well, I don't have any friends so that isn't saying much.'

She takes a step forward and I lurch towards her with the scissors, just far enough to be a warning.

'You won't hurt me because I know where Gina is.'

'And my mother?' I ask.

Faith merely shrugs. Could she have taken Mum as well as Gina? In Mum's text, she specifically mentioned Amy, but did Faith trick her? Are they working together?

I can't bear it: the not knowing; not understanding. 'Please, tell me. What did you do? Where is my family?'

'Your mother never deserved you or Gina. Everyone thinks the same. You only have to read those articles to know what the world thinks of her. I swear, every decision I made was because of how much I care for you. Once we started talking on Instagram, I knew what I had to do.'

'Kidnap my sister? Why?'

She shakes her head. 'I didn't take her.'

'Then who did?' Hot tears of frustration build in my eyes.

I just want this to be over. I want them back. 'Tell me, Faith. I want to know everything.' I pause, trying to find the words she wants to hear. 'Look, I can't promise anything, but perhaps if you tell me the truth now, we can figure things out together. If you tell me the truth, I might be able to forgive you.'

She sniffs heavily. 'I didn't kidnap her. I'm taking care of her for you.'

My heart leaps. 'Where is she?'

Faith turns around and walks out of the room. I start to follow her.

'This house is over one hundred years old,' she says. 'It's been one of my family's properties ever since it was built. The Clements family estate.' She snorts. 'Over the years we've had to sell many of the other properties across the country, but we kept hold of this one. You know how it is, one rogue brother or uncle gambles away half the family fortune and the rest goes on inheritance tax.' As we walk back towards the stairs, she gestures to the old paintings on the walls. Stony-faced men and women glare down at us in the gloomy space. 'They were a sociable bunch, not that you can tell from these. My grandfather and my father made a great many friends over the years. Friends in high places, friends in low places.' She turns to me. 'When you were found, and I saw what happened to you in the newspaper, there was one name that stood out to me. Hugh Barratt.'

The sound of his name in her mouth makes my blood run cold. But I don't interrupt her. We begin to ascend the stairs to the next level, and she continues.

'The man who abducted you was a friend of my father's. Daddy liked to invest in construction projects from time to time. I believe they worked together on several different things.'

'Faith,' I say quietly, trying not to spook her. 'Did Hugh hurt you too?'

At the top of the stairs she pauses to get her breath back, and also to compose herself. 'No.'

I decide not to probe further, but now I understand her obsession with my life.

'You know that I killed Hugh, don't you?' I add.

'Yes. You did what you had to do. Like I did what I had to do.'

As I follow her towards a dark, mahogany door, I realise what she means. She murdered her father.

'How did you do it?'

'He was old and ill. No one suspected that I'd hurried the process along. I held a pillow over his face.'

'I understand why you did it.'

Before she unlocks the door, she turns back to me and I see the tears dripping down her cheeks. 'I *know* you do. That's why we're meant to be a family together.'

'Please, Faith. I need to see Gina. Open the door.'

She wipes the tears away. 'Only if you make me a promise. That we'll all live here together. You must understand now, this is our destiny. We're linked. Forget about your mother, she's a shrew. Your dad cheated on her. None of them –'

'What did you say?'

Faith shrugs, turns back to the door and slots the key into the keyhole.

'Wait.' I grab her shoulder. 'What did you mean when you said my dad cheated on my mum? How would you even know that?'

'It's true.' She pulls away and opens the door. 'Just ask Amy Perry.'

The door swings open and Faith steps back. There's a king-sized bed opposite a large bay window. On the pink bedding a little girl plays innocently with Barbies. I almost drop the scissors. The air catches in my throat.

That little girl bounds her way over, almost tripping over her feet. She wraps her arms around my waist and starts to cry into my shirt.

'Denny,' she says. 'Are you here to save me?'

Chapter Forty-Three

AIDEN

I almost don't hear the door moving along the carpet above the sound of Gina's tears. But I do hear it, and my body reacts more quickly than my mind. First, I push Gina away, which I hate, but know I need to do. Then I spin around to see Faith quietly closing the door behind us. That's when I realise that she's trying to lock us both in.

First, I shove my foot between the door and the frame, getting to it just as she's about to close the door. She continues to tug the handle, trapping my foot between wood. It hurts, but I grit my teeth, grasp hold of the door with my right hand, and jerk it back. Faith stumbles forwards as I manage to make the momentum work for me and not her.

When she lets go, I push her into the hallway and hold up the scissors. She lifts her hands to protect herself. There's a blur of movement near my leg, but I'm so focused on Faith that I barely notice it. Neither does Faith. Out of the corner of my eye, I see Gina running down the stairs, but it seems that Faith hasn't seen her at all.

'What did you say about Amy Perry?' I ask, still brandishing the scissors.

'I said you should ask her about your dad.' She lifts her chin and her eyes flash. 'They had an affair, back before you were born.'

I frown, not sure whether to believe her or not. Is it even an affair if you're that young and not even married? 'How do you know about this?'

'Amy told me,' Faith says, smiling. 'Like I said, Hugh was friends with my father, but what you don't know is that I've been friends with Amy since Hugh brought her to our house for a visit five years ago. We were in touch again after you came back from the bunker.'

'Then you knew,' I say. 'You must have known that Hugh had kidnapped a child.'

'No, I never knew. My father only made friends with Hugh when he was interested in buying a chapel from our estate. You have to believe me. I hate Hugh for what he did to you. So does Amy.'

My head starts to spin with all of this new information and I'm not sure I know who or what to believe. 'You're wrong about that. Amy always knew.'

Faith falters. 'That isn't true.' She takes a step back, closer to the stairs. 'All Amy wanted to do was teach Emma a lesson. It was because of Emma that Amy lost her baby. Emma hurt her, you see. Emma bullied her at school, and then she pushed Amy and made her lose her baby.'

There's sweat forming on my palms and the handle of the scissors becomes greasier and more slippery. My arm aches from holding them up. But most of all, I'm confused. Mum can be fierce, but it's a protective fierceness, not a mean one. Even at an age younger than I am now I can't imagine her bullying someone. I definitely can't imagine her pushing Amy and making her miscarry. If that was true, why were Mum and Amy friends after school? Out of the corner of my eye, I see Gina scurrying along one of the corridors.

'Amy took Gina,' I say, trying to keep Faith's attention on me. 'Am I right?'

She nods.

'Where's Mum? Is she with Amy?'

Faith nods again.

'Where?'

But her eyes drop to the scissors in my hand. I know in that split second that she's going to try and take them from me.

When she lunges for me, I make the choice to throw them away. Her eyes track the trajectory of the weapon as it falls, and she makes her move towards them, but I block her way. The way we meet in the middle makes my thoughts turn straight to Hugh in the bunker when I hit him over and over. I put my hands up to defend myself and she screams, pushing me back towards the open door. Panic seizes me. Every limb grows heavier, my breath catches, my blood runs cold, but I know that I can't end up locked in that room. Not again. I can't allow it to happen again.

Before she can force me closer to the room, I shove her as hard as I can. The force of it makes her stumble, but as she tries to right herself, she steps on the scissors, which move beneath her feet. She loses her balance, landing heavily on the top stair. A scream rips from her throat as she tumbles over herself, rolling and flailing down the staircase. Her body bangs painfully into the wall, ricochets and continues down the next flight. I wince with every blow, every cry until finally Faith lands at a broken and twisted angle, her face bloodied by the fall. She stares up at me with glassy, unfocused eyes. The life has gone.

Gina calls tentatively up the stairs. 'Denny?'

'I'm OK,' I reply, with a hoarse voice.

'The police are coming,' she says.

Chapter Forty-Four

EMMA

I place two fingers on Amy's neck and feel for a pulse. It's there. I don't know whether I'm relieved or disappointed. But even though she's still alive, it doesn't mean she will ever wake up again. She could quietly die without ever regaining consciousness. I don't know.

The keys didn't help me but maybe she has a phone.

After taking a break, eating a little of the beef jerky and recovering from my previous exertion, I attempt to roll Amy over so that I can reach her other pocket. I twist Amy's body left and right to make sure she doesn't roll in the opposite direction. It's laborious work, but I finally get her into the position I want.

When I see the rectangular outline through her jeans pocket, my heart soars with new hope. My fingers wiggle greedily into the pocket to discover the hard, smooth surface. I get better purchase on it, sliding it gently from her jeans. I'm almost back in the bars when a set of fingers wraps around my wrist.

'What do you think you're doing?' she says, slurring slightly.

Without answering, I jam her hand against the metal bars. She lets go, but I also allow the phone to fall from my fingers. It bounces on its corner; drops back from the bars. We both lurch towards it at the same time. I'm hindered by the cage; she's hindered by her head injury. I get there first but can barely reach. My fingers stroke the surface. Amy's hand comes down. I let out a roar of frustration and somehow flick the phone towards me, grab it and retract my arm as fast as I can.

Amy is half up from the ground as I'm dialling 999. She has to pull herself up using the bars. Half her face is covered in blood, the hair matted to the wound. Her skin is milk-white, an alarming contrast to the red.

'There's no signal down here, Emma,' she says quietly.

I move the phone from my ear and look at the bars on the screen. There are none. I move to a different part of the cage and try again.

'Give up, Emma.'

But I won't. I try every part of the cage while keeping away from Amy. Whenever I move closer, one of her arms dangles through the bars, idly trying to catch me. We play this game over and over again as I continue to dial the emergency services.

'You're not going to win,' she says. 'You're going to die down here. You're never going to see your children again. This is it. Your final days on this earth.' She gently lowers herself down onto the floor and I do the same onto my mattress. I keep the phone next to me. 'Give up. Just give up.'

But I won't.

Chapter Forty-Five

AIDEN

I haven't told Mum this before, but I can admit it now. For a long time, I felt as though I was still in the bunker. My mind wouldn't come back from there. Sometimes I'd even hear Hugh laughing because he knew that he'd tricked me into thinking I was safe. When I walked in the countryside or went to the cinema or took Gina to the park, he'd be there in the back of my mind telling me that soon I would be going home to him, and those thoughts were dark, sour things that I couldn't shake.

I was a bitter, angry person. Though I rarely raised my voice, inside I would be screaming. And in therapy, that bitterness would come out. It took time, but eventually I stopped hearing Hugh's laughter and most of the bitterness ebbed away.

Now Gina's back, I feel like part of myself has returned. But there's still a piece of my family missing, and I need to find her.

'Tell me what happened,' I ask Gina. 'Tell me everything before the police get here.'

We're sitting on the bottom step of the stairs, staring at

the front door. I wanted to keep her away from Faith's dead body. No child should have to see something like that. She snuggles into my side as though we're on the sofa watching *X-Factor*.

'The lady told me Mummy wanted me to go with her. She said she was Mummy's friend.'

'Was it Faith?'

Gina shakes her head. 'No.'

Amy then, I think. It *was* Amy who kidnapped Gina.

'What happened after?'

'We walked a long way. I got scared. When I tried to run away, the lady said she'd hurt Mummy if I didn't do what I was told.'

'It's OK, Ginny, you're safe now. Nothing like that is ever going to happen again. What happened after you were walking. Did the lady give you to Faith?'

She nods her head.

'Did Faith hurt you?'

She shakes her head.

'Have you seen Mummy since you came to this house?'

She shakes her head again.

I ask her some more questions about whether Faith fed her properly. It seems, at least, that Faith did make sure Gina had enough to eat and kept her in the bedroom with the en-suite bathroom for the duration of her kidnapping. *About the size of the bunker.* My spine grows cold.

There are sirens and blue lights outside. I take Gina's hand and we look for the keys to the door to let the police in. I find them in the top drawer of a cabinet. Just before I unlock the door, I pull Gina aside.

'Did Faith mention anything about a church or a chapel?'

Gina shakes her head.

As I let the police in, I can't shake the feeling that Faith's throwaway comment about the chapel on her father's grounds was important. Could it link back to the plans I found in the Manchester flat? The ones Hugh drew up, that I scribbled on when I was a child. She said Hugh had been friends with her father for about eight years. That might coincide with the time Hugh decided he wanted a second bunker for another child. Could Mum be stuck in that building?

The PC registers shock when I give him mine and Gina's names. He goes to contact his station and I tell him to get in touch with DCI Stevenson.

'You did a good job calling the police, Ginny.' I rub her head, noticing how Faith has plaited her hair, like she's a doll.

'Mummy showed me how,' she replies. I almost laugh. I'd rolled my eyes every time Mum ran through an emergency drill, showing us both exactly how to call the police on a mobile and a house phone, but she'd been right after all.

Gradually, more and more police officers arrive at Faith's house. A black body bag is carried away. She'll never message me again, and I'll have to come to terms with that, but for now DCI Stevenson steps into the foyer.

'Is everything all right, Aiden? Gina?'

'She hasn't been hurt.' I tell him the story of how Amy kidnapped Gina and used her friendship with Faith to keep Gina here. It's my suspicion that Amy manipulated Faith, using plans that Hugh started while he was alive but never finished. 'Faith is the one who sent me those Instagram messages. I guess this is all my fault. I let her into our lives.'

'The thing is,' he says. 'She could've been good. She could have become a lifelong friend. Someone to pass the time with. She could've helped you at some point. It just so happens she was bad. There's no way of knowing. Don't beat yourself up about it. Perhaps we'll go over a few ways you can keep yourself clued up in future.'

I nod, relieved that he didn't give me a dressing down for being so dumb. I glance across at Gina, sitting at the kitchen table being distracted by one of the PCs showing her a magic trick with a fifty pence piece.

'Faith said something about Hugh wanting to buy a chapel on her father's estate. I don't know if Dad told you, but I found some old drawings from the bunker. There were plans on the back. Grandad looked at them and thought they looked like a church or a chapel or something. I think Hugh was building another place for a child and using Faith's father's estate. She hinted that he was abusive. Maybe it was some sort of arrangement.'

Stevenson's face pales. 'I'll have a unit search the grounds.'

'Can I come?' I ask.

He nods.

As we head outside, I realise that the Indian summer has broken, and it's now raining. A light drizzle, with a hint of warmth in the air. There's a damp smell that makes me think there'll be a much worse downpour soon. I remember the way water would run into the bunker. The mildew air that came first.

Faith's family home stretches into fields, some of which are heavy with dense crops of trees. We dodge through the trees looking for some sort of outbuilding. Every part of the house and its cellar has already been checked, but Stevenson believes some households used to own small chapels outside their main building. It seems to me that some people have too much and others too little. There's no rhyme or reason to who gets what. Nothing is fair or equal.

'Over here!'

The group turn left in unison and continue on beneath the thick canopy of trees. Once we come to a clearing, I see the small building.

The PC points to a lock on the front door. 'Anyone got bolt cutters?'

Once the appropriate tools are passed along, he snaps away the lock and the door opens with a creak.

Inside there's no electricity. The police turn on their torches, sweeping them across the floor, up the walls, the ceilings. I don't like the smell here. It's too damp, too earthy.

Stevenson stays close to me as we make our way between the old rows of pews. They're dusty. In disarray. There are puddles of water on some from the leaking roof. My stomach flips over. I want to call out to her, but my voice is lodged deep inside my throat.

'There are some stairs back here,' someone shouts.

The team continue down to the back of the church. I hold my breath. The officer who shouted goes down first.

With each step, my legs feel unsteady. I hear Hugh's voice laughing at me in my mind. *I've already killed her,* he says. But I won't listen to it. I found Gina safe and sound. I can find Mum, too.

By the time I reach the bottom step I know something is wrong. There would be voices by now, but there's been nothing but silence so far. I swing the torch back and forth, checking each wall, each dusty cavity. The officer says it for me.

'There's nothing here.'

Chapter Forty-Six

AIDEN

We arrive back in Bishoptown at midday. Stevenson drops us both at Dad's B&B, where there's a welcoming party for Gina. Even Josie is there. But none of that matters, because the one person Gina asks for isn't here and she doesn't understand why.

Grandma takes Gina for some lunch and a bath while I tell everyone what happened. No one speaks until the end. I hold my breath, waiting for them to tell me how stupid I am, how I messed everything up. No one does. Then Grandad pours everyone a whisky and we collapse into the sofas.

'Emma's still out there,' Dad says. 'She's still missing.'

Josie leans forward on the sofa. 'I got your email, Aiden. About the picture your investigator found. He said the person who took it was somewhere in the Midlands. Well, I remembered something. Hugh and I once went on a trip to the Midlands, about six or seven years ago.'

'Did he take you to a church?' I ask.

'Yes,' she says. 'I think he did. It wasn't a proper church, though. It was this old abandoned chapel in the woods.'

My heart begins to beat faster. Dad rests his elbows on his knees. Even Grandad is listening intently.

'Are the plans still here?' I ask Dad.

'Yes,' he says.

After he's gathered everything, we spread them out over the table along with the picture of Amy in the supermarket. Dad fetches his laptop and we load Google maps on the screen.

Josie points to the map. 'This is Lower Rothby, the village we stayed in.' She pinches the screen and zooms in. 'I think this is the shop from the photograph.' Josie leans back in her chair. 'I remember this strange building. We went walking in the woods and Hugh insisted we veer away from the path, which I thought strange at the time. It was as though he knew where we were going.' She pinches the map again, zooming in. 'These woods. We walked until we found this old, rundown chapel. The roof was sagging in and the doors were all crumbly. This was two years ago, so God knows what kind of condition it's in now.'

'Can you remember whereabouts in the woods it was?' Dad asks.

She shakes her head. 'I think we walked from the road here. But we were walking for a while. There was a half-built wall blocking it from the main path, but Hugh made me walk around it. I felt like I was trespassing. It was pretty isolated. Easy enough to hide someone.'

Another woods, another abandoned building. Another small village with a small population. This is Hugh. I close my eyes and picture him standing over me, smiling. *Hey, kiddo. Comfortable? Aren't you a lucky boy with the new mattress?* It's only when Dad pats my hand that I realise my fingernails are digging into the table.

My voice has grit in it when I speak. 'We need to go there. Now.'

Grandad says. 'You need some rest.'

But Dad nods to me. 'We should leave now.'

. . .

We're in Dad's car, silent except for the sound of the engine and the rain on the window. It's misty outside, with smears of yellow and red lights tracking up and down the wet motorway. In the backseat, Josie is taking a nap. I keep staring at the blur of the cat's eyes, Hugh's voice at the back of my mind. A laughing voice that repeats over and over that Mum is already dead.

'There's something I need to tell you,' Dad says, pulling me from my thoughts. He sniffs, wipes his nose. The skin around his nostrils and the corners of his eyes are red and sore. 'I should've told you earlier but I'm too much of a coward. I should've told you because I know you've been blaming yourself, and that's not fair. It's . . . it's actually all my fault. Years ago, before you were born, I cheated on your mum with . . . her.'

'I know.'

He glances sharply at me. 'You do?'

'Faith told me. I guess it's why Amy is so unhinged now.' I shrug my shoulders. I'm not sure I'm an expert on why anyone does anything.

'It shouldn't have happened,' he says. 'It was this stupid fling one weekend. I should've known better. I knew Amy had this weird obsession with me because she kept telling me that she loved me. Even then I knew it was wrong to use her, but I was a teenager and all I wanted was . . . well, you know.'

Teenage boys want sex. That's what everyone says, anyway. They're slaves to their hormones. So far I haven't been able to relate to any of this.

His voice drops to barely above a whisper. 'And then there was the baby.'

I turn to look at him. He sniffs again, holding back tears.

'I handled it badly. I've been a coward many times in my life, Aiden. Every single day I wish I was more like you.'

All I can do is shake my head. Why anyone would want to be like me, I don't understand.

'Faith said that Mum pushed Amy down the stairs and made her lose the baby.'

Dad glances at me, an incredulous expression on his face.

'What? Your mum doesn't even know Amy was ever pregnant, at least not as far as I know. No, it was me. I was the
arsehole. I asked Amy to have an abortion and she did.

'This is all because of what I did back then. She's
punishing me. First with you, helping Hugh in the way that
she did, and now with Emma and Gina. This is all my fault.'
He grimaces. 'I can't believe I never told anyone when you
were missing. What if it'd helped the police figure out where
you were? But I never suspected her of anything. She seemed
fine at the time. She never came across as unstable at all. I . . .
I'm so sorry Aiden.'

'Everyone thought I was dead,' I reply. My voice sounds
matter-of-fact, and, to be honest, I'm detached from the
words anyway. 'It wouldn't have made a difference. It just
would've upset Mum.'

I gaze out of the window, watching the rain fall. In the
backseat, Josie's head rests against the glass. I hope she didn't
hear Dad's conversation.

He sniffs a few more times and Josie stirs. From the
rear-view mirror I see her slowly realise where she is. The
backseat of a car with the son and ex-boyfriend of her
friend. People who were hurt by the man she loved at a
time that feels like a lifetime ago. In a way, because of the
past, because I was gone for so long, the three of us are
strangers.

The world is a stranger to me. Its bizarre customs, social
conventions, behaviours I don't understand, people who
wrinkle their noses when I ask questions, or who stare and
then look away when they recognise my face. People like
Faith, who do destructive things for attention, who bombard
me with messages, and cling to the most bizarre moments.
I'm not sure I'll ever understand it, but at least I get to
breathe in fresh air and see the sun.

And then, if I can save my family, perhaps I can stop
Hugh from laughing for good.

. . .

We arrive at our B&B mid-afternoon. I've been awake for hours and I'm hungry and tired. We head up to our rooms to dump our bags.

The rain is torrential, worse than I've ever seen it. When I close the door to my room, the sound blocks everything out. It hammers against the windows like pounding fists.

I remember how the rain sounded in the bunker. The muddy water constantly leaking through. Is rain running in through the chapel roof? Is it dripping onto Mum? I used to believe that the roof of the bunker would cave in and I would be washed away by the water. I would sit there and wait for it to happen, scared at first and then disappointed.

We reconvene ten minutes later, and Josie takes us to the shop that's in the photograph. The first thing we notice is that the cereal aisle matches perfectly with the picture. She grabs some snacks while Dad and I talk to the servers.

One, a woman in her fifties with blue eyes that won't stay still, nods thoughtfully. 'We've had police asking about her, too. I didn't know she was the one wanted for the kidnapping. It's not usually women, is it?'

'Do you know her?' Dad asks.

She shakes her head. 'I've seen her once or twice. She's not someone I'd recognise unless someone points her out to me.'

'But she's definitely been in here?

She nods. 'I noticed her buying a lot of water and I remember thinking it was selfish, what with the heatwave going on. It seemed like she was stocking up. Taking it all so others can't get it. People do it with toilet paper when it snows.'

We ask everyone in the shop but no one else recognises her.

We get back into the car and eat cold Cornish pasties and salt and vinegar crisps.

'I think we'll beat the police,' Dad says. 'Seems like they've been asking around the village, but I haven't heard anything else. We know that DCI Stevenson is arranging for the woods to be searched but that's about it.'

While Dad and I examine the paths on Google maps, Josie checks the weather on her phone.

'This is forecast for the rest of the day and all through the night,' Josie says, almost shouting to be heard. 'There's a flood warning.'

Because of the new weather conditions, we decide to stop at a hiking store and buy proper wellies, waterproof coats and hiking canes to help us over the terrain. The shop is in the main part of the village, run by one guy, about thirty, with a long straggly beard. We ask him about the church in the woods while we're there.

'Oh, yeah. I have heard of that. But it's not a church, it's a private chapel that used to belong to some rich person's estate. The estate isn't there anymore, but the chapel was bought by a builder a few years ago. As far as I know, he's turning it into a cabin in the woods, kinda thing. For people to rent if they have too much money and don't like camping.' He laughs. 'But if you're thinking of going to take photos or whatever, you should know that you'll be trespassing. It's not part of the main woods, it's private land. And I think it's quite far from the main path. Wouldn't want you guys to get lost out there in this weather. We've had some problems with flash flooding over the past few years.'

'Thanks,' Dad says, 'but that won't be a problem.' The guy behind the counter lifts an eyebrow.

He then glances at my face with a frown and I see the flicker of recognition in his eyes. He looks away again.

'Any chance the person who owned that estate is Faith's family?' Dad asks as we make our way back to the car.

'It's too much of a coincidence for it not to be,' I reply.

Chapter Forty-Seven

AMY

It begins with a change in the air. My top is no longer warm enough and goosepimples break out along my forearms. I see the little hairs standing on end.

At least that's what I think it is. It could also be my body reacting to the onslaught of a sedative and concussion at the same time.

The cold makes my fingers shake as I tighten the last stich and snip it close to the scalp. There. All done. All better. Now that it's done, I wrap my arms around my body and rub my upper arms until they warm. There's a gloom of dark clouds surrounding the church. Since Emma has my phone, I don't know the exact time. I can't even check the nanny cam because I need a phone to do it. I stand and move closer to one of the windows, peering out between the slats. All I see is the torrential thrashing down of rain.

Late September is finally catching up to us. Well, it doesn't matter, it'll be over soon. This was never an endeavour that would continue on into winter. I scoop up the box of pills and watch the water running in through the roof as I grind them up to put into the glass of cold apple juice. *Time to drink the Kool-Aid.*

Emma and I have one thing in common. We're underestimated at every turn. No one expected Emma to fight back the way she did. No one thought a pregnant woman could do what she did. And no one thought that I would fight back, either. Not Emma, that's for sure.

I brush my hair out of my face and begin to carry the apple juice down to the cage, debating whether to tell Emma about everything or not. Shall I tell her about Faith? Shall I tell her that her precious daughter is probably being spoiled rotten by a deluded little princess of an adult woman? Should I tell her that Faith has been contacting her son? And that sometimes I tell Faith what to say to him? Would it be satisfying to see the expression on her face for the final time?

No, not yet. There's been no contact from Faith for the last few days and I don't want to reveal too much too early. Perhaps it would be better for Emma to die without ever knowing where her daughter went.

I watch her sleep, all curled up on the mattress. Moving my unconscious body around really took it out of her. I glance at my smartphone clenched tightly between her fingers. I decide not to wake her, I simply place the glass on the floor inside the cage, and then sit down a few feet away from the bars so that I can watch.

It doesn't take long for her to wake. Raindrops begin to trickle into the cage, some hitting her on the mattress. The sight of it makes me frown. How bad is the rain? Not only is it coming in through the roof of the chapel, it's filtering down to the cellar.

Emma sits upright and stares at the phone in her hand. Then she looks at me.

'I brought you apple juice,' I say, nodding to the glass in the cage.

Emma regards it for a moment, but rather than take the glass, she starts fiddling with the phone again.

I let out a long sigh. 'I don't know how many times I've told you, there's no signal down here.'

'Shut up,' she snaps.

I watch in amusement as she cancels the call, moves around the cage and tries again. But it's when she dares to move closer to the front of the cage that I get to my feet. When the phone begins to ring, we both stare at each other at the same time.

As I try to reach for her, she bends down, misses my outstretched hand, grasps the apple juice and throws it in my face. I gasp in a breath, spitting out as much of the apple juice as I can.

'Hello? Hello?'

I wipe the juice from my eyes and try again to snatch the phone from her hands.

'If you can hear me, my name is Emma Price and I'm trapped –'

She doesn't get to finish the sentence; I reach through and swat the phone out of her hands. It lands with a crack on the stony floor. The same noise my head made when she knocked me out.

'They might be able to trace the call,' she says. 'There's hope. I can get out of here, and you're going to be arrested.'

I glance down at the apple juice on the ground. If she won't take her medicine, I'll just have to find another way to finish this.

Chapter Forty-Eight

AIDEN

At the car, we cut shopping tags from our new equipment and pull on waterproof boots and coats. The material crinkles and crackles as I zip everything up and smooth down the seams. We worked fast inside the shop, not bothering to try things on. The coat is too large for me, Dad's is slightly too small, but he can just about pull the zip up tight.

'Is everyone ready?' he asks.

I take a deep breath and nod. I don't know why, but since the man in the shop told us about the chapel, my lunch has been churning in my stomach. This is real now. And the weather being so awful adds another layer of urgency on top of everything. We've driven down here to find Mum and now we're going to discover if it's even possible to save her. Now we find out whether she's still alive after all.

Dad drives us to the edge of the woods and parks in an empty car park. No one wants to come out hiking in this weather. It's 4.30 p.m. and I feel like we've already wasted time. The sun will set around seven, giving us just three hours to find her.

No one speaks as we climb out of the car. What we need

to do will not be easy. For all we know we'll need to fight to get her back. My skin is cold all over and I want to fade away from myself into the silence where it's safe. But no, we have a task to do.

Dad limps around the car and bangs his walking stick against the tarmac. 'You two need to go on without me. I'm going to take a slower path while you both go on ahead.'

He hangs back while we move into the trees, obscured to me by the hood of my coat. Rain drips down my nose, over my lips. I have tunnel vision from the hood and can't even hear Josie walking beside me because of the noise. Rain on leaves, stones, soil. The wind. All of it muffled by my coat. A panicked thought flits through my mind: what if Mum's shouting for help and I can't hear her? I remember the hours I spent screaming until my throat went sore. Hugh hit me when he realised what I was doing, but he brought me throat lozenges in the end.

I open my mouth again, and scream. 'MUM!'

Josie's head turns to face me, her body contorting from the surprise of my scream. Then she relaxes and joins me. 'EMMA!'

We follow the path, intermittently shouting through the rain. It drums down, bouncing off my sleeves, dribbling into my jeans. Every now and then I have to ball my hands into fists and then relax them in order to get the feeling back. I yell as loud as I can. Josie cups her hands around her mouth and bellows. But there is only the sound of the wet weather in return.

'Do you remember how long you walked?' I ask.

Josie shakes her head.

I don't say it but I wonder how often Hugh did things like that. I wonder if he took Josie for walks in Rough Valley forest, taking her as close as he dared to my bunker, just for the thrill of it. My stomach lurches. I stop and pull in a deep breath.

'Are you OK?' she asks.

I nod my head and we continue. I keep shouting. The rain

drums down. We carry on walking for about an hour before Josie stops.

She points at a gap in the trees, where the ground slops down into a ravine.

'I remember almost falling down that slope.'

We head away from the path, towards the ravine. My feet slide down the slope, boots sinking deep into the mud. There's so much rain that the water gushes around us, turning the slope into a waterfall. I'm freezing cold inside my coat.

The deeper we go into the woods, the more I feel like I'm fading into myself, retreating into that dark place. I can't help it. This is too much like the rainy night I escaped from the bunker, I didn't feel the cold that night. Hugh's laughing voice has turned into a vision of him. I see him as large as he was when I was small, when he'd stand over me. I see him smiling, see him screaming, see him crying. See all of the parts of him that the woman walking next to me probably never saw. She never saw the light fade from his eyes or the blood escaping from the wound I inflicted.

Josie stops and I stop next to her. We both wobble, our balance altered by the sheer amount of mud. Her head turns from left to right. 'I don't know where we are.'

We take a few more tentative steps before taking out the map we brought with us. We already know that the chapel isn't marked, but we know the direction of the road, so we can figure out how to continue.

Josie's indecision slows us down as we carry on through the woods, and all the time the rain lashes down. When we stop to corroborate the map with what it says on Google, we notice a news alert about heavy flooding in the area.

'Mum might be underground,' I say, staring at the news. I don't know much about flooding, but I know I wouldn't want to be underground while it's happening. What if the old church isn't structurally sound? What if the building collapses on top of her?

A few minutes later, as we're negotiating our way through a patch of brambles, there's a rustling behind us. I spin around, on edge, to see Dad limping along.

'I tried to hurry,' he says, out of breath. 'The rain's getting worse.' He picks his way through the thorns, leaning heavily on his stick. I'm not sure if the tight line of his mouth is fear or pain, or possibly both.

'I don't even know if we're going the right way,' Josie says. 'It's hopeless. I can't remember anything.'

'We'll just keep going away from the road,' Dad says. 'That's all we can do.'

Chapter Forty-Nine

EMMA

She's been gone for what I think must be about thirty minutes. What is she doing up there? Has she run away and left me here alone?

Since she's been gone, the rain has started to pour down the walls in the vault. I look at the smashed phone on the ground, wishing I could try the emergency services again. It all happened so fast that I don't even know if the call connected. All I could do was shout down the line and hope someone on the other end could hear me. Do the operators on the emergency service lines track calls via GPS now?

I hear footsteps coming down the steps and rush to the back of the cage. Some of the battery powered lights flicker as water seeps into them. The upstairs of the chapel must be slowly flooding for this much water to be leaking down to the cellar.

Amy's skin is waxy and pale. Even though I can see that she's tended to her head injury as best she can, fresh blood dribbles from it, like sleepy morning drool. There's an edge to her expression. Determination has hardened her features. I rush to the mattress where I've hidden the shard of porcelain from Lily the doll.

Water splashes around her boots as she comes to the door of the cage and uses her key to get in. I'm in a state of shock. It's the first time I've seen the cage door open since I came here. Then my eyes drift to the long knife in her hand.

'You wouldn't take your medicine,' she says.

It dawns on me then. She'd put something in the apple juice. She tried to kill me.

'Just let me go,' I say, a pathetic hail-Mary pass. 'If you leave now you can get away.'

'I gave your child away.' Water runs down her nose, splashes across her lips as she speaks.

I lunge for her now, but she holds out the knife, stopping me in my tracks.

'Where's Gina?'

Amy just smiles. 'She's with a friend.'

I don't know what that means but it makes me sick to my stomach. Without the fear and rage running through me I'd probably lean over and puke. Instead I make an attempt at grabbing her wrist, trying to wrestle the knife from her hand. She twists away from me, slices the knife against my top. It rips the fabric but barely grazes the skin.

'You're not well, Amy. You've got a concussion, did you know that? Your movement is wobbly. Your skin is white. I think you've lost a lot of blood.'

She blinks, positions herself between me and the cage door. Below, the water gathers in puddles. The electric lights dim. The smartphone sits in water.

'I'm fine,' she says. She tries again to slash me with the knife, but this time I manage to grab her wrist while slicing her hand with the sharp porcelain. We both cry out at the same time, her from the wound, me from holding that sharp ceramic shiv. She drops the knife to the pooling flood water below. I take the opportunity to push past her out of the cage door, when above us there's an almighty groaning sound followed by a crash. In a split second, I realise that the roof of the building has collapsed. Rubble begins tumbling down the stairs and into the cellar. Parts of the vaulted ceiling begin to fall from the weight of the debris above. One of the electric lights is smashed. A chunk of plaster hits the top of the cage.

I hurry out of the cage, but the water is rising, now above my ankles. Amy collides with me from behind, shoving me to the ground. My face hits the dirty water and she holds it there. Slippery hands clutch my hair and face as I try to pry them away. My lungs burn from holding my breath. I want to gasp, but I know that I'll breathe water into my lungs.

My fingernails dig deep into flesh and finally she lets go. I pull my head out of the water and take in a deep breath.

'There's nowhere to go,' she says. 'The stairs are blocked.'

I wipe water from my eyes and examine the damage of the collapsed roof. Amy's right. Even if I stop her, I'll still have to fight my way through the debris to escape the building. I don't know the extent of the damage above us.

I sit down in the water and Amy watches silently.

'Giving up so soon, Price?'

'No,' I say. 'I'm thinking.' I pause for a moment. 'The police —'

'I think they're busy, Emma,' she says.

'If I die, you do too,' I remind her. 'If I can't get out, neither can you.'

She shrugs.

I ignore her and make my way towards the stairs. We still have some light, but it's dim, and making my way around the fallen debris is tricky. Water obscures most of it, and I find myself tripping on the stones underfoot.

Halfway to the stairs, the last light is knocked out by falling debris. A wave of water comes gushing down. I crawl through the dark. From somewhere in the darkness, Amy's hands pull at my ankles, but I kick back and don't feel them on me again.

Very little light filters down from the stairs, which is a bad sign. I move up a step and start removing old bricks, bits of wood, heavy chunks of plaster. Streams of dirty water wash over my arms as I work. I look at the sheer amount of time it's going to take to get out, and I'm not sure I'm going to make it. But I keep going anyway.

Chapter Fifty

AIDEN

A rumble of thunder reverberates through the woods. A moment later, there's another roar, and then the noise stops. We all halt in our tracks and turn to one another, rain dribbling down our noses.

'What was that?' Dad shouts above the downpour. 'It sounded like thunder, but . . . I don't know.'

The silence doesn't last for long. There's a third, low grumble followed by cracking and smashing, like someone is demolishing a building. Why would someone be demolishing a building in the middle of the woods?

And then it dawns on me.

Dad is the first to move. I break into a sprint, passing him and continuing on in the direction of the din. Behind me, Dad shouts something about calling the police. I yank back my hood so that I can see better. My feet slide out from underneath me and I fall into the muddy water. But I heave myself up, yanking my hands from the sucking mud. The wet ground tugs at my boots but luckily they aren't pulled all the way off. Still, it slows me down, and the delay feels agonising. I need to get there. I need to help them. What if . . .?

A root trips me and I tumble, jarring my shoulder against a tree. Every expletive Hugh ever yelled at me in the bunker runs through my mind as I stumble forward, ignoring the jolt of pain in my shoulder. The pain doesn't matter. Nothing matters except getting to that tumbling building because it just might be the place where Amy is keeping Mum.

When I hit a patch of harder ground, I start sprinting again, dodging through the trees until I find myself on a dirt track. Now I know I'm almost there. This track must lead to something. It's big enough for a car to drive down it. Sure enough the building comes into sight and I force my legs to keep going, despite the shock of what I'm seeing.

The chapel is broken in the middle. Two gables stand at either end with the roof almost completely collapsed. Panic makes my heart thud as I cross the track towards the sagging church. I yank open the door and fly into the wreckage.

And then I drop to my knees because I don't know where to start.

'Aiden?'

Josie jogs into the chapel. Her eyes roam over the rubble, broken bits of ceiling and rafters, and lifts a hand to her mouth. I know what she's thinking. She thinks Mum's dead, that this is the end, but I refuse to believe it. I climb back to my feet.

'She must be in here,' I say, and begin picking my way through the stones.

But Josie grabs my elbow. 'Wait. We could make it worse. We need to wait for the emergency services to decide how to proceed.'

I shake my head to tell her I *can't* stop. That I'm too close to finding them at last. But her words give me pause. What if she's right? I could dislodge the wrong stone that happens to crush my mother. My breath catches and frustrated tears of pain well in my eyes.

'Come on,' she says gently, leading me away.

I follow her closer to the door but can't seem to leave. 'What if she's underneath all of this? What if she can't breathe?'

'We wouldn't be able to help her.'

'No,' I mumble, mostly to myself. I was alone once, and I thought I would die alone without breathing in fresh air again. If I leave this place, she'll be alone, too. I can't let that happen. 'MUM!' My throat is raw as I shout her name. I climb over some fallen stones, not stepping too far into the middle of the building, where I can see the floor has caved in.

'EMMA!' Josie shouts, following me slowly, her hand close to my coat, ready to catch me if I fall.

There are muddy puddles of water everywhere. I bend down and put my ear to the rubble. Nothing. I move, going over the entire floor, picking my way gently, feeling for anything unstable. We call out and we listen.

Dad hurries into the building while we're going through this process. Eventually the rain begins to calm down to a gentler patter. We shout. We listen. Nothing.

'I've called the emergency services,' Dad says. Then he follows up with. 'Oh Jesus Christ. Oh, Emma, no.'

I tell him to be quiet and call her name again.

The chapel breathes, but there's no other sound, nothing human. Whenever I turn to face Josie, she has a grim frown on her face, one that suggests she's beginning to lose hope. I can almost see her thoughts counting down until she thinks it might be an appropriate time for her to tell me to leave.

Sure enough, she says quietly, 'Aiden . . .'

But I shake my head. 'I can't leave.'

I glance up at the opened roof. The building seems more stable now that the rain has turned into a fine drizzle, but it's still possible that more could fall. I look back down at the rubble. Hugh would keep his captive in a basement, wouldn't he? In a cage like the one I was in. Did Amy use the same framework? Could the cage have inadvertently saved her?

'We're not doing much to help here,' Josie continues.

'Five more minutes.'

She purses her lips, but she nods, and we all call her name another couple of times, and yet again the building breathes and creaks but there are no other sounds. Until . . . A cough. So quiet I can barely hear it. Followed by more coughing.

I make my way over to the back of the chapel, on the left next to the outer wall. I kneel down, press my ear to the rubble. I hear it. I hear the coughing, and my heart leaps into my mouth.

'Over here!' I shout, and Josie and Dad hurry to where I'm kneeling on the ground. Slowly, gently, we begin to move the bricks and debris, scoop away the build-up of broken plaster, until a hole forms. 'Mum?'

We wait. Dad passes me a torch and I shine it down into the hole.

Nothing.

Then another cough, followed by the tiniest glimpse of wiggling fingers coming through the debris.

We keep going, until we find an arm, an elbow, a face. I stagger back. Amy. Awake. Covered in slime.

Dad pulls me away from her before I do something I regret.

'Where is she?' I yell. 'Where's Mum?'

Somehow Amy pulls herself from the hole. There's blood all over her face, her eyes barely seem to focus on us, but she still pulls herself out from the debris while we stand there in a state of shock.

'No.' I fight against Dad as he holds me steady. 'You don't get to live while she dies.'

Amy coughs up some sort of brown sludge and staggers away from us, her body wobbling from side to side. It's Josie who takes hold of Amy's arm and holds her still.

Dad and I begin to move more of the debris. I work methodically, so focussed on my task that I barely even notice the emergency services finally begin to arrive.

Chapter Fifty-One

AIDEN

There's a roaring in my ears and the world sounds as though it's all underwater. I watch a paramedic and a police officer lead Amy away. I try not to look at her as someone else guides me away from the crumbling building. 'It isn't safe,' they're saying to me. I protest at first, but I leave with them eventually.

'But, Mum. She's under there. She's trapped.'

Dad puts an arm over my shoulder.

'They're looking for her, mate,' he says. His eyes are wet. There's dust and debris in his hair.

I glance around at all the men covered in dust, and it dawns on me that things have been happening at a much faster pace than I'd realised in my confusion. The fire department are here searching for mum in the wreckage, and DCI Stevenson is striding around in the background with a worried expression on his face.

The rain finally stops, and Dad sits down on a flat rock close to the chapel. Sunset comes and goes. Floodlights are constructed around the ruins. I wrap my arms across my body. Someone comes over to me with a takeaway cup filled with tea, before handing one to Dad.

'Do you think they'll find her?' I ask quietly.

Dad rearranges his weight and works his jaw. 'Yes, I think they'll find her.'

'But you're not sure if she'll be alive?'

'We found Amy alive,' he says. He smiles, but it's a smile that doesn't reach his eyes. I'm getting better at recognising those, but it just makes me sad.

'She's dead,' I say.

He shakes his head. 'Don't talk like that.'

'No, it's true. She's dead, I know she is. This is how the world works. You start to feel happy and then something comes along to take it all away. I was happy before Hugh took me. Then I started to be happy before Amy took Gina and Mum. So, she's dead. I know it.'

'Aiden, stop.' Dad runs his hand over his face. 'Please. There's always hope. Always.'

I want to punch something. The rock, one of the trees, anything.

'Did you feel that hope when you found Gina? You did, didn't you?'

'Yes,' I say, 'and that's exactly why Mum's dead. Because I was happy for a moment and now the world is going to take it all away again.'

Dad puts an arm over my shoulder and for once I don't move away. I just leave it there. I'm numb all over. Hollowed out and bone tired. Part of me wants to leave but I stay and watch the firefighters work. I just sit here and stare. I'm still sitting, feeling useless, when there's a shout from inside the church.

I drop the tea onto the grass below and hurry towards the shout, somehow ending up lost among a group of taller men. But I push through to the front just in time to see some of the searchers lifting what appears to be a long, dust-covered sack. It's only when the dust sloughs off that I see the features of a person. Mum. One of the men lifts her into his arms, where she lays, limp and lifeless.

Chapter Fifty-Two

AIDEN

In my darkest moments, the idea of giving up on life and love seems blissfully easily. The lifeless lump pulled from the dust and stones turned out to be alive, but only just. They took Mum to hospital and now it's three days later and she's still sleeping. In the days that followed the rescue, I became accustomed to hospital lights once more. It reminds me of the time I lived here for a while, after I escaped, locked inside my own mind. Mum is locked inside her mind, too. She can't speak either. She can't open her eyes or eat. She's unconscious, induced by the doctors, in order to allow her brain to heal. When the church collapsed, she was hit by the debris and suffered a brain injury.

There has been a meticulous process of unearthing and uncovering information since the day the chapel collapsed. Amy Perry is still in hospital following her own concussion. She's in police custody for the kidnap. She didn't take Gina for money or revenge; she took her as a way to lure my mother into her trap. But she used Faith's obsession with me in her favour, promising Faith that if she had Gina, I would follow, and somehow we'd all be a happy family without my mother around. Faith was so psychologically damaged after a traumatic childhood that she believed it.

I can't stop thinking about Faith and Amy, and why they did what they did. Whether they thought they would win, or if they didn't care if they lost. How did either of them think this wouldn't end with either their own death or an arrest? Or was that the point? That they truly cared so little for their own lives?

And I can't stop thinking about who I am and how I fit into this mess. Because I relate to that kind of reasoning. Sometimes I want to give up. I could happily let darkness win, drown in my anger and bitterness that all of this happened to *me*. I can't shake the idea that the world is punishing me, even though I don't know why. But now I know not to give in to those thoughts, because there's an alternative.

A girl, stolen from her family, younger than I was when I was taken, still knew how to call for help. I was a resilient child like Gina once; I can be again.

'When will Mummy wake up?' Gina asks. She and I are staying at Dad's until Mum gets better, but every day we end up coming here and she asks me the same question.

'I don't know,' I reply. 'When the doctors think she's better.'

Ginny places her little hand on top of Mum's paper-thin skin. I've never seen my mum so fragile.

'I want to tell her I'm OK,' she says softly.

'She knows.'

One day either Mum or I will have to explain to Gina why she was taken and what it all meant. I don't want to think about that, about the emotional toll it will take on her. But one thing I know about my little sister is that she's tough enough to cope. The women in my family are more resilient than any other people I know. Everyone tells me that I'm the survivor, but I don't feel like I even compare.

A few hours later, I take her to get some food and bump into DCI Stevenson, here to visit Mum.

'I wanted to let you know a little more about the case,' he says as we settle down with coffees in the canteen. I dropped

Gina off at the creche on the way there. 'You were right. Hugh bought the land owned by Faith's father, using cash. I had the Clements's house searched and found indecent images of children on a computer that I think belonged to Faith's father.'

The words still shock me, even after what I've been through. They still make me feel cold all over.

'Hugh Barratt and Clive Clements were persistently evil men, with a disease,' Stevenson says. 'They used their money and influence to do whatever they wanted to do. And I think Hugh was the kind of man to attract people like him. Maybe that's why Jake found his way to Bishoptown.' He taps the tabletop with his fingernail. 'But this isn't what the world is like. They're a tiny percentage. Tiny.'

'It doesn't feel like that anymore,' I say, and the bitterness creeps into my voice before I can stop it.

Stevenson nods slowly. 'I know why you feel like that. But I promise you, things are going to get better now.' There must be something hard in my expression, because he continues. 'Words are empty, aren't they? I'm sorry about how everything other people say sounds like platitudes. I'm sorry that this happened to you and your family. I like to think I know you all a bit better now. You're a good lad. Your sister is another good kid. And your mum, well, she's the best fighter I know, and stubborn too. You're surrounded by the best people.'

I nod my head. 'In my therapy sessions, we talk about how words heal. I don't think words are empty.'

'Good.' He pats my shoulder. 'Keep talking, and don't hold anything in. When I was a kid, I had an uncle who liked to hurt me. He used to give me a pound not to tell my mum and dad about what he did.'

I sit up straight, surprised.

'I didn't tell anyone for a long time. And you know what?'

I shake my head.

'All I did was think about how unfair it was that it happened, and no one knew. All I did was think about how it was my fault and I was stupid, and I hated myself.'

'I think those things too.'

'It does nothing good, Aiden. For me it just made me a victim over and over again. That's why I became a police officer, to get my revenge on my uncle, twenty times over.'

'Did it help?'

'No,' he says with a laugh. 'Because I kept on saying horrible things to myself. I drank too much, almost lost my wife.' He sighs. 'But when I started to talk about it, everything changed.' He pauses. 'This job can be pretty depressing at times, because I'm constantly meeting crappy people. But something else I learned was that those crappy people were hurt by other crappy people who were probably hurt by an older generation of crappy people. And the cycle goes back and back and back. It goes forward, too, until someone is strong enough to break it. That person breaks it because they forgive themselves, and the crappy arsehole who hurt them in the first place.'

'I don't know if I can do that.'

'Oh, you can,' he says, lowering his chin and nodding at me. 'Believe me, mate. If anyone can do it, you can. You just need a little bit of hope and a little bit of love.' He smiles and stands slowly, groaning at the weight of his older body. 'I think your family is due some good luck now. How's your Mum doing?'

'Still unconscious.'

'Let me know how she gets on. I'll come and visit again. If you need anything, give me a shout, OK?' Another firm nod, making sure I understand.

I mumble a thanks, still taking in his words. Still thinking about the cycle and the way to break it. Still thinking about forgiveness and blame and hatred and love. I pick up Gina from the creche and hold her hand to make sure she doesn't wander off. When I look down at her, I'm scared for her, and for me and for what the world will be like if Mum doesn't make it. I was so sure she was dead, but I was wrong. What else am I wrong about?

Do I dare to hope for the future?

Before entering Mum's room, I see people in white coats

through the frosted glass. They surround the bed, leaning over her. My heart skips a beat, I start to move forwards, but one of the nurses calls me back.

'They won't be a moment,' she says.

'What's going on? Why are there so many people in there?'

'She just woke up.'

Chapter Fifty-Three

EMMA

Rob stares at me with his dark eyes, pleading for forgiveness. I open my mouth to suggest we go for a walk in the woods. I have a bad headache and I want to clear it with fresh air. But then I realise that this isn't Rob at all. It's Aiden, my son. I close my eyes against the headache and see the midwife passing me a small bundle. I'm a child myself. Terrified of the future. Afraid that I won't be enough for him. But as that small bundle settles into my arms, all of those fears fade away and there's no one else in the room apart from me and him. My heart expands until it feels too big in my body. I need extra room for the love in my heart. It leaks out into the air and hangs around us like a cloud. It cannot be contained.

I open my eyes again and Aiden is still there. He's a man now, but everything comes flooding back. All of our experiences as a family, the fact that I struggle to think of him as a man and not the baby I held in my arms. No matter what has happened over the past few decades, Aiden is a full-grown, fully formed human being.

'Mum? Are you in pain? Do you want the nurse?'

My thoughts are muddled but now I see that I'm in a

hospital. I want to laugh at the question about pain. What I'm feeling now is pure joy. Pain has been and gone. I could never experience any pain worse than I've already felt. For the first time in a long time I feel untouchable. It's like me and Rob walking through Rough Valley, our hands entwined, the first touch of autumn on the leaves above us. Fifteen and the world at our feet. That's untouchable. It was foolish to think it, but it was how we felt.

Aiden still looks concerned and I realise that my reply came out quite slurred. Luckily a doctor comes in and I hear him explaining that my brain needs time to recover after the injury I suffered during the collapse of the chapel. Of course. The chapel. Amy. Gina. Gina!

I try to stretch my arm out to my son, but I can't seem to move it. My jaw works but the word is mumbled. My tongue feels thick in my mouth.

'I think she's saying Gina,' Aiden says.

I nod my head without any idea if my head actually moves.

'Gina is fine,' he says. 'She's perfect. I found her before we came to the chapel to search for you. Amy's been arrested. Everything is OK now.'

Untouchable joy continues to spread through my limbs like sunlight on skin. I close my eyes and bask in it.

I'm leaving the hospital today. Aiden and his grandparents are fussing around me, making sure I'm comfortable as I climb into the car. Rob's there too, and I'm not sure how I feel about that. At one point he takes hold of my hand, but I pull away. Guilt flashes in his eyes and he swallows deeply. Since I woke, he's visited the hospital every day, giving me advice based on his own experience with traumatic brain injuries. I've been grateful for it, but at the same time I can't quite process how I feel about him yet. Amy punished us all, but her hatred seemed to focus on me. Whatever she felt about Rob fizzled out, but that fierce jealousy she felt towards me burned and burned and burned.

Losing consciousness isn't like in the movies. You can't whack a person on the head to knock them out without consequences. Head injuries kill brain cells. I'll be a little bit less than I was. It'll take time to get used to that. Each morning, when I open my eyes, I remind myself that I'm still enough. I'm still me.

We go back to my parents' house, where our things from Manchester have arrived. We've decided not to run away from Bishoptown anymore. This is our home and it feels right to stay here. Sure, there are painful memories around every corner, but for the first time I feel like we're strong enough to face them. I hadn't realised that we were hiding in Manchester. With Amy out there, I hadn't allowed myself even a moment to relax. But now she was going to prison for a long time, and that emotional weight had been lifted.

Aiden's old school has offered me a job, which will be waiting for me when I'm ready to work again. We can start a new life here. A new, old life.

Gina chooses her room and she and Denny play together while I slowly put my belongings away. My fingers trail over the tin I use to store my paints. For the first time since I awoke from the coma, my heart pangs. What if I never recover the ability to paint? Tears sting my eyes and I clear my throat. What if. What if.

'Mum?'

I lift my chin to find Aiden hovering by the door. Despite the straighter stance he's had since the day at the chapel – the new-found confidence he exudes – he still looks awkward as hell standing there.

'You OK?'

He nods.

'I want to talk to you about something.'

This time my heart doesn't clench. I don't think the worst. My mind stays open, ready for the next challenge. I gesture for him to come in and sit down on the bed.

'What's on your mind, kiddo?'

'I sold three more paintings today.'

My jaw drops. '*Three*? That's incredible.' There's that

familiar panic seizing my heart. The realisation that my child has a life outside my own. I push it down. There's no place for those kinds of thoughts now.

'I've got quite a lot of money saved up now,' he says. 'So I can help out with the bills.'

I shake my head. 'There's no need.' Which is true. Jake's inheritance has been providing us with enough disposable income to pay bills and live comfortably. Especially with my old job back.

'Well, it's there. But I thought I might use it for something else if you don't want it. If that's OK.'

'What do you want to use the money for?' I ask.

'University,' he says.

I sense that he has more to say so I remain quiet.

'I know you don't approve,' he says. 'And I understand why. I know that I came back wrong, that I'm all broken up. I know that I'm delicate and my skin hates sunlight and my knees ache when it rains. I know my digestive system isn't great and my muscles are weak. I know that I have PTSD and have only just learned to sleep with the bedroom door closed. I know I didn't speak for weeks when I came back and that I still struggle to talk sometimes. And I know that I'm going to find it difficult to make friends. I know I don't like being touched. I don't know if I like girls or boys. I don't know if I'll ever want a . . . partner. I don't know who I am yet.' He pauses, pants because he's out of breath. 'And I know that sometimes I wish I was back in the bunker and how sick that is.' He pauses again, but I let him go on. 'But I'm working through it. Dr Anderton is helping me. Words heal. The more I do, the more I say or write or paint, the better I am. I think I'm ready to move on.'

I take his hands in mine and hold him closer. 'You didn't come back wrong. We're all broken, Aiden. And I don't just mean this family, I mean everyone. And you know what? That's what makes us all who we are. Even if you don't know who you are, I do. I know you're perfect. Perfectly strong, perfectly different, with a perfectly *good* heart. I think you're ready, too.'

'I can go?' he asks.

'You don't have to ask my permission anymore, kiddo. You're grown.'

He stares down at our hands and nods.

'I'm here if you need me.'

'OK,' he says.

Epilogue

EMMA

It takes a lot longer this time. There are brand new aches and pains since the last time my feet trod these paths, but I don't care. I'm with my family. The sun is shining and the wind is blowing back my hair. In my lungs is the Yorkshire air I know and love. I have good days and bad days. It's just over a year since the accident at the chapel, and my recovery is gradual. Today I feel strong, and we're walking back up the hill to the field where we like to sit and look at the clouds. The field that overlooks Bishoptown. Despite everything that's happened, this tiny village is my home again.

'You OK, Mum?' Aiden asks.

I'm a little breathless from the hill. 'I'll have a rest. You guys go on ahead.'

Aiden turns to his dad, but Rob waves his hand.

'I'll stop and keep your mum company,' he says.

We stand there for a moment, watching my daughter, now an even more precocious five-year-old, run on ahead, making rocket noises. Rob laughs and I do too. I steal a sideways glance at him and see him watching me, that slight hint of shame visible in the creases between his eyebrows. Our relationship isn't what it was, but we are still good friends.

'Do you think you'll ever forgive me for what I did?' he asks.

Forgiveness has been on my mind for a long time. Choosing not to forgive can be hard on the soul, but some acts are easier to forgive than others.

'Yes,' I reply, after a long pause.

He sighs. 'I sense a *but* coming.'

I smile. 'You always did know me better than anyone.' His eyes catch the sunlight, sparkling. 'I was locked in a cage when she told me. She'd just revealed a doll she'd named after the daughter she'd never borne. Amy was ill, evil and cruel, but when she told me what you did, I believed her. Right away, I believed her.'

'Because you know me,' he says.

'I do. Everything she said reminded me of the person you used to be.'

'An arsehole.'

I nod my head. 'That's one way of putting it. Another is selfish.'

His voice sounds sad as he says, 'It's true.'

The breeze tickles the hairs on the back of my neck as I take a moment to compose my thoughts. 'What I don't know is whether you're still that person anymore.'

'Neither do I,' he admits. 'But I'm trying not to be.' He smiles, and laughter lines crinkle in the corners of his eyes. We shared a lot of laughter together once, and a lot of tears.

I put a hand on his arm. He's good, I know he is, despite what he did twenty years ago. But in my heart, it feels as though I've already let him go. Still, we stand like that for a while, happy enough in each other's company. No matter what, he's the person who knows me better than everyone, and he's the father to my wonderful, complex son. My first love, but hopefully not my last.

Ginny runs around us all, screaming for Denny to play football with her, pulling us back to the world around us.

Staring down at Bishoptown, it strikes me that the

looming shadows of Hugh and Jake are still there, hanging over me. Even after Hugh's death, I couldn't rest and, in a sense, I was right not to rest, because I'd underestimated Amy's hatred. But what I did during that time had consequences for my family. I'd held them too close and smothered them, like every mother worries she will.

Now that Amy is behind a different set of bars, those shadows are a little smaller. They'll always exist, but we can work on making them smaller; on forcing them to stop blocking our light.

I allow my eyes to roam over every part of the view, the light and the shade. In the light I see golden trees, touched by autumn. In the shade I see the hint of winter to come. No matter what, the world continues on, and time keeps marching.

Aiden is at university now, studying for his art degree. His coffee table book is a bestseller, and he still sells paintings. He lives in a shared house in London during the week and comes home at the weekend. It terrifies me, and I think it scares him too sometimes, but he's doing it and I've finally found a way to let go of the constraints I had unknowingly placed on him.

Gina is the most resilient of us all. I keep watching her, waiting for signs of trauma. But aside from a few bad dreams, she's the same Gina as before. Sometimes she asks about Faith and where she is now. Even though I think she understands the evil things Amy and Faith did together, she has forgiven her captor without question, and I decided to do the same. Amy was both villain and victim within her life. I don't have it in me to hate her anymore. In fact, I don't have it in me to hate Hugh or Jake either.

When I lost Aiden, I discovered what it was like to lose control of my life. Everything spiralled until I thought I would lose my mind. Then he came back, and I learned how to take the control away from my abusive husband in order to save my loved ones. But I couldn't give up that control. I kept controlling my children, choking them with the love I felt for them, terrified of anything happening to them again. And then Gina was taken away from me. I rarely let her out of my sight, and she was still taken from me. All that control and I couldn't stop it from happening.

When I was trapped, Aiden found me. Aiden found Gina. Even Gina managed to call the police. I could do nothing. The best thing I could do for them was give up control. And now I'm doing it again. I'm letting them live. Letting them breathe. Giving them the space they need to become the people they are.

And what will I do while they are living? I can live for myself again. Now I can take my own breath, because we're safe. We're free.

THE END

* * *

Thank you for reading STOLEN GIRL! I hoped you enjoyed this continuation of Emma and Aiden's story. These characters mean a lot to me. Turn the page for one last instalment – AIDEN'S STORY, a short story set in between Silent Child and Stolen Girl.

If you enjoyed this book, you might like LITTLE ONE. Fran finds a child standing alone in the park. But when she reunites her with the family, she suspects little Esther might not be safe with them.

Aiden's Story

I guess this is me. I'm Aiden Price. I'm sixteen years old. The newspapers and the social media sites all call me the "Boy from the Bunker", which is true. That's who I am and where I came from. The bunker was my home for ten years, if you can call it a home. It isn't anymore, though. I live with Mum and Gina. We're selling Jake's house because Mum doesn't like it there.

After I escaped, I didn't talk for a long time and I think it scared everyone. Mum especially. They didn't know if I could read or write. They didn't know what was going on in my head. I guess I didn't know myself. If I'd spoken, I could've told everyone what happened, but I didn't want to. I was scared of what they'd say when they found Hugh. When they saw what I did to him.

Whenever he hit me, I always felt like it was wrong, so maybe I shouldn't have hit him when he gave me the bat. Before the bunker, when I was little, Mum and Dad both told me that hitting was wrong, but then I met Hugh and he broke all the rules I thought were true. I suppose I started to think that if he could break all the rules, I could too. And it seemed like the only way I could get out.

Anyway, Dr Anderton wants me to write down my story because she says it'll help me. I'm going through something

293

called cognitive behavioural therapy and it's all about changing my thoughts from negative ones (bad thoughts) to positive ones (good thoughts). I'm not supposed to think bad things about myself. I can't call myself stupid. I can't think I'm alone anymore, because I have Mum, Gina and Dr Anderton to help me. Part of that is writing about what happened to me. This is what she called "narrative writing".

But I don't really know what to write.

Dr Anderton doesn't like it when I don't answer her in our sessions. Sometimes I don't feel like talking again, it's like the world slips away and I'm back in the cage on my own. Back in my empty head. But Dr Anderton says that words heal. If I talk about what happened, I can move on.

The problem is, I forget things.

Or I don't want to remember. Is there a difference?

I don't want to start at the beginning, so I'll start somewhere else: the day Gina was born.

Hugh was there. At least, the shell of him. By the time I led Mum to the bunker, I'd already watched the light go out of his eyes, and the blood come out, so I know he wasn't really there. Mum started leaking and something was wrong. I said, "Mum, you're leaking", and her eyes went big and round like little moons in the dark. I had to help her up the steps and into the woods. She was breathing all wrong. Panicked. Gulping.

That was when the police officer came and he helped me get her back onto the road. I had to shove my fingers in my ears when the ambulance siren came close. I'm still getting used to all the noises. Mum says I was noisy before I was taken and I'm sure she's right. I remember that my favourite toys were the ones that made different sounds. Hugh used to bring me toys in the bunker, but they were silent.

I had to wait with the police officer while Gina was being born. DCI Stevenson. He's all right. His voice reminds me of Hugh's. Jake's did, too. I guess it's all the male ones. High voices make me feel strange, like I'm on a new planet. That's taken some getting used to. Sometimes Mum would talk to me or tell me to do something and I'd just want to run away, which is stupid now that I think about it. I wish I hadn't come home all wrong.

It took hours for Gina to arrive. For some of it I went and sat with Dad in a different part of the hospital. He was asleep and Grandma and Grandad were with him. Grandma kept crying and sometimes kissed me on the head. I wanted to stay with them but watching them made my stomach hurt a lot. I didn't like it at all. Everyone had a problem I couldn't fix. They can't fix my problems and I can't fix theirs. So I went back to sit with DCI Stevenson and he told me all about his police ID and the uniform he used to wear when he first joined. He bought me a hot chocolate and a Mars bar and I sat and waited. Then I heard Gina start to cry and the noise was just horrible. Even when the nurse asked me if I wanted to go in and see my little sister, I plugged my ears with my fingers and shook my head. But she waved me in, and I followed, expecting to turn around and run away as soon as I entered that room.

Mum's face was all sweaty and red, but she was grinning from ear to ear. She smiled when she looked at me. She had a bundle in her arms. The crying wasn't so bad anymore. Instead, Gina was making funny little noises in between the cries.

"This is your sister, Aiden," Mum said, moving her arms towards me so that I could see the little bundle's face.

It was all scrunched up and red. There was a bit of hair on her head but not much.

"She's a little delicate," Mum said. "There were complications because of the stress before I gave birth." I didn't understand what she meant at first, but then I remembered Jake. I remembered Mum throwing herself on him, hitting him, biting him. "It's okay, Aiden. She's fine. She's going to be just fine. But I have to give her back to the doctors in a moment. So, say hello now, and then you'll see her again later."

"Hello, Gina," I said, and I gently touched her nose with my finger. She gurgled and for a moment I felt like she was saying hello back.

I went to Grandma and Grandad's that night. Mum had

to stay overnight in the hospital and I was tired. It was strange not to sleep in the bunker or my room at Mum and Jake's, but it didn't take me long to go to drift off. The next day I went back and held Gina in the way Mum showed me. At first, I thought I might drop her, but I didn't. She was warm and a bit wriggly. But she gurgled again and seemed happy. I gave her back to Mum after a while because she seemed so fragile. I don't feel like I can even take care of myself. I don't know what I'm doing or who I am. How could I possibly make sure a little person like Gina wouldn't get hurt?

Dad woke up, too. But he couldn't talk properly and I didn't like it. I went to visit with Grandma and Grandad and watched him slur his words and drink from a straw. Jake killed part of his brain when he hit him, and the doctors had to help him learn to do things again, like walk and talk. I remember that I started my sessions with Dr Anderton not long after Gina was born, and she suggested that I saw myself in Dad. That I had to learn how to walk and talk again too. Or maybe I was like Gina, that I came out of the bunker wiped clean. A blank page. I wish.

When Mum was released from hospital, we all went to live in Jake's house. Gina's room was all set up. The place was as white and boring as ever, but now there was no Jake. No man's voice apart from my own, and I started to enjoy that feeling. That I could speak and contribute. I could sing to Gina or read her a book. I could tell Mum what I wanted to eat. I could tell her that I wanted the bedroom door open at night. That sunlight hurt my eyes. That too much milk made my stomach hurt. That I hated the white walls of the house.

One day Mum put Gina into the car seat, and we went to the next town over. Once I'd helped her with the pram, we went into a large, brown building and bought several cans of paint. "Choose as many colours as you want," Mum said. I walked up and down the aisle picking up the cans of paint that I wanted. Pastel blue. Cranberry Crush. Forest green. Peony pink. Sunshine yellow. And more. It took us ages to put them all into the car.

We also bought protective sheets and covered the carpets

and furniture. We made sure Gina was safely in her room with the windows open and we painted the house until every room was a different, bright colour.

"It might make it harder to sell," Mum said, wiping sweat from her forehead. "But I don't care."

She even let me paint my room with swirls and patterns. I painted it sky blue with orange swirls. Pink polka dots. But inside my wardrobe I painted black and grey stripes. I didn't tell Mum about that bit.

* * *

I had to rest for a while. My hand was starting to ache writing all this down. I did a bit of writing in the bunker, but not every day, and not as much as this. Mum is trying to teach me how to type on a keyboard but I'm slow at everything. I did a lot of drawing in the bunker so it's quicker for me to hold a pen. She says my handwriting is very neat and she seems surprised by this. She seems sad, too.

After Mum and Gina came out of hospital and we painted the house, we visited Dad a lot. He was starting to talk a bit better and could even get out of bed. I also had lots of appointments suddenly. I had to do these assessments now that I was talking again. That was when I met Dr Anderton, a psychologist who knows a lot about children who have been through the things I've been through.

I filled out lots of forms and saw a few doctors. I had dentist appointments and Mum bought me sunglasses so that my eyes don't ache when it's bright outside. Mum is always being given reports about my health and then she tries to explain it all to me. I don't think she tells me everything, but I guess it's because she thinks it might upset me. Do I need to know it all? I don't know. Maybe she'll tell me when I'm a bit older.

Mum is really tired right now. When Gina cries, she has to get out of bed and feed her. I know this because I hear her moving around in the night. But that doesn't bother me. I don't think I slept for long amounts of time in the bunker. I had a clock to tell the time, though it broke a lot. I knew if I'd stayed up 'til 3am, or woke up at 2am. I just had to look at the clock.

Grandma and Grandad babysit Gina every now and then. But when Gina is gone, Mum is even more stressed. She stares at the red skin on her hands and I can tell she wants to scratch it. Sometimes she bites her fingernails instead. I know how she feels. I have a spot at the back of my head that's gone bald because I keep scratching it. No one seems to have noticed yet though.

I guess that's everything that's happened since I came out of the bunker. Since Hugh died. Since… since I killed Hugh and escaped. That's everything that's happened to me since Gina was born. I started to talk. I met my little sister. I met Dr Anderton and lots of other doctors. Dad started to talk again, too. Mum got really tired, but she let me paint the house. She also bought me canvases and lots of acrylics so that I could paint in the garage. She bought me all the books I wanted. But she said that we can't stay in that house because it makes her sad.

I understand that. The bunker made me sad, too. But sometimes I want to go back there anyway. Sometimes I think that it's the only place I'll ever truly feel at home, and the thought that I can't ever go back makes my skin itch.

I remember the first moments in the bunker. It smelled down there at first but later I didn't notice it. Sometimes it would get too hot and Hugh would turn on the air pump. Sometimes water came in through little holes in the bricks. Hugh explained that the bricks needed holes so that I got fresh air. I don't think there was anything fresh about the air in the bunker, but he insisted it was.

For ten years, his was the only voice I knew. His face was the only face I saw. He was the only person in my life.

And I killed him.

* * *

I had another break, but not because my hands were aching this time. I just needed one. I've written all about Gina and Dad and Mum, but I haven't written much about Hugh or the bunker. That's the bit I know Dr Anderton wants me to write about, but it's the part I don't want to write.

One thing I will admit is that when I was in the bunker, I learned things. Hugh used to buy me books and they included textbooks about science or history. Once he bought me a huge Atlas of the world. It showed you all the oceans and the continents. And it showed you the rivers going across the continents, rivers like the Ouse – the one that Jake pushed me into. Though I didn't know Jake pushed me in until recently when he admitted it. I remembered running down from school to look at the flood, and I remember being on the riverbank, but I didn't remember falling in, just the sudden freezing cold chill on my skin and the pull of the current. Water in my mouth and up my nose. Moving my arms. Not feeling my fingers.

Even now when I think about it, the cold creeps underneath my skin. Even my bones turn cold.

Yes, I studied those books while I was there. Hugh used to bring me pens and paper. Nothing that I could sharpen, though. I didn't notice that until I was older, and he was still bringing me felt tips and crayons. Eventually he brought me pens I could write properly with, but they always had a soft nib. I think I was twelve when I realised that was because he thought I might hurt him. It never occurred to me to fight back until that point, and I felt stupid for not trying. For a while I thought Mum would be disappointed in me because I didn't try hard enough. I only tried to escape once. That was the day Hugh broke my leg.

He'd fallen asleep on the floor of the bunker. I remember rolling out of my mattress onto my feet. They were bare, and the concrete was cold. I saw the edge of Hugh's pocket. Even though it was night-time, the electric light was still on. I figured that his keys must be in that pocket and if I could put my hand in there without him noticing, I could unlock the bars and run out. I hadn't run for I don't know how long, but I knew I could do it if I forced myself to.

He was snoring a little bit, which was good because I was breathing heavily. My body was shaking. I leaned over and stretched and my fingers twitched as I got closer. I slipped my fingers into his pocket but as I was searching for the keys his eyes opened and he grabbed my wrist.

"What do you think you're doing, mate?"

Mate. Always mate. He talked softly most of the time and acted like he was still Uncle Hugh, the person I knew before the bunker.

"Nothing." I tried to pull myself away, but he held tight.

Still with his fingers tightly wrapped around my wrist, he manoeuvred himself into an upright position. "You were looking for the keys." His eyebrows bunched together, and I saw a spasm cross his face. I'd seen that before. It always happened before he got mad.

He'd shouted at me before. When I cried and asked for my mum and dad, he would get angry and shout. *Don't I bring you everything you need? Don't I look after you? I spend all my free time maintaining this fucking place and you've got no gratitude for me at all. Why do I even bother? I should let you rot down here. I should walk away and never come back. How would you like that?* He often threatened to leave me there and never come back. He told me I'd starve or freeze to death if he didn't keep bringing me electric heaters and blankets and all those other things I needed. That he wouldn't put traps down for rats or that he'd take the air pump away.

"I wasn't," I said, hoping I could lie my way out of this. "I wanted to play with them, that's all."

"You were trying to escape." He twisted my arm as he stood, and I cried out. "Fucking ungrateful shit."

I was used to the language by this point. He would yell and swear at me all the time, but I wasn't used to what happened next, the way he beat me and threw me around until something broke.

* * *

I had to take a break again, sorry. I don't remember a lot about breaking my leg. I think I passed out. I can't remember which bone it was, only that it was my lower leg. And I remember Hugh running out of the bunker. That was when I passed out. When I woke up, he was bandaging me. He had lots of medical things that he attached to it. He made soothing noises and injected my arm with something that made me feel a lot better. I went to sleep again.

* * *

My leg still hurts sometimes, but the doctors said it healed well considering the circumstances. I overheard Josie tell Mum that Hugh wanted to be a paediatrician once, and began studying medicine at university before he dropped out and set up a company with his brother. I guess he knew what to do when he broke my bone. No, not broke, fractured. That's right. But my leg still hurts sometimes, especially when it's cold.

The broken leg was one of the worst moments and it hurt more than anything has ever hurt. I don't like to think about it very often, but I do dream about it sometimes. But while I am thinking about it, maybe I should write down the routine I started in the bunker, because after a few years I realised that I needed to stay strong. I hated, *hated* not being able to run around, so I figured out a new way of using my muscles. Especially when I learned more about muscles from the science textbooks.

I didn't sleep at regular times, but when I slept for a longish period of time and felt well rested, I would get up, drink water, and eat something. Usually a breakfast bar or something like that – Hugh didn't bring a lot of fruit or veg because it would attract mice and flies. Then I would do as many star jumps as I could. I'd count them every time. I could do over one hundred star jumps at a time. Then, depending on how sweaty I was, I'd climb the iron bars, up and down, up and down until my arms ached. I'd stretch my legs and my arms, my back and my neck. I'd seen Dad doing sit ups and press ups. I wasn't sure how to do it right, but I did those until my muscles felt sore. And then I'd read, draw or write. If it was hot, I'd use the hand-held air pump. I'd check the toilet and sink was clean. I'd shoo the spiders out of my cage.

As I got older, I did more star jumps and sit ups, but I never looked as muscley as Dad. I didn't understand what I was doing wrong. And then it finally dawned on me that no matter what I did, I couldn't exercise properly in this tiny space. My diet wasn't nutritious enough to create muscles. I never got to use my legs outside of the cage. For a while, I stopped, and there were black thoughts, ones that Dr Anderton wouldn't approve of. I thought maybe I could drink cleaning products to kill myself. Mum had always told me they were poisonous. But by this time, I was old enough to realise that the small amount Hugh left me in the cage prob-ably wouldn't kill me, just make me sick.

And then he kept talking about my mum, about her marrying someone called Jake. He showed me pictures and videos. I heard her voice saying *I do*. I thought that perhaps I should keep trying to be strong and maybe one day I could get out. That if I did, she'd be proud.

It happened. I did it. I think she's proud. Happy, anyway, although she's scared, too.

But I'm not proud. I hate what I did.

* * *

I had a therapy session today and Dr Anderton asked me how I was getting on with my narrative writing. I said that I was doing it and that I was writing about what life was like in the bunker. She asked me how it was making me feel, and I said it was making me sad.

"Perhaps in time, when you've written everything you want to write, you'll begin to feel better," she said.

I shrugged, because I can't imagine that happening.

"Once it's on the page you can leave it on the page. Maybe it will help you move forward."

"Because words heal?"

"That's right," she said, and she smiled.

For the rest of the hour we drew pictures. I have to admit that I do feel better after drawing. But Dr Anderton keeps reminding me that I can't get lost in drawing and painting, I also have to face difficult problems by talking or writing. She reminds me to use my words.

After I wrote about Hugh breaking my leg I didn't speak for a full day. Mum went to bed in tears. She thought I wasn't going to speak again. But I did. And I didn't even mean to, I asked her if I could have toast for breakfast and she went all tense before she smiled. I'm not sure how that makes me feel, because sometimes I think I just frighten her because I'm so weird.

It can be overwhelming outside the house. People want to take photographs of me because I sell newspapers or whatever. There's lots of noise. Even in our village there's people and cars and noise. So, I stay inside and watch television. The teenagers on TV are so much bigger than me and they talk all the time. They never stop talking or joking or laughing. They have girlfriends and they play sports and they dance and do all these things that I don't. I'm not normal and I'll never be normal because a man took my life away. It makes me so mad. Sometimes I want to hit him again. I want him to be alive so that I can keep hitting him until I'm no longer mad.

That's why I'm not proud of myself, because I'm a bad person. I'm violent. I'm horrible. I'm fucking ungrateful just like Hugh always said. I want to go back to my cage, to lock myself in and never come out. That's what I want. I don't deserve to be around Mum or Gina. I don't deserve family.

* * *

I had to take a break again. I got so mad. I had to put the pen down, take some deep breaths, get out of my bedroom and do something else. Painting seems to be the only thing that calms me down when I'm mad.

I probably shouldn't tell Dr Anderton this but sometimes I

use the computer and search for results about the kind of person I am. I want to know what happens to people who have experienced the kind of things I've experienced. Do you know what I learned? I learned that a high percentage go on to do those things to other people.

Dr Anderton wants me to talk about all of my feelings, from how angry I am, to how sad I feel, or even how happy I am to not be in the bunker anymore. But there are other feelings that she wants me to talk about that I don't think I can. Not yet. And those are very complicated. They involve things I don't really remember, because when they were happening to me, I went to another place. I focused on a spot on the wall, or I pretended I was back in the village with my friends, playing football with Billy and Oscar from school.

* * *

My bed is soft at night, now. The air in my room is fresh, and I always leave the door open so that the air remains like that. I don't often open the window, just every now and then. Sometimes I stand by the open window for a moment, feel the cool breeze on my skin and look at the street below. There are times when my heart almost seizes inside my chest because I suddenly realise how big the world is. I don't always like remembering the size of the world.

It's weird, but at night I like to wrap myself in the duvet. Head to toe. I like the darkness. I couldn't always control the lights in the bunker, because some were outside my cage, but when the lights went out it was pitch black. The kind of black I haven't seen since. The darkness doesn't frighten me because nothing bad ever happened in the dark. Of course, I was afraid the first time. I wondered what it would be like for a rat to crawl on me, or for a spider to drop from the ceiling. Nothing like that ever happened. Darkness usually meant the generator needed a new battery. It also meant that Hugh wasn't there, which meant nothing could hurt me. Unless a rat nipped at my toes, but then I'd been through much worse already.

I like the darkness before I sleep. I like knowing that Hugh isn't there and that he won't hurt me ever again. But I don't like my dreams.

* * *

I had a break because I didn't want to write about my dreams.

I still don't, but I'm going to try.

In my dreams I feel his breath against my skin, his large hands on my arms. I see him in many different ways. Sometimes they are harmless memories, like him reading me a story, cutting my hair, cutting my nails, turning up with Indian food. Sometimes they are the in-between memories where I'm scared but he's not hurting me. The way he'd rant about his wife, his brother, his friends. The way his face would screw up as he spewed out vile things about the world. The way he'd change his voice to imitate other people.

At one point he started setting me homework. I'd write essays on different subjects. He'd either nod his head in approval or laugh. Whatever it was, at the end, he'd burn the pages. He burned a lot of my writing. But I kept most of my drawings. Those I stuck on the wall or hid under my mattress. But words were too much for him. Perhaps they felt too real.

"Do you see how kind I am to you?" he said one day. "Look at the books I bring you! Look at how much I'm teaching you about the world. I'm better than a father, aren't I? Aren't I, Aiden?"

"Yes."

"Good boy."

All of this turns up in my dreams, often broken up, or out of order. They're hazy. Hugh's face changes. At times his hair has greys in it, other times it doesn't. Or I'm younger in my dream than I was in real life. It doesn't matter, though, because I always wake up sweating.

I won't write about the worst of it, no matter what Dr Anderton says. I know that words heal but I don't even know how to put it into words. So how can I heal myself?

Sometimes I imagined I was in a completely different part of the world, like Mum and me used to do when we were playing. The Great Wall of China. The Eiffel Tower. The playground at school. The campsite I went to on holiday with Mum and Dad. Mum's wedding, the one Hugh showed me a video of. I went to all of those places during the worst moments. That's where I was. But my dreams don't understand. They keep showing me clips of it like something on a film. I hate it. It was so bad that for a while I tried not to sleep at all, but I got too tired. Dr Anderton says it's healthy to have at least seven hours of sleep at night. I'm not sure she's right. I would rather not sleep if I can. I'd love to never have to see any of those things again.

But the worst dream of all isn't one where Hugh is hurting me. No, it's very different. It's the dream I have of Hugh's death. It's me holding the bat. It's me hitting him.

The bat was meant for me because I was getting too old to keep in the bunker. I see Hugh now like I'm there again, his eyes wet with tears, hand wrapped around the handle of the bat, his body trembling all over. He's going to kill me. But now there's a flicker in his eyes. He's thinking about what it'll be like to take another child, I can tell. He's thinking about going through it all again. And now he's thinking about how he can't help himself, even though there are times he wants to stop. He's thinking about the time he almost let me go, when he opened up the cage door and closed his eyes. But when I actually went to leave he slammed the door shut and started to cry.

And now he's thinking about it all being pointless. That it needs to stop. Now he's thinking about the only way this can end. Now he's thinking about giving up, giving everything up.

He gives me the weapon. He eggs me on.

I look down at the piece of wood in my right hand, and for a moment I'm not sure whether I know what to do with it. But I've been hit before and I know the parts that are the softest, most vulnerable. I lift it up above my head and swing it, hard.

I'm hitting him, over and over and over until his skull

cracks open. I'm there again, watching the blood spurt from his wounds. Fuck. I'm there. I head the crack of bone. I'm there watching the stillness of his body. The light fade from his eyes. The thoughts leave his body.

I'm there.

* * *

I had to stop again. I was shaking. You can see the wobbly pen marks. My words are scrawled all over, missing the lines completely. But it was like I was there again, watching it happen for real.

Dr Anderton, how could you make me relive these things? I don't understand how it helps me. It just makes me feel bad. I'm so mad at you right now that I want to do something, like, I don't know, hit a wall. Stab a pen into my leg. Why are you making me do this?

* * *

That was yesterday and I think I'm okay now. I spent the evening helping Mum entertain Gina. She's eight months old now and can pull herself up. It's like watching Dad learn to walk again.

I feel really crappy today, like I'm nothing but black and grey lines fused together. That's what I painted earlier, lots of black and grey lines in the shape of a boy. When I was finished, I left it on my bedroom floor to dry. But as I was getting up, I knocked over some yellow paint and it splashed onto the canvas. I was mad at first, but then I kinda liked it. It reminded me of what Mum says, about light coming in through the cracks.

But it only made me feel better for a moment, so Mum asked me if I wanted to go for a walk with her. We made our way out into the countryside where it was quiet, with Gina in a carrier on Mum's back. We walked until my bad leg ached and then we sat down on the grass, which was slightly damp, and we ate sandwiches and didn't really talk much. Mum asked me how my writing was going, and I told her that it made me think things that I don't want to remember anymore. She said she loved me and that we'd get through it together.

Mum says love a lot. She likes to remind me that she loves me. But I'm not sure I understand that word. Hugh used to say it too. But being in the bunker wasn't love. Being hurt wasn't love. And what if I don't love anyone or anything? What if I'm numb forever? Or worse, what if I'm a bad person?

Families are supposed to love each other but I didn't see my family for ten years. The only way I saw them was through photos and videos that Hugh showed me on his phone. Smiling images of them living their life without me, believing that I was dead. How do I match up the smiling picture of Mum and Jake with the Mum who takes me on a walk and tells me she loves me? Who tells me that light comes in through the dark cracks within us? That promises me that everything will be all right?

It all comes back to one thing that I know is true: I don't know her. I'm getting to know her now, but I haven't lived with her for years. She might not be the person I remember.

Because I was six when I was taken, I had happy memories from before. Yes, I remember family holidays. I remember going to school. I remember Christmas and the presents I got. I remember Mum painting. She laughed a lot more, then. We used to chase each other. I remember all of those things and I try to hold them in my memory and never let them go. But while I was inside the bunker, they began to seem like something that never happened. Did we really make up games together or did I make it up in my head? Did I dream the picnic in the park or was it real?

I was alone so much that my mind often played tricks on me. That was why I read so many books, it was the only way to stop my mind from drifting. Otherwise everything distorted. Everything twisted up until I couldn't recognise it.

The sandwiches were good. We didn't talk all that much and I think Mum got a bit frustrated because I kept shrugging and answering with one word. But Gina was funny, making silly noises and faces.

We went through the outskirts of the woods on the way home and all the trees were turning brown for autumn. I ignored my leg and kicked up the leaves to make Gina laugh. Mum smiled, too, and it seemed so different to when Hugh used to smile. It's like she's looking at the things she values the most, or like she's warm from head to toe. I ached from walking, but it was the kind of ache that I like. It made me tired, but it reminded me that I was free to walk.

Now I'm about to get into bed and I think maybe I'll sleep well tonight.

* * *

I decided to read a fantasy book today. It's a chilly October day, but I went into the garden and sat on one of the garden chairs with a book about a hero with a pet dragon. I put a blanket over my knees and Mum made me a cup of tea to keep my hands warm. The dragon starts off small and cute, and then he gets bigger and the hero has to find things to feed the dragon with. Goats, sheep, wolves… until he realises that the dragon wants to eat people. The more the hero feeds the dragon, the bigger the dragon gets and the more dangerous it is.

Eventually the hero realises he has to feed the dragon people, because nothing else will fill its belly. But when the hero does feed the dragon people, the dragon realises he doesn't need his master, and flies away to hunt alone. The dragon wreaks so much violence that the hero has to decide whether to kill the dragon or let it live and keep on hurting others.

Sometimes I wonder whether I have a dragon inside me that I'm feeding. There's an angry monster inside me and if I feed it with negative thoughts, it'll keep getting bigger until I start to hurt other people. But my response to that is that my life has been so unfair. Why shouldn't I be angry? And if I am angry, how do I stop feeding the dragon? Dr Anderton says that I can do that by turning my negative thoughts into positive ones. Words heal. The more I write them down, the more I can let them go. The less they go round and round in my head until that dragon grows up to be a beast.

And maybe she's right, because since I wrote about Hugh and the way I hit him over the head until he... No, I should say – since I wrote about the way I killed Hugh – I've felt lighter, in a way, like the dragon is a bit smaller.

Since my last entry, we've been walking a lot. Mum likes to point out some of the trees as we stroll. She said that we can buy a book so that we can identify them better. And plants. I think she believes that I should spend more time outside because I was in the bunker for so long. Maybe she's right. Maybe I do need to look at the sky more and listen to the birds. Maybe these things are as healing as words. Maybe they help turn the negative thoughts into positives.

The walks are helping me, but I still feel overwhelmed by the world outside of the bunker. Especially people and the way they stare at me. Or the sound of loud cars. Ambulances and fire engines. The brightness of the sun. But with each passing day, they become a little bit more bearable. Both Mum and Dr Anderton tell me that I'm adjusting well. Mum says I'm a good son and a good big brother and that I should be kind to myself at all times.

It's nice today. There is a slight chill in the air, like nighttime in the bunker, and the sun is hidden behind some clouds so it doesn't hurt my eyes. It seems like it might rain, but for now the weather holds. I can sit here and read my book, thinking about ways to stop feeding the dragon. The hero slays the dragon in the end. It's not exactly a happy ending, he'll forever miss his dragon, and he won't ever be able to stop thinking about the moment he killed it, but in the end, killing it saved him. And now he can move on and go ahead and live his life without a monster to feed.

About the Author

Sarah A. Denzil is a British suspense writer from Derbyshire. Her books include SILENT CHILD, which has topped Kindle charts in the UK, US, and Australia. SAVING APRIL and THE BROKEN ONES are both top thirty bestsellers in the US and UK Amazon charts.

Combined, her self-published and published books, along with audiobooks and foreign translations, have sold over one million copies worldwide.

Sarah lives in Yorkshire with her husband, enjoying the scenic countryside and rather unpredictable weather. She loves to write moody, psychological books with plenty of twists and turns.

www.sarahadenzil.com

Writing as Sarah Dalton - http://www.sarahdaltonbooks.com/